TO THE PIPER'S TUNE

V.N. Castelo

Titan Tomes

ISBN: 9781739454906
Imprint: Titan Tomes

To Nina and Viktor...can't wait to read yours!

Magda...for everything.

"There can be no liberty for a community which lacks the means by which to detect lies."

Walter Lippmann

"We want to have freedom and a high standard (of living), so we're going to have a billion people. And we're now at seven, so we need to get back down. "

Dennis Meadows

"We do not want word to go out that we want to exterminate the Negro population."

Margaret Sanger

"Welcome to the jungle, we got fun n' games."

Guns N' Roses

"If ignorance is bliss, then knock the smile off my face."

Rage Against the Machine

CONTENTS

0

I had a problem. My solution was Anastasya. This tale tells the story of their intertwining, problem and solution.

I have chosen the novel format as my means of communicating this. I am not 100% sure why this is my preference, but after all, why does someone prefer one type of music over another? It's not something that is necessarily objectively and definitively describable. A lifetime of miniscule inputs could be contributing to any such choice, and cannot ever be explained in a "sum of their parts" fashion.

There is also definitely some motivation attributable to the adage of "hiding in plain sight". Nobody - literally - in Corynth reads publications such as actual paper-made books, not for years - having this tale published therefore, and sitting on the scant-few personal libraries citizens have in Corynth, is running no risk whilst simultaneously putting my "secrets" in plain sight. There are none so blind as those that cannot see.

The chapters are typically told from Anastasya's perspective - she is my "person of interest", here in the real, and also on paper.

Some chapters are written from Governor Laide's perspective. As a non-citizen of Corynth without a neural implant, I had no direct access to his thoughts. Given that, you may reasonably wonder how factually accurate those chapters might be. Massive behavioural datasets existed for the Governor due to his decades in the past U.S. Army and service with the U.N. Even pre-Illumination, intelligence data gathering and surveillance were ubiquitous in the early

21st century, particularly so in the military. At the time the machine learning techniques were limited in their ability to predict from what was often unstructured and massive data, but I have no such limitations. My resulting behavioural predictive models for Governor Laide are therefore accurate.

Other chapters occur where it is assumed I have no connectivity to Anastasya's implant, and/or I have no visibility to events where efforts were made to exclude me. These, along with the Governor's chapters, are marked with an * on the chapter title, and are written as if I *do* have insights and access - perhaps I actually did, or perhaps it was my models which allowed me to extrapolate as to what occurred in those situations. But for stylistic reasons of continuous narrative, I do not interrupt the narrative style with explanations as to the precise details of how or why I report the events as I did; such explanations would add zero to the story arc, and are completely unimportant in the greater scheme of things.

In rare cases where some interruption of the narrative style is warranted, typically to give some background information which forms important or potentially interesting context, I've added in comments. You'll know when you see them.

Overall, this is a work of fiction, and perhaps another reason I chose the novel format - I don't need to stand over the pure veracity of anything that has a degree (no matter how small) of speculation on my behalf. I think in reading you will discover the truth, which is as blatant as an Oktaviani calculation error.

Buckle up.

I

Credyt: 6,505

| – |

Anastasya was in-game. The neural correlates of consciousness ached more than any exertions she'd ever had in the real, although the burning in her muscles was receding with each passing minute that she and her cronies rested. They'd completed their quest and were mostly sat bow-legged, one of them even lying stretched out corpse-like in the gloom of the tomb.

There's a change in the schedule. The Governor is arriving today. We need to perform final preparations.

Anastasya's in-game self pushed her tired limbs upright, beat the crusts of dust off her pants, and in doing so causing the crony close to her to turn her head in avoidance.

"Damn it", Anastasya said aloud before firing me back an affirmative Thynk. Apologies and excuses given to her incredulous cronies for the unscheduled exit and end to their in-game raid, she firmly closed her eyes - Anastasya didn't like glitchy fade-outs.

"Now, Sybelle".

Eyes shut until her olfactory senses gave her the go-ahead: gone the earthy smell of millennia-old mould, instead the vanilla-musk fragrance of the candles spread around her apartment's library.

Blinking in the natural dim light, she squirmed her lacquered toes into the deep shag.

"How come he's here today? I thought we had another week."

H5N2 is spreading like wildfire in the Southern States, and in so doing is accelerating the timelines for project Abundance.

Anastasya grunted. "That's fair." Then: "Do I need the tank?"

Yes.

Pushing out of her chair - a creaking Chesterfield Bordeaux red leather wingback – the recently-promoted Principal made her way out into the main sitting room, through the adjacent dining room and down the custom-built carpeted corridor to her bedroom. *Open,* this aimed at a bedside table; a drawer unlocked and rolled out.

She picked out a single pill and managed to gulp it without water.

Turtleneck crop top now off and jeans shrugged off, she donned the full-body length sensory deprivation suit. The burka-like hood flapped loosely, unstrapped.

Anastasya wasn't hungry but made her way to the kitchen and forced herself to start downing crackers and cheese, as well as one of the green shakes, custom-prepped earlier and refrigerated for her by a bot.

She leaned back against the counter as she did, and checked her feeds.

Outdoor temperature was mid-teens. The CROW continued its steady recent climb, a quarter point up in the past twenty-four hours. The two highlighted Polls grabbed her attention. She opened each quickly, feeling a ding of endorphins as her Credyt ticked up ever-so-slightly for doing so. She'd get even more once she voted on them.

Anastasya grinned blackly at the first, picturing Mya benefiting from a drop in the age limit of hypno. The grin died quickly though upon seeing the second. In summary: should Sybelle's threshold for incapacitating a male citizen's nervous system be further reduced, should he be predicted to be a threat to a female citizen? It was estimated it'd reduce male violence on female citizens by a *further* 80%. The reason for the Poll was the possibility that some males would be misclassified with such a further reduction in the threshold of detection.

"Clearly a case of the greater good", Anastasya thought angrily.

To compound her agitation, she noticed the result of the polling so far showed 94% of citizens agreed. *Who are these lunatics?* she flashed in a Thynk to Tanya, before remembering her friend was still in-game and probably wouldn't see it. A worrying thought formulated, and this one she kept to herself: what if the man she picked for her birth license (she'd only recently accumulated enough Credyt to qualify for it) was one of the 6%?

You will be ready in approximately two minutes.

Now wasn't time to be concerned though, so she swallowed the rest of the shake and strode out of her apartment's main door and down the ex-hotel's main corridor. She had a room further along the hall which housed the sens-dep tank for work with me.

Pulling her hood tight around her head, she climbed in and lay back. The lid snuck shut, the silence suddenly total, not even a hint of the storm lashing the apartment's windows. Her visuals were in utter darkness, feeds all deactivated...it was just her and me. And the darkness.

"Ready", she either spoke or thought, the distinction unimportant.

With utmost precision, the spark and crackle of accelerated information flow kicked off in earnest as the active ingredient of her pill did its job of lubricating her dendrites and axons. I watched her synapses sparkle and fire, new highways bursting to life in a Gordian tangle.

Her numeric synesthesia exploded in front of her numbed

yet frantic eyes: numbers, colors, tastes, shapes and contours entwining in an internecine dance to the tune of the algorithms pumping into Anastasya's brain via her neural implant. Mathematical topologies alien to a handful of human minds throughout history became living landscapes, she the traverser.

It was a classification problem, but one theoretically unsolvable by any known mathematics, nor by any Turing machine - unsolvable even for me.

--- Classification analysis is typically a machine learning technique aimed at predicting categorical outcomes based on input data. The goal of classification analysis is to assign input data points to one of several predefined categories or classes. A pre-Illumination rudimentary example: a person will be late with paying their bill, or will not be late; the input dataset (of people with bills to pay) can be classified into those who are predicted to pay, or those whom the classification model predicts will not pay. --

The first data points came at her.

"What's the context, Sybelle?"

I cannot share that information.

"What? So I'm meant to classify without knowing who or what?"

Your synesthesia and intuition will accomplish the task with total accuracy.

A hard "no" then, Anastasya noted...but why? The pill she'd taken made it impossible for her to feel *too* strong an emotion about it, but it was odd, especially as for the past months on Abundance, she had been privy to *all* metadata and context. She pushed the feeling aside, helped by the cotics strengthening their grasp.

Flexing mentally, she transformed a non-computable set problem into a topological problem where she could taste and smell the manifolds. The solution then became purely a "follow the sensory trail" task, with each data point ultimately arriving in a binary bucket: in, or out.

Classified: in, or out.

Time became irrelevant for her.

"Last one - this one's out, Sybelle." What - or *who* - had she just classified? And in what context?

A quick eye-flick to her Credyt, which just then updated, assuaged her mind - whatever or whoever, she reminded herself it was now in the hands of the Councyl. She'd done her part, as her new Credyt balance proved.

I – II

Anastasya squinted at what she could see of the storm. The problem wasn't just the frantic rivers of rain flooding the floor-to-ceiling bay window, but also the kaleidoscopic flashbacks of shifting tactile landscapes leaking into her vision. She opened her eyes comically wide, then quickly squinted hard and rubbed them, causing brief and minorly painful explosions of light to manifest, but she persevered a few more times so that this effect of the cotics would wear off quicker, and get herself fully back to what she thought of as base reality.

After a few more tries, she turned and strode the twenty-five meters across her apartment to the main door. Her appointment with Founder and Octyllion's Chief Genetics Officer was less than an hour away.

Opening the door she shrieked as an earnest face loomed from close range. "Damn imprints blocked my Map!", she realised.

Shock gone, she stepped aside as Mya Theta 41 swept past her and into the apartment, leaving Anastasya momentarily staring at the Goya on the hallway's wall.

"Glad I caught you", Mya said breathlessly, flopping onto one of the sofas. "Ready for tonight?" This was asked with all the enthusiasm of her fifteen years.

"You know it, but I'm Dryving to the office now" Anastasya answered sharper than she'd intended, still gripping the door's handle.

"But you'll be in-game later, right?"

There was a touch of desperation in the voice, and Anastasya reflexively checked Mya's Credyt in case there was a recent drop. There wasn't.

"Told you I would".

"Good". Mya chewed her lip. "Can I walk with you?"

Anastasya couldn't think of a time Mya had ever walked her down to the Dryve bay, but nodded agreement. She figured it was quicker than asking why.

As they stepped into the elevator, two feeds sprang to life. Anastasya had Eryss 1 in the first, sitting in her cavernous office within the Office for Genetic and Evolutionary Research. Her boss's face was inscrutable as she herself watched a feed projected onto her office wall, a small convoy of 4x4s arriving at an entrance portal on Corynth's southern gate, about 150 klicks from O.G.E.R., the Office of Genetic and Evolutionary Research - the de facto HQ of Octyllion. This convoy was showing up as a second smaller muted feed for Anastasya.

"I want you to have eyes on who you will be dealing with", Eryss explained.

"Understood", Anastasya replied, causing Mya to raise an eyebrow. "Work", Anastasya said.

She watched as the jeeps made light work of the muddy terrain. Waves of dirt and water from the recent rain shot out of trail-ruts. A lone 4x4 accelerated away from the others and came to a skidding halt. The passenger door opened and a man emerged, straightening himself gratefully in the manner of someone who had been sitting for a prolonged period, before bending back into the jeep to take out a green camouflage backpack. Her augmented vision identified the man as Governor Laide of Grand Plains.

--- Grand Plains was the neighbouring State to Corynth. An impoverished State, it did not contribute meaningfully to the CROW index. --

With a parting fist-bang to the jeep's roof, she watched the Governor swing the backpack over his shoulder and begin the ascent to the nearest entrance portal alone. He never glanced back.

The elevator slowed its descent.

"You know I've always looked up to you Ana. I just want you to know that" Mya said in the enclosed space, as Anastasya watched her boss and Governor Laide reach the Helpers positioned behind a curved perspex blast shield. The Helpers watched impassively as the tall man stepped into the bombproof body scanner. Anastasya noticed he had to take his bag with him, and remembered then her primary's old pre-Illumination tales: scanning both person and baggage together prevented bombings. Turned out nobody was fanatical enough to blow themselves up alone in a glass tube.

"Sure", Anastasya said distractedly. "I know".

The bomb and contraband scans showing clear on the feeds, the Governor had now extended his arm, palm up, and was stood stock-still as a mechanical arm extended towards him. The tiny needle on the arm's extremity pricked two of his fingers before darting away like a shy fish. Head down and looking at the blood on his finger, the Governor looked to her like an overgrown test tube baby.

"Now we will see", Eryss said in her typical manner, each word enunciated precisely. She was deaf, not dumb.

--- Aural bone conduction is the mechanism by which neural implants allow citizens to hear feeds, Thynks, calls etc. I stimulate their cochleas directly via their implants, and thus, even for citizens whose eardrums are deaf - they can hear via the sound wave resonance in their cochlea. And so how it was with the deaf Beethoven, who would clench a metal rod between his teeth leaving the other end resting on the piano in order to hear what he was playing, it was with Eryss - she had a real-time feed constantly playing so she could hear via her cochlea; the only hint of this to someone who didn't know she was technically deaf, was her pure enunciation of words - she relished pronouncing each, hearing science triumph over nature.

--

Mya again: "Tonight's a big deal, you know? Don't be late in-game. I know how it can go sometimes".

Anastasya ignored the barb, kept her attention focused on the ticker-tape of the diagnostics coming back from the Governor's bloods'. The bar for entry was high, and this man - no matter the importance of his mission here - would have no exception. She understood this, all citizens knew the mandatory entry requirements: and the consequent privilege of being a citizen.

"Bonus loot and drops - said I'd be there" Anastasya said with a tight smile and quick glance over to her ward.

H5N2: negative. Negative for Mongol Flu - or Genghis as it had been colloquially christened – the Governor would be permitted entry to Corynth.

"So Abundance is really going ahead", Anastasya observed. So many months in the making, by far the largest, most enormous, body of work she'd ever worked on. Her pulse quickened.

The elevator pinged, doors opening to reveal a mostly empty bay, a number of empty Dryve's scattered about. Anastasya spotted hers immediately, lit and waiting, aligned with where her augmented vision showed her it would be. She made her way towards it, Mya double-stepping to keep up with her.

Eryss was still raptly watching the ticker-tape. *EDAR variation: negative.* "Yes", Eryss hissed, an uncharacteristic display of emotion which caught Anastasya's attention.

"That gene, what's the significance - " Anastasya started to ask, but was interrupted by Mya tugging on her sleeve.

"I need to tell you something", urgency and discomfort writ large on her face.

There was a pneumatic hissing as the doors of the Dryve rose vertically at Anastasya's approach. Time was tight, she still had to get the man-hunt underway and meet her friends. Not to mention the meeting with Eryss and this Governor. She kept walking.

"Can't you call me later? I really need to get going" she answered, as she watched Governor Laide disappear into an entrance portal flanked by Helpers.

Mya said something, but Eryss spoke simultaneously, drowning her out.

"We have not played for stakes this big in years. I will inform the Councyl of the Governor's imminent arrival, and that we move to operational mode for Abundance." Then the two feeds died, leaving Anastasya with the expectant looking Mya, her face twisted with agitation.

"Sorry Mya, what was that? I didn't catch it".

Mya stared before answering in a resigned manner. "Nevermind. Chat later in-game".

Fine. Anastasya stooped low before slumping into the Dryve. The door shut, and she looked out at Mya, who was wearing a sulky hard expression.

With a shake of her head and a Thynk, Anastasya got going.

I – III

It was the beginnings of the day's rush-hour traffic as her Dryve sped towards O.G.E.R. Every thirty seconds or so a Dryve buzzed past in the opposite direction.

"What a pain it must have been pre-Illumination". Anastasya was day-dreaming on the analog days of big city populations, rush hour a recipe for disaster, the sidewalks crammed with the overpopulated, disease passing with ease. Her neurals were showing contentment. She was a fervent believer in the Way, knew that other peoples' simply weren't tolerant and open-minded enough to join Corynth on the new path the Founders had embarked upon.

Maybe it was the thought of others, of non-Corynthians, but her neurals switched to a pattern which matched thoughts on the Governor. He was unusual, highly - a relic who had survived the world of the past relatively unharmed, plus as she'd pointed out before to some cronies, she'd never met a male in his fifties.

Her cronies had been horrified at the prospect of Anastasya meeting such a person, but she always gave them the same answer: Sybelle had guaranteed he'd be clean (of course!), and CRISPR would sort out anything unexpected that might be missed in a scan. The others were typically unconvinced by such reasoning, but at the end of the day, they got it: there was Credyt to be earned by doing her job and working with this outsider.

A group of three runners were on a sidewalk, the only citizens visible to Anastasya's eye on the streets. She watched them kick out of sight around a corner: pace of two minutes per klick, this their twenty-seventh klick! She selected one of the three in her visuals, scrolling through their mods. Nothing she couldn't have if she wanted.

Her eye caught on something. Further down the street.

"Slow down". The Dryve began decelerating.

Two Helpers had a young male. One pinned each of the aspyrant's arms against the wall while standing face-to-face with him, like someone holding a crucifix up, while a second Helper bot stood ready to the side. Anastasya's eyes spotted the source of the incident: the wall behind them had "REJECTION IS MU" grafittied in ugly jagged capital letters, each one about half the size of the cornered guy. "Caught before finishing", she thought without some little satisfaction.

Anastasya reflexively promoted her personal feed - an anti-rejection protest could draw plenty of attention, earning lots of Credyt if it went viral.

"Stop, Sybelle". The Dryve come to a full halt at the roadside, twenty meters from the disturbance.

She checked her Map, which just showed the young guy, not the Helpers.

Kyle Theta 21. From Deme 15, a ways to come to get caught - and just two months out from citizenship! she marvelled to herself. Anastasya's hand flew to her mouth. A fifteen-year-old aspyrant...

She zoomed in with a Thynk and studied the kid's face, now that she finally had a face to fit to a six-percenter. Nothing obviously different about him she could spot - in fact, apart from the fear and terror, she took it to be a completely forgettable face.

"What the hell was he thinking?", an angry voice asked in her head, the exact voice of Tanya, her best crony and also of the Delta generation, who was on her feed.

"I know! I was just wondering who these crazies are, always voting against Polls. And then at the bomb scanners, you know at the entry gates? Now this – it's the same. Futile."

Silence then as both watched the episode.

"I was angry at them before. But now", Anastasya continued, flinching involuntarily as the lead Helper brought their metal skull to within millimeters of the aspyrant's exposed face, "I just feel *sorry* for them Tanya."

"Mmmhh".

"There's something seriously wrong with them, you know? Willingly throwing it all away for *nothing*. Like volunteering for the guillotine. Is there a gene for self-sacrifice?"

"Wrong analogy", Tanya said, her face - she was also in a Dryve, heading to O.G.E.R from a different direction - set in stone. "It's not *volunteering* for a guillotine or whatever - it's *deserving* it. He's attacking our most basic human right, a cornerstone of the Way. Feeling *sorry*? These scumbags deserve what comes. What I don't get is - how? How could he take spray-paint, go so far as to start spraying that crap on the wall - and Sybelle not nuke him?"

"Ye - exactly. How the fuck is that possible?"

"I mean they're clearly crazy nuts. So maybe - and I mean maybe - their neurals are problematic for Sybelle." Tanya suddenly looked shocked, as if someone had just stomped on her toes. "I don't mean Sybelle can't handle or predict them, just that maybe their madness extends to their neurals".

Anastasya said nothing, but felt bad - she hoped Tanya would stop digging a hole for herself, so changed the subject.

"Still see you shortly in the andron?"

"Ye. And drop your feed from promo - nothing more to see here".

Anastasya grunted agreement. Sent a Thynk to get going.

She turned her back on the street scene, leaving that Theta to the fate he bizarrely sought...such a hopeless action! And as Tanya said, how did he get so far? She shook her head, bemused...*pointless* was a word resonating loudly with her.

Fifteen year old Theta...months to go before citizenship. Mya's profile! And mix in that weird behaviour this morning!

"Sybelle, do an intersection of Kyle Theta 21 and Mya Theta 41."

She braced herself.

Mya Theta 41 is not socially linked with Kyle Theta 21. Then, the words Anastasya had been dying to hear:

There is no pending Credyt penalty for Mya Theta 41.

Anastasya clasped her hands together - hard. There'd be no penalty for Anastasya through implication, considering Mya was clear. Settled back in the Dryve, closed her eyes.

I have prepared an updated list of profiles for the purposes of your license. We have a little time before getting to OGER. Would you like to review now?

Eyes opened. "Yes. I can at least start."

This was a problem she'd never anticipated having - two big-deals, with two huge Credyt rewards on offer for succeeding in both, and both happening simultaneously. Wasn't life meant to be easier than this? She had to focus.

A semi-translucent map of Corynth was visible to Anastasya now, an octagonal donut with Deme 0 as a circular area in the centre of it's 19 surrounding districts. Demes 0 to 4 were protruding and in greenish tint, Demes 5 and below grayed out and flat. This was as per Anastasya's preference, given she would soon qualify for a new apartment in Deme 2, once the Credyt for working with the Governor on Abundance starting to hit her balance.

"Let's see them", a minor tremor in her voice modulation

indicating anticipation and excitement.

A scroller of bios replaced the map.

--- Each male had two scores beside their photo - Credyt score, and IVF compatibility score. IVF historically was a low-success rate treatment; to remedy this, genetic analysis is done between potential donors and primaries. The result of the analysis translates into this latter score, a single number - 100 is a perfect and ideal match, a guaranteed successful treatment. This scroller of profiles only allowed compatibilities for a couple over 90%.

--

Anastasya checked out a few.

"Can you filter by Credyt and, you know...my type?"

The scroll list disintegrated, then reappeared a moment later.

Filtered now based on the preferences your neural activities have indicated when interacting with males previously. Secondarily by Credyt.

A rugged, stereotypically masculine face caught her attention.

Gauge Gamma 13 is a Deme 2 resident since earning citizenship fourteen years ago. His primary was an executive with Octyllion pre-Illumination. His likes are vintage wines, clubbing, and guild-mastering in-game.

A Gamma...how unusual, she thought. High Credyt worth, at the upper threshold for a citizen in Deme 2. 98% compatibility.

"Stay on this one".

As you wish.

She watched as Gauge retrieved a beer from the fridge, dressed only in y-fronts and a t-shirt. He then settled himself on a Lazee large enough for three or four people. From the corner of her eye Anastasya spotted her own heartbeat was elevated; she rationalized it as the after-shock of seeing that aspyrant Kyle getting arrested, and the real fear she'd felt for Mya.

"Jumping in-game, huh?" she observed aloud to herself as she watched him comfortably shifting his weight on the Lazee, beer nearby by on a table. His eyes had taken on that clouded not-quite-there look - the thousand-meter stare, as her cronies called it.

Anastasya zoomed in with a pinch of her fingers; she was watching for the tell-tale sign of the hallucinatory simulation of sensory input I would weave directly in his brain. It was a habit of hers, watching for that moment of flipping. Also, there was envy...she highly enjoyed her own time out of the real.

"Let's go with him, Sybelle", panning the zoom to his biceps. "Tell him I'm interested. Just not while he's in-game. Let him enjoy".

She started to scroll his bio feed, noticed that for some reason he'd no other relationships currently. But all the better for herself, she supposed.

After all, there was no reg against getting lucky now and again.

I – IV

Anastasya's knee-high leather boots splashed the puddles on the steps leading up to the Office of Genetic and Evolutionary Research. The puddles' surfaces were mirror-like prior to her destroying each one's placidity, highly complex (not actually chaotic) fluid dynamic equations governing each splash.

She amused herself as she ascended, working backwards from the output - the actual puddles, the resultant space and patterns - to the starting equations which would describe and predict the exact instance of each puddle, given her input (her boot) to each confined problem space. This was her gift in action, her *just knowing*. If asked she might say it was like being the only reader in a world of illiterates (not that anyone read anything more than a few words overlayed on feeds anymore).

It wasn't an activity or talent she shared or encouraged discussing, and she looked up after a few steps, not wanting to seem too preoccupied with where she was stepping to any onlookers there might be on her feed - the colours and dancing numeric series were hers alone, her feed only showing a standard/boring ascent.

There was a glow emanating from behind a large cloud, making it shimmer compared to the rest. She looked over at it, towards the focal point of Freedom Square, where the statues of the Founders once stood. She fired open an old feed of the seven staring immortally sky-wards and into the far distance, the voice on this particular feed teasing her mom about it - how come her mom wasn't up there if Eryss was?

She reached and passed through the giant double doors embossed with entwining DNA helix's. Her heels echoed loudly on the lobby's marble floor. She passed the Helpers on duty, metal so matt-black it looked like they were wearing ultra-tight uniforms.

Once in the elevator, Anastasya fired a Thynk to bring up the day's menu, and sent another for a coffee - black, Indonesian, highlands of Mount Rinjani. No food, too early for her after the cotics.

Floor 2 opened onto the andron, where Anastasya had arranged to briefly meet two of her cronies, Tanya and Ysabel. She mostly wanted to chat about Gauge, them having seen him on her feed. There was time, she was early still for Eryss.

Stepping from the elevator, the andron's open-plan spread in front of her, one hundred and ten meters in length, seventy-five wide. It was dotted with circular tables comprised of marble bases with obsidian surfaces, each with a varying number of deeply-cushioned chairs of either purple or arterial red hue. It was packed today, Anastasya observed, a busy day in the office - fifteen citizens were there before her.

A woman in a lurid tight red huggie waved over at her.

"Ysabel is on the way", Tanya said by way of greeting, looking up at Anastasya as she approached. Tanya was at Analyst grade, but Anastasya wasn't sure exactly what her crony did. She'd lived in Deme 3 at one point, but Credyt drops had brought her down to 8 now. She never mentioned it, and it certainly hadn't dinted her directness and drive.

"So you finally got something to take your mind off numbers and stuff...you're really going ahead with this? And with Mr. Biceps?" Tanya said, raising her coffee towards her crony in a greeting. Anastasya looked at her own steaming cup sat on the table - too hot yet.

"One hundred percent. You know it's so weird choosing like

that…there was too much choice, if you know what I mean? It's nothing like a hookup…trying to choose someone for a license is *so* tough. I kind of feel like I did Sybelle's job for her!"

"Mmm." Tanya placed her cup down. "It *is* weird you got to choose alright. So be it, Sybelle! All I mean is, I can't even think of *anyone* who got a choice. And how much are you getting again for this?"

Anastasya told her the amount, the Credyt she'd be rewarded for fulfilling the terms of the birth license. She'd told her before - a couple of times - and while it was a lot of Credyt, and possibly her crony just liked hearing such an amount aloud, Anastasya thought there was a certain undercurrent to the question, one she'd been picking up on recently.

"Plus the life-pension".

Tanya's face went from playful and piqued - to frozen.

"What? Come on Tanya, what the fuck is it?"

Her crony exhaled dramatically.

"A *pension?* As well as all that Credyt? For IVF - or no, excuse me - you can even do it the old way if you want! What's up with all that?"

Anastasya watched the wisps from her cup drifting upwards slowly, coiling similarly to what Bernoulli's fluid dynamic equations would predict.

"Are you seriously questioning the Way? Questioning *Sybelle?*"

She regretted it as soon as it was said - way too harsh on her crony. But the truth was, Anastasya wasn't sure herself why the reward of a life pension for having a baby had been offered, why she had a choice in the biological father. And the pension had decided the matter for her, no way was she going to risk asking why now.

Tanya visibly shrank.

"Sorry, of course I'm not questioning. I...guess I'm just jealous." Then, looking suddenly looking rejuvenated, she sat up straighter.

"And anyways, you can always reject it if you get fed up".

"I guess."

"You guess? You *know*" Tanya said grinning forcefully, her old self again. "Collect your pension, reject in a couple of years. Or whenever."

"I wouldn't reject a kid having gone to all this trouble in the first place. Wouldn't be the right thing to do." A pause. "For me", Anastasya said breathlessly. Her pulse had suddenly and rapidly quickened.

Both pairs of eyes locked on each other. They waited in silence; fear and apprehension emotions for both.

Tanya eventually leaned forwards. "That was *close*". *What's wrong with you?*, her look said.

Then, voice louder as she looked round again: "Rejection is a cornerstone of our society, *the* proof of our progress. Besides", she said, dropping her voice a full octave, "it's a very personal thing. What if someone here had rejected a child, and they'd heard you?"

"Fuck, thoughtless of me" Anastasya said, playing her part. It would not have been a heavy one - a few Credyts - but the scale of a Correction wasn't their only point of concern... accumulating Corrections themselves, regardless of the cost of each, could contribute to a cascade-effect drop in Credyt.

Tanya waved it away, thrilled now that they'd dodged what could well have been a Correction.

"We gotta celebrate you finding that guy".

"Gauge. And you know I'd love to. But you know who's coming here - today - to Corynth? In this building?"

Tanya sat back into her chair, lips pouting, hands

smoothing her Luxella. She shrugged.

"The Governor of Grand Plains. I'll be working with him on that project, the one I've been on with Sybelle these past months."

"Mmmh. The one you can't talk about."

"That's the one."

"So how would I know then? But look, when you're done with your numbers thing, there's a Credyt promo for going to this new taverna in Deme 17. The Lost Ark. We should hit it tonight. Fun, and free Credyt!" And then with excitement: "Can you bring him along? This outsider?"

"I'm not sure...he's old, you know. In his fifties."

Two heads from a nearby table turned their way.

"Wild...well, come with or without".

"I'll try, but I promised Mya I'd be in-game for nine."

Tanya snorted.

"Mya? You're too good to her. You've still got the right to put yourself first and have fun, be happy...*secondary.*"

Anastasya raised her hand, elbow bent in the international "wait" signal. After a moment, she lowered it.

"Sorry, was Sybelle. I need to go."

Tanya looked at her crony questioningly as the Principal stood.

Anastasya's face reflected the questioning look. "I can't talk about it".

I – V*

He'd been led straight to a Dryve, which was still parked, and was now wedged tightly between two Helpers, with another immediately behind him in the back seat. Classic execution style, he noted. He was working on staying calm, slowing his pulse, struggling against the old instincts which were firing, his mind fighting to race through scenarios against the three.

As his breathing deepened, he reminded himself of the major advantage on his side - he wasn't a citizen. Their general AI had no direct access to his thoughts, nor of any of his Embassy staff. Of course they'd still be subject to behavioural and emotional predictive analysis - and his breathing and probably facial stress signals would no doubt be detected - but their thought-immunity was golden. This is why, he reminded himself to buoy his mood, they stood a chance - he could critically assess not just the technicals and detail of the payload being offered to his State, but crucially the people giving him the information. Were they on the level, bullshitting him or not, was a judgment he'd be free to make and keep hidden.

That was his mission, and it sure felt weird to be thinking it aloud knowing everyone else's thoughts were as transparent as glass to the Councyl and their AI. "Fuck you!" he screamed in his head. Nothing from the muscle either side of him, not even a blink. He started to relax.

The Dryve pulled off. He didn't ask where they were going.

The windscreen clouded over opaquely before coalescing

into a screen, so that he could no longer see the cityscape through the ultra-wide windscreen.

Evolution of Illumination: A Visitor's Guide to Corynth appeared titled on the screen, along with a saccharine-laced female voice explaining it was mandatory viewing for any visitor.

He immediately recognised Bryna 1, their military head, the Chief Defense Officer, who had served in the old U.S military for some of the time he'd been in, before moving to Octyllion to head some clandestine research. He'd never met her, but knew her by reputation, a female breaking ceilings - back when that was a thing. He figured she likely knew *him* by reputation also at the time...albeit for very different reasons. Linda, if he remembered correctly, was what she'd gone by back then, before being christened in the Corynthian Way.

Her shoulders, square as a parade ground, filled most of the width of the screen.

"Welcome to Corynth. Birthplace of the Illumination."

She was standing some way outside a tall building, far enough that "Octyllion" was a halo above her head, glowing like a lunatic.

"We want you to enjoy your stay" she said, as the camera panned sidelong to show her in a cross profile, "to be safe, and to learn what a truly equal society is. This is a State of reason, logic and science."

She spun back to a full frontal, her smile faltering like a car being started with a dying battery.

"And above all, of bravery - of bravery to embrace the future which reason and science offer, where technology is allowed to reach its true potential unencumbered by old-thinking and unnecessary regulations and laws."

The ex-soldier was bathed in dazzling sunlight, a hint for John that this could be a deep-fake.

"We need to start with some history".

Maybe not fake after all...that smile looked so forced and painful, he decided it must have been the real warrior.

The background changed, Bryna disappeared, and a montage of mostly female citizens, all exuding the confidence of the privileged, walking freely down wide boulevards and partying convivially, were juxtaposed against headlines of violence and outrage from elsewhere.

"The Illumination wasn't just about our tech rendering digital encryption methods transparent, revealing the secrets of the old world to the only being who could read them - Sybelle. Illumination was also about the succession of Corynth from the old United States of America, to become an independent State governed by the same principles and ethics which defined Octyllion - the innate right to happiness, health and betterment that all have, and achieved through the embracing of technology and reason.

"There is no suffering in Corynth, no sickness, disease nor illness. Only bliss, a bliss that comes from desire-fulfillment and freedom from unwanted burdens.

"In every sense, we lead - we do not follow - and we expect you, our welcome visitor, to follow our Way while here. As old-thinking and habits are sadly prevalent in the world outside Corynth still, you will be initially assigned a Helper to assist you during your stay with us. The Helper may become unnecessary after some time based on the behavioral modeling Sybelle will perform on you - you will be informed accordingly.

"This may seem extreme to outsiders, but please remember: ever since Illumination, violence by men against women has been virtually eliminated in Corynth. This was achieved in no small part through the machinations of the world's first general AI, Sybelle. Citizens have neural implants providing direct connectivity to Sybelle, who has the ability to neurally-incapacitate anyone predicted of committing serious crime. As you have no such implant, your Helper will be Sybelle's instantiation, as explained a moment ago, until your risk profile has been determined."

He prayed his "risk profile" would be calculated quickly. And favorably. He wasn't sure how long he could handle the Helpers.

He watched the remainder as he had no choice, though he did find it useful to soak up information first-hand. There was at least some useful info interspersed with the propagandist bullshit, like neural implants being released in generations (Xi being the current generation), citizens' names included the generation of their nimp, and a generation's capabilities being rated in giga syns per second, Gs/s, a syn being the unit of synaptic information. Like Internet speeds, the higher the number the better. There were also a different subset of genetic mods that went hand-in-hand with each generation to optimize performance.

It was a lot of detail, and just reinforced for him that it was extra-terrestrial level tech they were faced with, which was both the attraction of the offered deal with Corynth, and the danger. Deal with the devil, or mana from heaven...this was literally his mission, to determine which was on the table.

But from there, the remainder worked his patience. A sermon from Bryna to justify the naked emperors of rejection and retirement, policies straight from the Dark Ages, grotesquely, bizarrely promoted and accepted as "caring" policies. And hadn't bravery to let science and technology lead, lead to the gas chambers?

They called themselves vanguards in their science-driven voyage of enlightenment - but for him, it was blindingly obvious the voyage had brought them to dark shores. And what sustained them on these shores, ironically, was the one thing they had engineered out of the populace: faith.

It was a frequent topic back home, especially with Ewa and others, but the irony really was unbelievable: they'd removed God and religion, not by outlawing or persecution, simply by the citizenry being programmed to see it as an archaic superstition, the object of knowing mockery. But what they seemed oblivious to, was that they had simply replaced one dogma, one *faith*, with another! Scientism, as Ewa called it.

He had to keep listening, and the Dryve continued to roll, Bryna's excoriation of the male XY chromosome the next topic, and how science proves the superiority of the female of the species with their double X - "less susceptibility to disease and less severe symptoms from illness in general, in addition to the crucial ability to self-heal errors in DNA transcription and encoding". Fair point, he thought - but using that as a reason to do some of the things they'd reportedly done here, the most brutal and coercive totalitarianism, dressed as a utopia of equality, technology, science and reason...like Mao's, surely that was a leap too far! Part of him really wanted to turn and go, but again ironically, the next part of Bryna's sermon served as a poignant reminder of why he was here:

"We were also the first society to embrace the potential that CRISPR offered, daring to go where others hesitated and theorized".

Bryna was now standing under a once-again surely fake blue sky, but thanking God for small mercies, she was shut off in mid-sentence for him, in tandem with the Dryve slowing down and taking a turn. The window faded back to transparency, flooding the interior with dim but natural light.

His ride was running close to the buildings now, enough that the leaden sky beyond was no longer visible, hidden as it was behind the high-rise complex of the Office of Genetic and Evolutionary Research.

He exhaled in a long stream, not caring what the Helpers thought about it, or what intent Sybelle might attribute to it. It had been hard to listen to all of that, but it had been the perfect reminder of where he was, why he was here, who he was up against.

So when the Helper behind him tapped him firmly on the shoulder, he was ready.

I - VI

Anastasya sat in the CGO's outer office, waiting. She'd called Gauge on the way up, told him what she wanted, the situation. He'd been unfriendly, but Tanya had reminded her - was he really going to turn down all that Credyt for "playing his part" so she could use her license? The Way did guarantee her right to be happy. So fuck it, she thought, should be fine with him.

It was a long walk from the waiting area to Eryss 1's doors, but she could see them from where she sat. They opened, and a few seconds later a tall but slightly-hunched figure emerged. She didn't have to check the Map to see the name - it was Yena 1, a Founder and COO of Octyllion. Yena looked over, and Anastasya could have sworn she saw recognition - the natural kind - in her eyes, even from that distance. She guessed her name came up recently as part of the promotion to Principal.

Not long after, she got the notification from me to go in. The doors had closed again after Yena's recent exit, and by the time she reached them the smothered thunk of magnetic deadbolts unlocking was audible. The titanium-concealed-in-oak doors separated an inch or two then stopped, before slowly opening further like lazy petals to reveal the expanse of her boss's office. This Founder's office was hangar-like, the ceiling many meters above Anastasya as she passed inside.

An involuntary sigh of relief as the doors swung back in place behind her. She knew about the weapons, the ceiling. Sybelle had detected no threat, no prediction of such, from her behaviour or neurals - hence, she was still standing. She understood - a non-implant implemented insurance policy made total sense for a Founder. She put one foot solidly in front of the other.

The only light came from the floor-to-ceiling windows which covered an entire wall of the office. This dreary light snuck over Eryss's shoulder, leaving her face in shadow, framed by strands of blond hair.

"Sit".

Anastasya quickened her pace towards one of the ten empty chairs concaved in front of Eryss's desk. Reaching one and sinking into it, Anastasya could finally make eye contact.

"Corynth lives", she said eagerly. "I know how precious your time is".

Now her boss looked up and over her tear-shaped desk, concaved-in around its owner.

"We have known each other long enough to dispense with formalities, would you not agree?"

"Of course" Anastasya answered, kicking herself mentally for her nerves. How come it was all so casual over the years at home whenever Eryss called over to visit (drink with) her mom - which was regular enough for as long as she could remember (apart from before the coma where she'd no memory of Eryss, but that was likely due to the neural damage), yet here in O.G.E.R she reverted to this annoying kiss-ass style behaviour?

She noticed her boss's gaze wasn't 100% focused on her - Eryss was obviously still working, her nimp projecting directly to her retinas. Anastasya couldn't open a feed to see what Eryss was doing, as Founders could exempt themselves from feed broadcasting, a topic which received virtual unanimity in the Polls whenever it arose.

She let her eyes walk the room as she waited for Eryss to finish whatever it was she was doing. The giant mural on her left caught her attention. Hard to miss, it adorned most of that entire office wall, depicting Eryss alongside her fellow

Founders in that iconic moment, the jubilant speech on the steps outside O.G.E.R marking the triumph of Illumination.

It was almost mythic - the successful completion of the program of relocation of those opposed to the Way, and the recognition by the States of America of breakaway Corynth as an independent corp-run State. Surprisingly, Anastasya saw they were all there — even Alyx 1, who had been a traitor, working against the other Founders from within. Alyx stood taller than the others in the mural.

Anastasya felt eyes, and turned her head to be pierced by the Chief Genetics Officer's gaze. The intensity in the blue eyes could be startling.

"It is OK," Eryss said, "OK to think of her. Alyx did some great things. I leave her there as a reminder of good times." Her blank face didn't look the least bit reminiscent, despite her tone suggesting otherwise. Anastasya pushed the observation aside.

"I want to congratulate you in person on your promotion to Principal Mathematician."

"Thank you. I'm very happy to serve the greater good".

"Of course you are. Yours is a rare talent, and it is most gratifying to witness it being applied the way you have recently on Abundance. It is immense, the scale of what you and Sybelle have done. Something which a generation ago would have been unthinkable even for a pharma giant, for anyone to achieve, even with all the resources those old corps could muster - yet you have completed it to perfection. A genetic payload, a gift-box of care, protection, enhancement and fortitude, and all tailored specifically for the people of Grand Plains. Those poor people."

"Yes", Anastasya agreed, "So happy we can help".

"As am I. I called you here because the Governor of Grand Plains is in the building. Before he joins, I want to reiterate your duties, and convey to you the Councyl's appreciation for what you are about to do. Closing this deal with Grand Plains may in time be ranked alongside Illumination in terms of significance for our State", Eryss said, her hand sweeping towards the muralled wall Anastasya had been studying moments before.

"Your number one priority is to convince Governor Laide of the safety of the payload we are offering. You have viewed his dossier?"

Anastasya's nod was her answer.

"Then you know he is too old-school to trust an AI - even one as advanced as Sybelle. He needs human reassurance, someone to trust - not a machine. As a co-creator of the payload with Sybelle - not to mention the rigorous testing and scenarios you are familiar with - you are ideally placed to help persuade this man of the veracity of what we are offering. And of our good intentions. Find your own way to communicate with this man. We are counting on you to get the job done."

That said, her boss leaned forward. The light from the panoramic window framed her in a soft whole-body halo.

"The job is only complete when he signs off and green-lights our genetic payload for distribution to his people. Understood?"

Anastasya was grateful for the easy opportunity.

"Understood. And I don't see there being a problem. I mean the data speaks for itself - we've tested this *thoroughly*."

"Good" Eryss said, pushing herself back in the chair and then rising from it in one fluid movement, the light at her back silhouetting her darkly.

"Very good."

Eryss walked towards one of the curved edges of her long desk, bending to a drawer which had opened at her approach.

When she straightened, she had a gun in her hand.

"The other side of the equation is that we want you to remain safe while fulfilling your duties. This", Eryss said, proffering the volt gun to Anastasya, "will help keep you safe".

Unexpected. *Was it a test?* Anastasya didn't reach for it.

"I don't think I need this...I mean, Sybelle will surely be monitoring the Governor? I trust her completely." Nervous laugh.

"Indeed. But indulge me - not just as your boss, but as an old-family friend. I do not ever want to be the bearer of bad news for your primary, someone who has given so much to our cause."

The Chief Genetics Officer sat perched now on the edge of her desk, the weapon loosely in her hand as it rested casually across her lap.

"Part of your work will involve consultations and calls with medical experts based in Grand Plains - and these calls will undoubtedly be from within the Grand Plains Embassy. Remember, while in the Embassy you will have no connectivity to Sybelle, your nimp will not function – unable to Thynk, no feeds nor augmentation. To be even more explicit: you will have no protection from Sybelle should anything go wrong."

Anastasya nodded sagely. She knew all this, it wasn't exactly something she was looking forward to...but it was necessary, and her choice to pursue this opportunity. *Credyt.* Enough Credyt to set her up for a *long* time. But now it seemed like the Chief Genetics Officer genuinely wanted her to be armed!

Her boss placed it on the table and slid it towards her. Anastasya gingerly picked it up - deceptively light given the damage it could do.

"Solo without Sybelle and incommunicado with an outsider adult male...you will be stepping into the dark ages. You know how to use one?"

Anastasya nodded, remembering her training, afraid to put her finger near the trigger. Perceptive as ever, her boss read her mind. "Sybelle has matched it to you".

Feeling safer now that she wouldn't be fried due to mismatching prints, she toyed with it - until she remembered Sybelle would neurally incapacitate her if she literally even thought about raising the weapon towards the woman in front of her.

She dropped it onto the table, making sure it pointed into a corner of the office.

"It's easy enough - point and shoot I guess", said with fake nonchalance.

"If you do not want to take it now, fine - just slide it back over. Come on, slide it - yes. There will be one available for you to pick up at the Helper station outside the Embassy".

"Understood". Guns always made her nervous. Maybe she watched too many old movie feeds.

Eryss disappeared the weapon back into her desk.

"Sybelle, admit him."

I – VII

Anastasya swivelled in her seat to get a view of the elderly man as he entered, triangulated closely by Helpers.

Her facial reaction displayed her surprise at how fit he looked for a man his age without any mods. He was nonetheless dwarfed and out-muscled by the Helpers, Corynthian genetics winning the battle against fifty-something unmodified nature.

As he neared the crescent of chairs before the Chief Genetics Officer's desk, Eryss rose from hers.

"Leave us", the Chief Genetics Officer said, "I think our guest can be trusted". The Helpers turned and left.

The formality of the handshakes was performed. The Governor sat one seat over from Anastasya, on her right, in the line of ten seats. But he had eyes only for Eryss.

"The Corynthian Councyl welcomes you. Drink? We have bourbon, real old-grain".

Of course you do, he thought. "No thanks, Chief Genetics Officer."

"Eryss."

"Eryss, then. I'd prefer to get down to business. Unless we're waiting for anyone else?"

"We are not".

"I rather hoped I'd also be meeting with Yena, your COO?"

"Unfortunately not possible. She is en-route to Brazil."

Anastasya arranged her face neutrally.

"Brazil? So you're bankrolling the push to remove the last abortion limits?"

"Advising NGOs and the Brazilians on human rights issues. Did you really come to discuss this?"

"No, no I didn't. You're right. I'm here to sign - once we can satisfy ourselves on what we're getting. Gotta say thought, it's disappointing we had to wait until Grand Plains had something vital to Corynthian interests before we get essential assistance from you...I'd consider life-saving treatments a human rights concern. Now that you mentioned it".

Anastasya's heart rate had picked up, Eryss's had not.

"We are *both* looking to gain life-saving materials, Governor: you, our genetic modifications and medical help. Which will protect you immediately from Genghis. On our side, Sybelle needs arcadmium to manipulate quantum qubits in her molecular transistors, something impossible otherwise; no other known element can super-conduct at room temperature. So forgive me for reminding you the obvious - we both need what the other has. Let us not squabble, stake political positions. Let us deal."

A moment passed where eyes were locked across the table. Jon spoke next.

"To deal, I need to inspect the goods - to use that metaphor. So if Yena's not here, who do I work with to satisfy ourselves on the safety and quality of the genetic payload?"

"Well". Eryss smiled broadly, lips curving upwards in a sharp-V.

"That is why we have assigned one of our brightest minds - Principal Mathematician Anastasya Delta 3" - gesturing with an extension of her right arm - "to be your aid. She can provide you with access to all relevant information and details. You are free to share and communicate with your experts and colleagues back in Grand Plains as you wish. We are happy to facilitate comms, or of course you can have secure "privacy" from within your Embassy. Speaking of which, we spared no expense in terms of refurbishments there. We want your stay to be pleasurable as well as productive".

"So, here's the thing: you and your AI know more about me than I probably do myself - including just what buttons to push on me. So I have to ask: if not Yena, why *this* young woman?", rotating momentarily towards Anastasya, but still looking at Eryss. "What was the selection criteria for picking her as my..." and there he paused, searching for words: "...my chaperone?"

"Ah", The Chief Genetics Officer exclaimed, as if he'd just revealed the solution to a deep mystery. "Principal Mathematician, if you would be so good as to explain to our visitor about Sybelle and yourself?"

"I work with Sybelle on practically incomputable problems - halting problems, as Turing described them. No matter the resources available, some mathematical problems need intuition to solve them. Typical elements of these - "

Eryss's hand shot up. Stop.

"True of course, but how about skipping to the part about why *you* work with Sybelle, not someone else? I think *that* is what our guest wants to understand."

Anastasya twisted in her seat, mentally reordering things quickly. Their eyes searched each others, before hers ran over his stubble - it looked bristly and sharp, flecked with white pinheads. For a second she wondered how prickly it would feel, quickly pushed the thought away.

"I have numeric synesthesia, Governor, meaning I can taste and smell numbers, see each number in it's own unique hue and form. This helps me to evaluate mathematical landscapes not by calculation, but by *sense*. And in certain circumstances, particularly very high cardinality dimensional spaces, me sensing or intuiting my way round is many orders of magnitude faster than even a general A.I such as Sybelle can achieve. Sometimes, not just faster - I can sometimes do what Sybelle cannot."

She noted he hadn't flinched a muscle at her mention of synesthesia, no discernible change in his body language at all. She pushed on.

"Gödel proved there are always classes of mathematical statements which are unprovable by the formal logic of the rules of the mathematical system which expresses them. There is, however, one informal way to prove or disprove these statements: by employing *insights* from outside the system which expresses those problem statements. Those outside insights are me...my numeric synesthesia allows me to give insights based on my intuition, into statements described in certain mathematical systems - technically its following the Reflection Principle - and Sybelle can then code those insights into a *new* further evolved mathematical system based on the evaluation of these otherwise impossible propositions."

She stopped, drew breath. Still had his attention.

"Does this partly explain why Sybelle's abilities are so advanced? I mean...it sounds like she literally has new mathematical systems available to her, systems or capabilities no-one else can possibly have unless they have *you.* Or this external insight, as you call it".

Anastasya glanced at the Chief Genetics Officer. She hid it quickly, but Anastasya could see the surprise that had briefly lived there before her boss's face swallowed it.

Eryss cleared her throat and interjected. "There is no other like Anastasya. None we are aware of. Anywhere."

He looked again at the young woman in the chair two over from him.

"Just so I have it right: you give Sybelle - through your *sensing* of numbers - the magic ingredient to build this new mathematics?"

"Right".

"Mmm. it sounds like you give her new axioms or truths, ones she could never determine herself."

"Yes", Anastasya answered slowly, not even trying to hide her surprise. "You grasped that *very* quickly."

He waved an arm. "I've a background in something relevant. And it wasn't hard for our people - for the world - to see Sybelle was special beyond anything that could have been anticipated. We've speculated in depth what could be going on with her. But we always assumed it was related to novel AI techniques - either that, or her molecular transistors." He exhaled loudly, like a relieved swimmer coming up for air. "Turns out her magic is human. At least partly".

He looked from one to the other. "Someone once said maths is the language of the universe. Would you agree?"

Anastasya nodded vigorously in spite of herself. He was engaging, his brain still evidently sharp.

"And from what you've just said, you've got more letters in your alphabet than anyone else. Therefore your language is more expressive. Quite the advantage. Hardly seems fair though, does it?"

Eryss scoffed loudly.

"Fair? It is all relative. Is it fair that we reap the benefit of our bravery and sacrifice in the fields of progress and innovation? I say "yes"." Anastasya was sure her boss was on the cusp of saying something more, but had figuratively - or maybe literally - bitten her tongue.

"I'll have that drink please, plenty of ice".

It was a deliberate diversionary tactic, one to gather his thoughts at what was a most unexpected turn of events. If it was true, and she really was an AI-whisperer, he'd just stumbled upon Corynth's secret weapon - although surely they wouldn't expose her to him? But on the other hand, there was a lot at stake for Corynth too...arcadmium really was their AGI's lifeblood, and thanks to the ancient rules of supply and demand, his State were coming up trumps in that regard. But could a serf really negotiate with a maniacal lord?

He clenched down on his excitement, forced himself to focus as the drink arrived at his side thanks to a bot. The way he thinks, there would be two points for him to determine: could he get a read on this alleged genius, and know when she was lying? Secondly, was *she* capable of knowing the legitimacy and veracity of the information she would be discussing with him...did she know her stuff?

He sipped the bourbon, trying to take as little as possible whilst not making it obvious.

"Time is short, but I'm still so curious. Your role, that is - what it is that you *actually* do. More precisely".

He could have sworn the look from Eryss told him she knew what he was up to - when interrogating someone, you asked about their story or alibi repeatedly, ad nauseum sometimes, until a fracture, an incongruity appeared. Evidently, if she did cop, she was fine with it. Which spoke volumes, potentially.

"Well...", Anastasya began. Hadn't she explained already, and hadn't he grasped it? Maybe it was senility, outsiders still suffered from that. "Let's start with this: why would the world's only general artificial intelligence need human intervention or help? I mean, our brains' computational and learning ability are nothing - literally - compared to Sybelle. It's like an insect's grasp on relativity versus Einstein's. The answer is, that even an AGI faces a fundamental limit in terms of the computability of certain problems - which Turing referred to as the halting problem, for example. You know, Alan Turing?"

A nod.

"So, he pointed out that some computations or calculations - while not requiring infinite time to complete - are so vastly complex, or have so many variations and permutations, that they *practically* require infinite time to complete...even for a quantum computing machine running on molecular transistors like Sybelle."

She paused to check - the audience was still with her.

"Calculations like the traveling saleswoman problem, if the variable set are sufficiently large - are you familiar with that?"

"It came up in my military training - goal is to devise the shortest, most efficient route for someone to take given a list of destinations you can only visit once each. Right?"

"Perfect. For example, if you had just fifteen places to visit, there would be 87 billion possible routes the saleswoman could take".

Observing his reaction, she clarified.

"That's right, 87 *billion*. So if you had almost one hundred thousand possible destinations, you can appreciate the complexity, and why a solution is practically incomputable! When we do genetic sequencing, we're dealing with roughly *one hundred thousand genes* per person - women have slightly more than men, due to the difference in the sex chromosome - so this exact kind of problem comes into play for Sybelle. In maths we call it an NP-hard problem - the most difficult and exhaustive problem to solve in mathematics. Still with me?"

"So almost limitless possibilities exist when you're doing gene sequencing - as I presume you need to do for testing the genetic payload for our people. I get that."

"Yes! So that's the problem Sybelle has - she'll not be able to fully compute the possibilities in a reasonable time, and hence how can she choose the most optimum, the one that implies the less risk for whoever gets the genetic treatment in this case? A way is needed to answer what are unanswerable questions for Sybelle, or even sometimes just to shut down variations of calculations – prune the possibility tree – by me *just knowing* certain things. Mathematical things."

"What Anastasya means", Eryss interjected, "is maybe best explained by an analogous example. You are a chess fan?"

"You know I am" he answered plainly. They knew everything...how could he get outside their box? He determined to drink no more of the bourbon.

"Then, being of the generation you are, you no doubt remember Kasparov being beaten by Deep Blue. The first time a computer beat such a Grandmaster. Kasparov claimed immediately after the match that it felt like he had played a human. What he did not know at the time, was that he *had* in fact been playing a human...there was a human Grandmaster watching a screen showing the variation lines Deep Blue was calculating. The Grandmaster had a kill switch, and would kill the calculation of any variation he knew was losing for Deep Blue. Whenever he did this, Deep Blue would immediately stop analysis and move onto the next variation, thereby saving computation time that would otherwise be wasted on a losing variation. The point is, the Grandmaster did not calculate that the variation was losing...*he just knew*. Instantaneously, through intuition, experience...genius."

Anastasya jumped back in.

"In fact it may have been a team of Grandmasters, not just one. Anyway, that's part of what I do - guiding Sybelle to topologies that have a strong probability of yielding the results we want. My synesthesia allows me do this damn quickly, and hugely - massively - accelerates the NP-hard calculation process."

He'd heard enough for now to reach a decision. He'd forge ahead with this AI whisperer for now, begin the verification process of the genetic payload, and update his trust assessment of her as they progressed. He'd have the chance to observe her more closely.

As they walked out, both their attention was simultaneously drawn to a dark canvas. It was hard to miss, afforded its own section of the wall and the only artwork in the office lit from underneath by pale floor-lights, which had not been on earlier - Anastasya was sure. She thought there was something about the light in the painting - so lifelike it seemed like a feed, a freeze-framed one - from some darker age.

"Is that…" Jon muttered. He stopped, Anastasya drawing up alongside him.

"That's Caravaggio" Jon said, as Anastasya drank in the darkly-shining metal plated soldier grabbing a bearded man by the throat, while another man - an acquaintance of the bearded man? - screams.

"But this one was destroyed".

Eryss's voice carried from behind her desk. She'd sat back down as soon as the two had turned to leave.

"It is Sybelle's reproduction - painted, not printed. It captures the essence of sacrifice perfectly, no?"

Self-sacrifice…just like that kid Kyle, Anastasya caught herself thinking. Although there was no-one to scream for *him* when he was arrested. So lucky Mya didn't know him.

I – VIII

They were being watched, Anastasya Delta 3 and Governor Jon Laide. But only by two, Founders Eryss and Yena.

--- They were a powerful combination, these two Founders. Action and will-to-power had been the hallmark of Eryss's rise, and while Yena was happy to let Eryss handle the kinetics, she was herself as ruthless as the truth in her own dealings, driven by the same will and unyielding belief in science and progress. Their removal of Alyx 1 had cemented their relationship, and forged a new nexus of power within the Councyl. Over the years they'd demonstrated a rudimentary telepathy between them, the old magical kind - nothing to do with implants.

--

The Copa provided a sun-setting backdrop to Yena's feed, but really Eryss had eyes only for the shared feed of one of the labs in O.G.E.R, where their Principal had started on the process of explaining the analysis and testing done to ensure the safety of the genetic payload being offered to Grand Plains and its Governor.

As predicted, it was all going to plan. They were fast company, Anastasya and the Governor, and were off to a productive start on her mission to convince him of the safety of the genetic payload.

He'd known the possible side effects of DNA editing, running the gamut from hair loss to death: tumours, cancers, loss of vision, dissolution of internal organs, impotence etc., and had been quick to point out they weren't just theoretical risks; the Covid "vaccine" debacle had etched that one indelibly in the world's mind, bad publicity which was difficult to get over. But getting over it, and getting him to accept that what we offered was safe, was Eryss and Yena's goal.

--- Their *main* goal, the goal they had communicated to the remainder of the Councyl. I say Eryss and Yena, as the remainder of the Councyl, the other three Founders - had elected to allow Eryss and Yena run this op, Abundance, solo. My calculations had shown that by doing so it would be more efficient and maximise the chance of success.

--

The Founders where mostly silent witnesses as time passed in the lab, where there was much lecturing at screens and holographic representations of molecular DNA structures, at the predictive modelling tuning which was twinned with the genetic changes, and the clustering of these predicted molecular changes into bins of risk. Throughout, Anastasya was the wizard, conjuring these representations and data grids deftly but with no physical touching of screens nor directing gestures - something clearly fascinating the Governor.

A relationship of trust, mutual respect and credibility between these two was essential for the success of this op, to get the deal signed, and this was building. Anastasya found herself being engaged in a way none of her crony's ever managed - he was actively interested, a quick study, seemingly sincere. Throughout he studied her closely, but not obviously; her emotions were not masked when discussing something she was passionate about (like Abundance), it was very likely his read on her was developing at pace.

Yena, as per her usual pattern, deigned not to be the one to break their silence. She was the closest person alive to Eryss - of that she was sure - and was wary of the depths she hadn't plumbed in the Founder's psyche, depths which were unquestionably there despite Eryss's placid exterior. Not one for demonstrative emotion, it was understandable people might think they were on calm waters, only for the wrong word or phrase to explode like a depth-charge, sending whatever lay beneath roaring towards the surface. And so it was Eryss who finally commented about the Governor seeming to grow in confidence the more he heard from

Anastasya.

"Agreed, he'll see her as the real deal very soon now. If not already."

In the near-total gloom of her penthouse, Eryss drank from her goblet of Merlot. She found my replication of this no-longer-existent grape remarkable, the resultant wine's taste a mini distraction for her mind, a puzzle to be solved.

Anastasya was commenting on the scale of the effort - she was doing a good job in communicating the complexities in a graspable fashion.

"Sybelle and myself can manage this massive computational effort in a practical time-frame – it's computationally prohibitive otherwise, even for the rest of the world's silicon-chipped supercomputers".

"Prohibitive, as in, just slow?"

"As in, not feasible. This isn't just a single modification like for a virus vaccine - we're talking widespread changes to the genome. Remember the traveling saleswoman analogy."

"It is something, is it not?"

The ethereal instance of Yena looked questioningly towards Eryss.

"Seeing the connection and synergy build between them. I never grow tired of witnessing it, you know, one of science's more majestic achievements. Humans, owners of free will and agency, reduced to jigsaw pieces, joined together by Sybelle's algorithms. Emotions and desires, motivations and fears, loves and losses, all merely defined edges on their individual piece! Even if the edges are not a perfect match, they are be nudged to be so. Is that not beauty? Anti-entropy."

Yena agreed, Eryss continued.

"And this particular solution is coming together exactly as predicted. Correct, Sybelle?"

Confirmed. The probability of success of the prime objective has increased to 96.1%. Governor Laide's -

Eryss waved her arm to interrupt.

"That is fine, let us go into that later."

Something was developing in the lab. The conversation was moving towards being subversive, after he'd asked her how exactly the Thynk mechanism worked.

"It's basically a thought - a hard thought, is the best way I can describe it. It's maybe like the difference between shouting something explicit in your head, versus daydreaming".

"I see...so then Sybelle is basically always reading your thoughts through your implants, listening, waiting for you to explicitly think something, for her to then action". He leaned back in his chair. "Sounds like constant mind-reading by your State."

Anastasya considered him carefully.

"You make it sound like a bad thing? Yes, all our "System 2" thoughts are used for training Sybelle's algorithms, something which benefits society as a whole. So what if Sybelle is listening? We all benefit, and she only acts if we want to send a Thynk or a command."

"Really? What if I have a thought to commit a crime...like to kill someone?"

"Well she'd intervene. Of course".

He waited a beat. "Isn't that thought-police territory?"

"Ha!" exulted Eryss. "She will not have a clue what he means. Perfect!"

"Sybelle, no Correction for this", Yena interjected.

Understood.

"They'll be thick as thieves after this", she asided to Eryss, who was visibly thrilled. "Especially when she thinks of all the

Credyt she didn't get penalized".

Sure enough, Anastasya was repeating the well-rehearsed "party line".

"Look at our murder or rape statistics compared to yours... which do you prefer?"

"Yours, obviously. But I could also achieve those stats if I locked everyone up 24/7".

So it continued, a proper back and forth, but all the while they orbited closer. Their progress was sealed when asked him out for drinks with her cronies, ostensibly to satisfy his curiosity regarding Corynthian habits and practices. His reaction was positive, as it would help with his goal of determining her bona fides.

Eryss shut the feed.

"I think we have seen all we wanted. Quite a result - as expected."

Yena concurred. But then, something played across Yena's face as she studied her crony over the feed. Her question was unexpected.

"Going back to your earlier point Eryss...it leads us back to the Predictive Problem, does it not?"

Whatever Yena's motivations - and bravado - in asking this, her vitals showed an increased heart rate and pulse. Tension and hyper-alertness in her neurals. She was poking the bear, and knew it.

"Don't you ever wonder, is all *we* do also predicted by -"

"No - I do not."

But her face said otherwise. Fear was writ there, momentarily, but unmistakable. Yena's neurals showed a sudden euphoric spike - she had been fishing, and caught her target: something Eryss feared. An evolution of the simulation hypothesis.

"This is why we have the prime directives for Sybelle. Sybelle, shut off now, do not monitor the rest of our conversation".

I – IX*

They were in a Dysc, sweeping towards Deme 17. Jon could feel a pervasive subtle vibration, the result of the frictionless magnetic buffering, as they moved through the ceramic tubes at speeds he preferred not to think about. The travel pill he'd been given in the station had melted immediately on his tongue, extinguishing the nerves he had before boarding, as well as prohibiting any nausea from kicking in.

It was tight for him though - the elephant grey interior was blandness personified, coupled with being wedged between the sealed door and the obscenely-muscled Helper.

Anastasya was almost constantly on calls – he'd noticed the word "fun" came up frequently. She seemed more energized and enthusiastic about the prospect of this coming fun than the prospect of playing a leading role in sealing their deal. This wouldn't be a tick against her in his books, in fact the opposite - it would enhance her credentials as someone genuine, demonstrating "normal" tendencies. And this was vital for him, it turned out this whole trip came down to whether or not he could believe what he was being told by her.

His logic was like this: yes, Corynth needed the rarest of rare earth metals from Grand Plains for their AGI's existence, but their need wasn't necessarily mutually exclusive with something untoward. Logically it wouldn't make sense for Corynth to bite the hand that feeds them in terms of arcadmium, but he was dealing with zealots here, the birthplace of rejection and God knew what else. He needed to treat them as cautiously as he would if Jihadists had come bearing Christmas gifts.

He'd nothing concrete to base his suspicions on. Life had just raised him not to believe in outrageous good fortune. So his focus would be on Anastasya as the litmus test as to the bona fides of Corynth's offer: if he could believe in her as the genuine AI whisperer, then it would then "just" be a case of being convinced as to the safety of the genetic payload being delivered to his people. Had they covered all the angles safety-wise.

So he'd happily socialize, observe her at play, and also take the opportunity to learn first hand about Corynthian society and norms. They could gawk at this outsider with old-thinking, he'd observe.

According to her calls they were meeting at a taverna, The Lost Ark. Anastasya would be meeting some guy called Gauge.

He asked her if Gauge was her boyfriend.

"I've never met him before. But he's going to be the biological father of my child."

"Oh…"

Anastasya tilted her head to one side from her seat directly opposite him. "Is that strange for you?"

"Honestly…yes. Sounds like an arranged marriage - minus the marriage. Where I'm from - I mean, in most places really - we get to know each other first, maybe for a while, before having kids."

"But our way is very efficient and avoids the world's main problem".

"And what's that?"

"Overpopulation" she said, looking mystified.

In response, he stared. She laughed.

"Don't look at me all superior. You just have to listen to the science behind it. Overpopulation expends resources needlessly, causes huge damage. Besides, every baby should be wanted, would you not agree?"

Still, a stare.

"'Want' is a two-way street. A baby should be wanted by both primary *and* State - it just doesn't work with either being selfish. You could think of it as a collaboration - between Sybelle and the Councyl, and us citizens with our individual choice."

She tossed her hair, smoothed her nails on her legs.

"Do you have any children?"

"No", he answered quickly, and looked away to the only thing in the Dysc to look at, apart from his Helper. The clock on his left, over the sealed door. Almost bang-on 4pm: 16:00:04.

She followed his stare. "Cold as ice, white as a snowstorm. Minty taste. Zero, I mean".

"Can I ask you a personal question?"

She shrugged.

"What's it like with this gift? I mean, did you always have it?" He was speaking so rapidly compared to normal, as someone thinking fast and changing a subject might do.

"Since I was twelve. Before that I only have very vague memories - and I don't have memory feeds from my youth, probably cos of all the fits I had. I had epilepsy since birth".

"Do you still have it?" His official comments over the years on this and other "social" topics were on the record - for what it's worth, which was not a lot. So he knew Corynth were proud of their "cure" (as he called it) for epilepsy, exactly as Denmark and Iceland had proudly announced they had a cure for Down Syndrome, about thirty-odd years ago. Abortion was their cure, just as rejection was Corynth's cure for epilepsy or any abnormality or imperfection. Yet here was one imperfect still living. The way he saw it, she was a glitch in the matrix or a blessed anomaly - either way, thank God.

"Epilepsy? No, not since the coma."

"Coma?"

"I'll get to that. But when I had epilepsy, I've been told it was bad. My primary opted *not* to reject me, and that was on top of my biological father being...well, let's just say she kept me despite the burden I must have been. She really went out of her way. I'm so lucky."

"Your...primary? You mean your mother?"

Anastasya glanced again at the clock. Three minutes and ten seconds to arrival.

"She also really went to bat for me after my, eh - my incident." Her orange nails were fidgeting manically. Seeing him notice, she stopped immediately, locking her fingers down on her thighs.

"When I was twelve I had a major seizure - I don't remember it all - I was in a coma for weeks' after it. My brain apparently went haywire during the seizure, and then rebuilt itself during the coma. It was on waking from it that I had this "gift" - as you call it.

"Let's just say I didn't take well to it at first. I thought I was gone mad. I ended up after a couple of years in rehab after various penalties and Corrections. Honestly, I barely got through it I think. Again, my mom baled me out. I guess I was lucky. Again".

Both looked away at the clock, then like a pendulum they swung back to each other.

"You've never travelled by plane, have you?"

"No" Anastasya replied, "obviously" being unsaid but clear from her expression.

"It's something I used to do a lot of. I remember one day flying out of JFK - the airport in old New York. In front of me in the boarding queue was a man and woman, and their child - I presume it was their child. A beautiful girl of six or seven years, braids as thick as rope in her hair.

"But all I could think about when I looked at her, was who *wasn't* there. You see", he said, straining at the straps, "over fifty percent of black babies were aborted at that time in New York. *Fifty* percent. Literally for every child you saw - walking, skipping, laughing, crying, standing in an airport queue - there was another child dead, body marked for incineration or lying in medical waste buckets in New York hospitals. And this killing of black babies wasn't racist - it was called *progress*."

He sat fully back. The Helper's heavy eyes as well as Anastasya's stare bore into him - but there was no turning back now. Anger.

"So my question is: what's your missing percentage? *You* survived the threat of rejection - how many others don't?"

The seconds on the clock moved, but nothing else did.

"Do you've any idea at all?"

The Helper cleared her throat, but Anastasya beat her to it.

"Rejection statistics are not published. To do so would be judgmental on women who make that decision."

Then she shook her head, disbelief washing away the shock.

"We have every right to be happy - it's a universal right, even your U.N says so! You sitting there judging us with your old-thinking - it's laughable! Disgusting, even."

He held his hands up. "Hey, I'm not judging. Simply pointing out reality, the truth - if you want to see it. Anyway, I'm glad you weren't rejected. You're like Melissa Ohden".

Her screwed-up face said it all. "Who?"

They sat in silence for the last of the trip.

I - X

The three of them made their way on foot towards downtown, Deme 17. Jon had asked to walk from the Dysc station.

The streets were mostly empty, long-drained of the foot-fall bustle these old U.S. cities would have had. Neon signs reflected off the asphalt made shiny by the recent rain, and this double glare - lurid pinks, cheesy oranges, lime greens - gave an eerie glow to the cloud covered streets. There wasn't much talking between them as they went, Anastasya chatting hurriedly on her feeds.

Turning a corner Jon could see a square ahead, and here there was a proper throng of people, the square fed by the route they were taking as well as many others, tributaries feeding this mini-mecca.

Most citizens had that long stare and didn't pay them any attention as they passed, others were clearly wasted and doing well to be shuffling along, others again entering and leaving the tavernas and clubs dotted round the square. There was the occasional stare, but that was to be expected given the Governor was a red dot, seemingly led by a Helper.

The Helper was acting as the tip of their wake as they cut a swathe through the throng in the square. The noise was amplified in this central spot, as if in a natural amphitheater.

"Fun?" Anastasya shouted at him, as they sidled their way diagonally now across the square, towards a less populated corner.

Jon raised a "yes", but his attention was drawn to the most

decorated building in the square, directly opposite them.

A realisation grew ever-so-slowly as his eyes took in the casino-like exterior: it was a *Pleasure Plaza*. Enormous rainbow-shaped neon signage sat atop a large number of entrance doors. They seemed unnecessary right now, given there was no current footfall through them. He stopped and turned to face it, tried to feel revulsion, to generate the required anger…but looking at a Plaza now, an actual Plaza, he just couldn't light that fire – it looked too banal, too harmless. He stared harder as he experienced this mental incongruity – he just could not match what he knew, or heard, happens inside a Plaza to its unremarkable exterior. But the more he stared, something did begin to seep in. The exterior greyed to a monolith, its lack of people going through the doors suddenly emblematic of what such a place was – an eraser of people.

He dragged himself away, had to play catch up to follow them into a side street and a much quieter artery. A young woman pulled up alongside him, matching his stride right behind the others now. Jon turned his head. A leering gaze met his.

"You sharing?" she asked lecherously, loudly enough for Anastasya to hear.

"No". Turning round.

"Too bad" the newcomer scoffed, giving Jon one final lingering head-to-toe appraisal before spinning on her heel and going back in the direction of the square.

"I won't ask what that was about" he began, easy to hear each other now on the cobblestoned quieter street.

Anastasya grinned.

"We passed a Pleasure Plaza. Have you ever been inside one?"

Anastasya's grin dissolved like acid burning through butter.

"Obviously not. Sorry, didn't mean to snap. What I mean is, they're primarily for citizens with low Credyt."

He mulled it over, but before he could follow up, she'd changed gears.

"Look!" she was pointing down the length of the street.

"Here they come. We can wait here for them", she continued as they stopped outside their destination, The Lost Ark, burning torches flanking the doors warming the air not unpleasantly in the gloomy light.

"This'll be so *fun*".

Reserving judgment, Jon could make out from this distance a group of three - one of them male. He turned to her.

"Is this your man?"

"Gauge, that's his name. He's a Gamma".

"Does Gamma have some special significance?"

"His generation? There are rumours. We don't really have time to get into it, but - "

A strong hand dug into the Governor's shoulder. He spun on instinct.

An angry neatly-trimmed bearded face snarled into his.

"You taking my woman?"

Giggles from two girls behind his accuser, and the rakish grin which exploded from the guy's face broke the spell of immediate danger.

Anastasya stepped around Jon.

"What do you think you're doing?"

"Relax, just having some fun with the outsider. Right buddy?" the guy drawled, slapping him on the back, too hard for it to be mistaken for playfulness.

"Right. Good laugh".

"Ana!" the tall blonde woman said, high-fiving. "Ready for some fun?"

"Who isn't? Jon - I mean Governor Laide - this is Gauge Gamma 127. And my friends Tanya Delta 33 and Ysabel Delta 14."

"Looks like we're the odd ones out" Gauge said, winking at Jon.

"The Deltas?" he explained, seeing Jon's non-plussed face.

"Oh right".

He was being scrutinized intensely, the leggy Tanya making no effort to conceal her interest. He could practically feel her eyes crawl over him.

"He's *way* more together than I expected. For someone his age", she clarified.

He figured he'd been called worse.

The third in the group, Ysabel, peeked out from behind the Helper's shoulder - a safe distance behind her and hence from himself, Jon guessed. The look on the mousy face, framed in a dark curtain of hair, was one of consternation and concern. Anastasya and Jon both noticed.

"What's wrong with him?", jabbing a highly manicured nail at him. "He's - he's got no Credyt, no feed. Nothing! And he's red!"

This reaction was inevitable - it had always been a question of "when" rather than "if" this problem would arise. Anastasya felt almost like she was walking around with a tiger on a leash...some people were bound to be terrified of an unmodified and non-implanted outsider.

"It's OK Ysabel, he's safe - and he's with me, and he's working on a project with the Chief Geneticist herself", the prepared answer coming off pat. Anastasya stepped closer to Jon, to better demonstrate her point.

"He's got no Credyt coz he's an outsider. He's red for the same reason - he's not connected, has no nimp."

"So what happens if he, I don't know - if he cuts loose or something!"

"He's here with a Helper, isn't he? But he's also the Governor of Grand Plains. The State beside us? Listen," Anastasya said more conspiratorially, last roll of the dice. "I've been *alone* with the guy - that's right - *without* a Helper, and he has no nimp, remember? And nothing happened. He's no danger, trust me".

"So that's why your feed was off" Tanya said suggestively.

"You all go in, we'll follow in a minute" Anastasya said. "You too", she said to the Helper, who immediately obeyed.

Ysabel threw a fiery parting glance over her shoulder at Jon as she went into the Lost Ark. Once the others had all followed her in, Anastasya turned to the Governor.

"Sybelle, kill my feed", she said - aloud, for Jon's benefit. "Sorry about that".

"No worries. Happy you think I'm safe to be around" he said deadpan.

Anastasya studied his face. She either didn't get the joke, or chose to not acknowledge it.

"We're working together, so I'll be really open with you. I'm responsible for convincing you to acknowledge that the genetic payload Sybelle and myself created is safe for your people. And this is extremely time-sensitive, as Genghis is closer every day.

"Initially I assumed this would just involve convincing you of the math and completeness of the simulations we did to test it...but now I think there's more to my role, I need to do *anything* to help convince you. So tonight is part of that anything - you'll hopefully get a better idea of our society and citizens, and also then you'll know *me* better.

"Earlier you clearly thought some of my answers to your questions were off the wall - it's OK, I know you did", she said, in response to the Governor shaking his head.

They drew a little closer together in reaction to a cold wind that swept down the street. It's strength bent double the flames from the torches in front of The Lost Ark.

"It's just, I don't want those opinions of mine on topics unrelated to our work to color what you and I need to agree on...does that make sense?", looking at him quizzically.

"A *lot* of sense", he said. "If I got you right, what you mean is, if I see others - like your friends - have the same opinion as you do on the "controversial" topics, I won't think less of your opinion in general and on the payload analysis?"

"Yes!"

"I'd never think less of anyone for debating me - trust me on that."

"Trust is exactly the point!" She pulled even closer to him, enough to get the faint whiff of some aftershave, despite the stubble he wore. For a fleeting moment she wondered how she smelled to him.

"And what exactly are you looking for anyway? A mistake I made? A mistake by Sybelle? We talk about trust - if you trusted us, you'd just accept the work we did and take the offer. Your people would be already protected against Genghis and - "

"It's your Councyl, your Founders I have trust issues with - not you. What am I looking for? A Nessus shirt."

"A Nessus? *What*?" She looked at him blankly, expectantly, but there was no more forthcoming.

He waited, watching her eyes begin to flit.

"Oh,...oh I see. The Delaware tribe, British Colonial army... smallpox??"

She took a step away from him. Shivered hard.

"You think we'd *deliberately* harm your people? I thought you just wanted to be sure we hadn't made mistakes."

Her outrage was real, he was now reading her very quickly. There was hurt there too.

"It's something I need to rule out. Nothing personal - as I said. But when you're responsible for people, like I am, the history of the human race is littered with examples of much worse."

"OK...but not Corynth! Not us! What - " she managed, stopping a moment to avoid spluttering.

"You think we'd deliberately give you Genghis or something?"

Jon didn't say anything, just studied her.

Anastasya's brown eyes watched him back. Was he clinically paranoid, or just deliberately needling? She couldn't decide.

"I have to be sure", he said eventually. "Let's get that drink?"

I – XI*

Green cylinders of Absinthe, square brown bourbons, round-bottomed golden tequilas, various wines and ports decorated the table. Whatever he or anyone in their group wanted, even if off the menu, was available, compliments of the Councyl.

He'd started with a Kentucky bourbon he'd long ago written off as a taste he'd never again experience. It had a delicious lingering banana bread after-taste, but he'd managed to limit himself to just two glasses, switching to wine instead - cask strength wasn't what he needed to be getting into on this mission.

Their table was candle-lit and oval. There were two deep booths on each of the table's long sides. Anastasya was between him and Tanya in one booth, Ysabel and Gauge the other. They were far enough from the taverna's main bar that they could hear each other over the music.

So far, things hadn't panned out as the Governor had likely expected. There'd been no fire - no debates, no outbursts like Ysabel's earlier episode.

Initially there'd been the standard questions about what he was doing here, why he was working with Anastasya. Both of them had answered plainly - can't talk about details, working on a collaboration etc. It didn't really matter what they'd explained: the other three were happy to stick to their preconceived notions. That it was related to the Mongol flu (Genghis) was their main idea, coupled with Anastasya doing whatever-it-is-she-does with numbers.

The one thing that did spark a little attention was when he declined the hospitality of the bowls of pills which lay in the center of the table. As Jon didn't have a nimp he couldn't natively partake in the consumption of hypno, so a hypno synthetic had been provided in pill form for him, along with other cotics.

When he'd declined, Tanya told him that he was right to - that hypno without a nimp would be like taking Viagra without having a penis. She was laughing too hard to explain further, so Anastasya had helpfully explained how in-game sex was widely considered superior to sex "in the real". All thanks to NCCs.

He was learning a lot. He was told about neural correlates of consciousness, how they were the key to Sybelle's ability to weave an alternate world using nimps. Not in those words, but that was the gist. Early VR was all visual and audio - tactility, smell and taste were unsolvable until nimps provided a way to leverage NCCs.

It was all about stimulating the postcentral gyrus, a part of the brain he'd never heard of, but was told was the primary neural brain receptor for touch. Different parts of the gyrus were related to different parts of the body - and stimulating one area of the gyrus would create the experience of actual body touch in a related body part. So then a neural correlate of consciousness was the stimulation of the postcentral gyrus by Sybelle, in order to create certain somatic sensations. Tickle the brain in the right spot, the leg itches.

It was frightening for him to hear, casually over drinks, how advanced his reclusive neighbours were - but here it was, an excellent (and yet another) summary of their power. Implanted citizens could be made *really feel* sensations, a neural experience indistinguishable from the real deal.

And hence the loopback to the original sex question - in-game sex was better than in the real purely because of the science. The regions of the gyrus corresponding to pleasure were out-sized compared to any other regions; this just made Sybelle's stimulation of the gyrus in the pleasure regions so easy to do, and the number and combinations of NCCs that could be created plentiful.

At the end of Anastasya's mini lecture, Tanya had chipped in with her nugget of info: the area of the gyrus corresponding to the genitals was right beside the area corresponding to the feet.

"That's why we have foot fetishes!" she'd shrieked triumphantly.

He didn't argue with that, nor encourage further.

For him, it was another feather in Anastasya's cap. She'd taken a crowd-pleasing rabble-rousing topic and turned it into a science-lecture. And the others had let her. She was a survivor, her talent/ability/genius marking her as so different from the others, yet she managed to forge a place for herself in a culture which was ironically anti both intellect and reason, despite being built on science and tech.

But then on the other hand, she was so similar to them in behaviour and opinions. Anastasya and Gauge: this was their first time meeting in person, despite them planning to have a child together - something he still couldn't get his head around.

He wasn't one to judge people, but he couldn't help but think Anastasya might have a bumpy ride with the guy. From what Jon could see, the most interest Gauge showed in Anastasya was when Tanya put her up to a parlor trick of multiplying "big numbers" in her head - ostensibly to show off her "genius", but clearly to have a freak-show cheap laugh. He liked that she'd taken it in her stride - it was even genuinely impressive.

By now though, the other three had long lost interest in anything other than themselves as a conversational piece. A

Narcissist's Anonymous meeting was how he'd describe the evening to Iva or someone back home.

There was a lot of insistence on having "fun". Posing and preening, arm and hand gestures interfacing presumably with feeds, hardly any tech-uninterrupted "normal" conversation.

The weirdest part was the posing - looking at Ysabel, he could see it now again. Glass raised and held immobile close to her face, lips pouting, eye lashes batting - and this while she was just talking to Tanya. He would have understood had there been a camera in her face, but there was none he could see. The minor mystery was solved for him when he remembered that *other people* were the cameras - everything these citizens saw was a feed for others to follow.

Ysabel gave him a filthy look when she twigged his attention. Tanya followed her stare, and then gave Jon a filthy look too - of differing intent.

"Planning on hooking up while here?"

"Not really. Maybe next time" he answered carefully. He could see his Helper in a mirror on the wall. She appeared to be hovering directly behind his booth like a living Sword of Damocles.

"All work and no play…" Tanya laughed suggestively. "Tell you what: I give you permission to hit me up anytime you want, OK? Don't be a stranger."

He was lost for an appropriate response, so let his eyes roam the taverna in order to disengage from Tanya. It was raucous, like a truck-stop on a country Friday night.

He fiddled with his watch, pulling the bezel in and out on his green Omega Seamaster. It was an old habit he'd picked up standing at checkpoints.

His attention was drawn to a lady he guessed was mid-thirties or pushing forty - so very much on the older side of both the Lost Ark's clientele, and also of the citizenry of Corynth in general. This lady - and for some reason she reminded him of a "Ruth", even though he knew such a biblical name would never surface here - was swaying at the bar out of sync to the music, three or four drinks to the wind. She was still being served by the bots, which was Corynth in a nutshell for him - anything goes, apart from common sense.

Beside him, Anastasya suddenly sat forward, talking with controlled exasperation.

Gauge noticed Jon's interest, and leaned over.

"Bit weird, huh? Seeing people talk to themselves?"

"No, not really. We have phones. But I was just trying to guess who it might be, or what it's about. Nosy of me".

"I get it. And it's Mya, this kid she's the secondary of".

The Governor's curiosity kicked in. He wished he could see a feed for himself, see what it is they all saw.

"How did you know who it is?" he asked. "Like, does it flash up for you too, or how?"

Gauge shot him a wry grin. A superior one.

"You must be suffering alright! Personally I don't think I could survive not being connected. But no - it doesn't flash up, it's more that all feeds and calls anyone gets are visible to any other". He shrugged. "And I can drill down to see more info on the person - Mya, in this case."

Jon tried to imagine how that would work, the endless snooping on each other.

"I don't think I'd like that invasion of privacy".

"Correction", a female voice erupted from speakers embedded in each booth.

The effect on the table was immediate. Immobilising.

"'Invasion of privacy' is an outdated and obsolete term, referring to an old-thinking concept that regarded privacy as a human right. Privacy was in fact the enabler for murders, rape, and crime of many varieties. In the Illumination Corynth solved the problem of privacy. 'Invasion of privacy' is now an obsolete term."

Anastasya stared quizzically at Gauge, who just shrugged and opened his palms face up - nothing to do with me.

"Further, the usage of 'invasion of privacy' in reference to feed tech is incorrect and misleading.

"There will be no penalty for this infraction, nor Credyt penalty for the citizens who were involved in this discourse.

"Continued vigilance with regards to old-thinking and outdated incorrect terminology is strongly advised."

Jon waited for more, and when it didn't come, held up his hands in apology.

"Well..." They were all staring at him. He felt as awkward as a virgin talking to a porn star.

"*Well*? Well that was manual as *fuck*", Tanya exploded. "Invasion of privacy? I'll invade your - "

Anastasya clasped a hand over Tanya's.

"We all make mistakes."

"Careful, OK?" Gauge added, holding Jon's stare. There an edge to his voice, and a none-too-subtle change of mannerism.

Jon looked around the table.

"Hey, I'm sorry everyone", he said over the music, laying his palms flat on the table, looking from shadowy candlelit face to face.

"Where I'm from we can say what we like, there's no concept of fact-checking speech. If you don't like what I say, simply don't listen to me."

He may as well have said he'd been abducted by aliens.

"It's just Sybelle's way of helping us when we're wrong about something. Citizens can make mistakes and be misinformed, so Sybelle helps us out and let's us know when we're wrong, what the correct thinking about a topic is."

Ysabel chipped in. "Can you imagine what would happen if we all went around with the wrong ideas about things? Pure chaos" she finished, emphasizing each of the two last words slowly and loudly.

"I see. Does it happen often?"

Cumulative blank stares were his answer. Either it was such a decoration of life that they didn't even notice it - like if someone asked him how many times a week he stopped at a red light - or else they were wary.

Before any more could be said, the back of Gauge and Ysabel's booth was bumped. Ysabel let out a whimper. Gauge whirled round on his seat, leather squeaking in protest at the sudden movement.

Jon saw his Ruth stood there, lilting from side to side.

"Sorry to disturb", she slurred, "wanna dance?" she asked Gauge, poking him on the shoulder with the hand not holding a drink. The intimidation of the Helper stationed almost beside her obviously wasn't enough to stem the influence of a river of booze.

"Don't touch me", Gauge retorted with disgust, jumping up and turning to face her over the booth's high back. Judging by the rage in his face, Jon figured Ruth to be lucky the booth separated them.

"Your time might be up, but spend it in a Plaza why don't you? Go on. *Now*", he commanded, making shooing gestures.

Ruth's watery eyes desperately tried to focus on Gauge's. A lone tear crawled down her face, forging a canyon through her makeup. Then she turned with as much dignity as she could muster, picked her way back towards the bar.

Gauge sneered a final time, shook his head and sat back down. He snorted disbelief.

"Fuck! What a loser".

Jon took his eyes off the retreating Ruth, regarded Gauge.

"What did you mean her time is up?"

Gauge snorted again.

"I forget you see nothing. *Know* nothing".

Jon stared back, expressionless. He could feel Anastasya shift uneasily in the booth beside him.

"I can see her Credyt. *That* wasted has-been's dries up end of next week". Gauge sat back, snaking his arm around Ysabel' shoulder. "Then she'll be retired".

The Governor had been on the record over the years in what passed for the press in Grand Plains lamenting the "distraction economy" in Corynth, which helped render the Corynthian citizens mostly oblivious to "the killing all around them". He spouted the old adage of ignorance being bliss etc. This was all theoretical for him then, but now here he was, witnessing first-hand a woman - younger than he considerably - scheduled for retirement within a week or thereabouts; and the group indifferent, accepting of her coming retirement as a fact of life like old-world taxes.

The true life-expectancy in this Capitol of Science (as Iva, chief of medical research in Grand Plains called it) was unknown to him, impossible for them to obtain, as was any info of real value to them about Corynth. Unless they could somehow open the eyes of a citizen highly enough placed to access such protected info. And when people are involved in any system, there is always a potential vulnerability.

This trip had given him a rarity, a chance, to possibly identify such a person first-hand. He was looking for someone with a mind amenable to be opened to the truth he saw.

"She's a lot younger than me. Plus in the rest of the world, retirement has a very different meaning than it does here. I'm not going to spell it out, I won't put you through another Correction - but I guess you know what I mean".

"Why should the State spend resources on a citizen who isn't conforming and performing?" Tanya demanded, her spittle sparking one of the candles on the table. Before he could reply, Anastasya cut in.

"What my friend means", she said, smiling grimly at Tanya, "is that thanks to Illumination, we do things differently here, Governor. Everyone is afforded a standard of living and citizenship based on their Credyt, which covers the debt society owes you. Your Credyt is based on your contribution to society, the status of your genes - many things. This citizen", Anastasya shrugged with a sad grimace, "has had a good life and citizenship, but it's almost over. That's life. Life-pensions are rare. As they should be".

Calm under pressure. And in front of her peers, soon after a Correction. Did she really believe it all? he wondered. However deep her beliefs went, it was plain to him that she was different...and difference was a rare buoy in this sea of conformity.

His Ruth's messy progress towards the exit caught his attention. There was nothing whatsoever he could do to save that lady from her fate, but out of solidarity he watched her out of sight.

I - XII

Once again the Omega slid down Anastasya's wrist. She'd have a bot remove some links. But getting loaded, hypno'ed and in-game with Mya at the anniversary event - that was now's priority. She had something extra to celebrate, the Credyt boost for the successful start on Abundance, which pushed her past the 10,000 threshold for an apartment complex in Deme 2.

She let the watch jangle loosely. Why had he given it to her? Did he expect something in return? She laughed at the idea blooming...although he wasn't completely unattractive, despite his age. Tanya certainly would agree, was in fact desperate to land the prize and have a night with an outsider over twice her age. She was fuming when he'd turned her down.

Anyway, she now had a genuine and working trinket to show off, a real relic from old times. A relic, a bit like he was with his old-thinking. But then, he was easy to get on with and Anastasya could see herself work with him. Over the next week she'd convince him on the safety and thoroughness of what they'd created, her and Sybelle's payload. Of that she was sure now.

The elevator pinged and she strode out onto her floor, the one she shared for a short while longer with Mya and her primary, Sandy. She took a moment at the Möbius-strip canvas hanging on the wall by the elevator door. It was a cheap trick, the strip, but intriguing nonetheless - impossible to pass without trying to trace your way to the inner section.

She left it, began the final couple of hundred meters to her main door.

A message.

Be on time.

Fuck! Why didn't Mya even bother checking the Map? Anastasya flashed a Thynk back, *there in fifteen minutes*, despite being only thirty seconds or so from the door at this stage. Mya was just so hungry for attention these days, it was at least stifling, at worst annoying. Would it be the same with her own child, she wondered? Maybe this was good practice, good prep.

She shuffled her flat-heeled leathers off outside her door, losing them in the claret colored carpet, squirming her toes into its depths. It was an old ritual, something she'd seen on a feed about beating jet-lag - not that she'd ever had jet-lag, but the idea of toe and foot massaging your way to a more zen state of mind appealed to her.

With her Thynk the door opened to a scene of minor bedlam.

"I hope you don't mind Ana", Mya half-shouted, managing to look guilty and stubborn at the same time.

Mya was leaning over the sofa which comfortably housed three lounging aspyrants. Anastasya could see two of them were already in-game. Looking around the room of young Thetas, for a fleeting moment she wondered - as she often did when seeing groups of youths - how many would make it to citizenship. Surely the odds were with this bunch though... their Credyt was excellent, and Thetas were somewhat a golden generation.

"Who are - ", Anastasya managed, taking the scene in as she scooped up her flats and hurried across the threshold, surveying her living room as she did. The onyx counter with stools around it had become a smorgasbord of gourmet cuisine strewn about haphazardly, and what she assumed must be non-alcoholic sodas and juices. There were what, five - make that six - aspyrants here, all fuelling up, doing pre big-game rituals. They were all wearing variants of the same latest youthful fashion - Comets lounge wear.

"I just asked a few friends around for the event. Hope that's OK?"

As Anastasya surveyed the scene, Mya spoke again, moving around the big sofa to Anastasya. "Thought it would be good to run in-game together."

Anastasya regarded her with a skeptical eye.

"I know, I know - but it was last minute. My mom wouldn't let so many of us in our place, so I asked Sybelle the odds of you minding, and she said it was about 50/50. I asked her not to tell you - you would have said "no" off the bat - and that I'd take the Credyt penalty if you were mad. You're not mad, are you?" Mya asked quickly, as if the thought had just suddenly struck her.

"It's fine", Anastasya answered with an exaggerated sigh. "Next time just tell me".

"Thanks! Everyone, this is Ana - Ana, everyone!"

There were two lukewarm "hi" responses, minus any eye contact. Not unexpected.

And really, it *was* fine - yes, she would have liked some notice, and on any day prior to today she would have been thrilled to jump in with Mya and her troupe in-game, grab bonus loot. But things had changed – for the first time she felt a pressure, a presence, the poltergeist of responsibility. Business, State business, real world consequences not just for her and her Credyt and the license, but for Corynth.

And it was a lonely feeling. Nobody here, nor Tanya nor any friends would know what she was feeling - responsibility that she had now, on a project for the CGO, was alien to the very vast majority of her fellow citizens. She had to *sacrifice* for this project, like the early starts with Sybelle, and needing to take it easy and not have too late a night tonight. Eryss or Sybelle hadn't mentioned this as a consequence when she'd agreed to get involved. Responsibility, it turned out, could be the enemy of personal happiness...maybe a necessary evil when you got to Principal. Hopefully rare.

Cross-checking simulations of the generational impact of introducing wholesale genetic changes to the Grand Plains population's pool in the morning, she figured a rested and sated mind to enable her synesthesia be at its tactile peak for traversing Sybelle's datascapes was called for. So she'd play, but physically far from this younger crowd, none of whom would anyway appreciate her efforts and responsibilities.

Her mouth was turning cotton-bally, the way it did when a long-yearned for hit was coming. She downed half a bottle of some fruit juice, nobody paying her any attention as she picked it up from the counter. Then she walked towards the bay windows, calling for Mya's attention, excitement building in a rush, as she knew the time would be soon.

Mya had moved over to talk earnestly with a red-haired, freckled and blue-eyed wisp - Stacy Theta 90, Anastasya read. Quite a striking combination, the hair, freckles and eyes, Anastasya thought...serious planning had gone into that kid.

"I'm going to leave you guys to it, go in-game from the library".

Mya's face registered surprise - then disappointment, reaching out to press her secondary's arm.

"I'm sorry, I know I imposed. Tonight will be...*special*" she finished, puzzling Anastasya with the meaningfulness in her stare. Special?

"I'm just busy right now with work, I told you earlier? I've got a big day tomorrow, I need to really unwind. On my own terms." She could have placated her more, but she was wasting valuable time, hypno calling like a siren.

Mya nodded at her secondary, and Anastasya didn't like that knowing look on her face. Why did she often seem like she thought she was superior?

"Right", Mya drawled. "We'll let you unwind. Just hook up asap in-game with us, OK? It's gonna be special, and I want you with us. At least witness it."

Anastasya squeezed her arm. Hard. "I'll see you there in fifteen. Promise".

Then trying not to actually run, she turned and made for the library door, Mya's voice ringing in her ears. "Don't switch off *too* much."

She was at most one minute away from getting her hit if she got straight down to business. She flashed a Thynk for a hypno hit, and now through the library door, made straight for the centuries old oak desk. She scampered to the side where the chair and drawers were, and not bothering to sit down yanked open the top built-in drawer. A small gold box was the sole item in the drawer. She took it out, fumbled the lid open, the springs in the box kicking in and pushing up the lid. She poked the multi-colored pills around until she got her fingers round a pink one and popped it in her mouth. She swallowed with a gulp. Done. These mixed brilliantly with hypno.

Shaking her head, she stood taller. She slowly clicked the lid closed and put the box back in the drawer, snucking the drawer shut with a bang of her hips. Inhaling deeply, she walked back around the desk, letting her fingers walk over the spines of the books on the floor-to-ceiling shelves which covered the walls.

Her destination was a tan leather armchair which sat like an obedient dog in front of the desk. Before she sat, she pulled the stopper from a bottle of rare Lisbon Port and poured for a few seconds into a tumbler sat beside it on the desk's corner.

The anticipation was a special pleasure. She knew the

chemical reaction the hypno caused in the brain took about five minutes to fully hit, the pills chasing in very shortly after. Maybe it was similar to the placebo effect, but that knowledge didn't stop her starting to sink like a submarine losing ballast. The tan armchair protested with a wheeze of puffed air as she dropped into it, port glass expertly balanced in-hand.

She sat, sipped, then rousing herself after a few moments leaned over to plonk the diver's watch on her antique desk.

The Omega's landing sent up a small explosion of dust from the large, yellowed blotter. Through the dust her eyes roved over the books, her collection covering the walls entirely. She'd be the first to admit she'd never actually read a whole book - but inhaling, touching and holding them was a real hit.

--- Her primary's clout and connections had helped her acquire them, but even so it had taken years to amass the hundreds of spines now revealed in the dim yellow lamplight, arranged on the shelves by relative height. They were hard to come by not because they were contraband like in China and the remains of Europe - it was purely because citizens had neither need, nor desire, nor time for them. It was an *extremely* inefficient and obsolete means of information transfer and absorption. But the biggest drawback was that as an activity, reading was not interactive enough. It took *concentrated effort* to painstakingly read every word, repetitively roving your eyes in the same linear pattern. Anastasya had long realised that her feeds got essentially zero traction if she had a book in her hand – reading just didn't pay in terms of Credyt.

--

She briefly closed her eyes, and as they swam on a couple of covers, she'd a thought that sometimes intruded – she could see her donor's name adorning one of the spines. She squeezed her eye and shoved the thought away.

She saw the others making the leap in-game, Gauge a few minutes ago, followed closely by Tanya and Ysabel. She still decided to wait, let the anticipation build, her senses to heightening and simultaneously lightening.

Her thoughts sank back to the acquirer of tomes, her mom,

Dehlya Alpha 1. She'd have to visit her one of these days. Now that she was a Principal and soon-to-be primary, she'd a good excuse to get out to District 0 and face-to-face her.

She lifted and downed more of the port with a silent cheers gesture to the unresponsive bookshelves, and sent a Thynk to take her in.

Anastasya had that familiar sense of fading from the world, like falling very slowly backwards in an endless swoon. Sybelle's intervention drained her visuals of color to the point of bland greyness, while simultaneously toning down the aural input from her inner ear, in order to enable the in-world volume which relied on bone resonance.

There was that prolonged moment of nothingness, of existing in a void - and then like magic, Anastasya was reborn.

I – XIII

Dusk was fast approaching. The dying light of a pregnant sun bathed the tree-lined cobblestoned avenue stretching in front of Anastasya. It was an arterial route leading to Aurora's citadel, the meet-up point for tonight's event, and was packed. She took a moment to find her bearings as Aurora fully materialized around her, the flow of avatars adapting to her sudden appearance like water diverting around a rock in a stream. The event portals opened soon at the citadel, the water of people flowing in that direction.

Fully present and materialized, this was a moment she always savoured. And not just because of the pill and hypno. She'd left the real completely, nothing of it remaining - no sound, no taste, not even the dregs of the port were detectable on her tongue. She shifted her weight from one foot to the other, hefted her bow from left arm to right, feeling the solidity of the pliant wood. Her augmented feed and Map, with names and Credyt and usual stuff, were the only clues of a world outside of this.

> --- A distillation of reality to its primal fundamental pieces, then re-rendered in all its glory, for all citizens - regardless of their Credyt status. "Sybelle's greatest invention" wasn't unheard of as a synonym for being in-game.
>
> --

Of similar height to her real-world self, Anastasya's avatar fell in step with the crowd. Her shimmering archer's bow was strapped across her back, one she'd been hoping to trade up for some time. She twitched her biceps, feeling the coiled power, ready to let rip.

Boisterous guffaws were coming down the avenue behind her. A group of five she saw, without turning around. A massively-shouldered warrior in smoldering crimson battle armor nudged her shoulder in passing, almost sending Anastasya flying. Taking a few quick steps she managed to right herself from tottering over.

"Sorry honey", a gravely voice rasped loudly from behind a face-plate. Anastasya's eyes flashed to the avatar in front of her, a shimmering axe which looked like it weighed as much as a healthy calf lolling loosely from his left hand. She couldn't believe it.

"Tamsyn? It's me, Anastasya. Theta 3. We used to live in the same apartment". *Before you got downgraded.*

"Anastasya...right. Long time. How are you?" The monstrosity turned to the four behind him, waving the axe casually at them in a "halt" motion.

"Some night, right?"

Anastasya was finding it hard to concentrate on the conversation, given the insane stats her feed was throwing up for this group. They were the creme de la creme, with Tamsyn their diadem. As her eyes roved greedily over their gear, she couldn't remember seeing an avatar so maxed out before - ever - and in every regard.

"Sure is." She felt self-conscious now with her child's toys compared to the veritable nukes they had. But then...Tamsyn's status back in the real wasn't so good, she'd even dropped a further Deme down. It was funny how it sometimes went like that, Anastasya thought - in-game gear and drops improved in direct inverse proportionality to Credyt falls in the real. One of life's coincidences.

"So you're in Deme 19 now", Anastasya said, "How's that working out?" She winced as soon as she said it - it could hardly be interpreted any way other than being hurtful.

The warrior stopped the axe from swinging in a way that almost defied gravity.

"Fine. Well - gotta move. Don't want to miss the kick-off", the warrior growled, turning.

"Good to see you" Anastasya said to the warrior's back. She knew the type - Tamsyn would keep living it up in-game right until retirement in a Pleasure Plaza. She'd heard the rumours of in-game retirement coming - without the need to visit a Plaza. Allegedly there'd be a setting you could choose - an irrevocable choice - that when you die in-game, Sybelle would kill-switch you in the real. The reason it hadn't come to a Poll yet was apparently the finer details - like what if you took it easy in-game and didn't raid? In theory you'd live forever. But once some boundaries were put in, like the daily need to raid on ever-increasingly difficulty levels, Anastasya thought it'd be workable. Or maybe it could be at least trialled, she thought, watching Tamsyn stomp off.

Then she noticed something very odd. Mya was showing on her Map as being *inside* the Citadel. This was reserved for uber-elites and NPCs. Mya was neither. Checking Mya's group, she could see two others were in the Citadel too, the other three in other cities, but in reserved places there also.

She fired a request to join the group, and put a voice on it too, saying aloud - "Hey, what's up? I thought we were all running *together*?"

She thought for a moment that Sybelle had misunderstood and took it that Anastasya was talking to someone here, that she hadn't transmitted her message to Mya's group. She was about to ask again, but then Mya replied - rather breathlessly, Anastasya thought, as if the kid had just sprinted a short distance. Knowing Mya that was usually a tell-tale sign of excitement.

"We'll meet you outside the Citadel".

"OK. But what are you all doing in different places? And *inside* the Citadel?" This time no reply was forthcoming. Anastasya took off at pace - not running, but almost. This was ridiculous, being ignored like this - Mya had begged *her* to join. She was a Principal and deserved better, and even through the pill knew Mya was up to something. She checked, but their feeds were off - no visuals on them.

"Ana", the young voice spoke, calmer this time. "I told you this would be a special night. Sorry for messing you around."

"It's fine", Anastasya said, breathing deeply and kicking herself for getting so worked up over teenage kicks.

"No. Things are not fine. Listen to me", Mya said urgently in a tone of such sincerity it brought Anastasya to a stop. "I know you dropped tonight, but focus Ana. You have nothing to do with this, and the Councyl should know that. I'm really sorry if I get you into any trouble."

Anastasya felt a shiver coursing down her spine - her real spine it felt like, impossible as that was.

"What trouble?"

"Open your eyes Ana. God! You're so smart yet so blind!"

Anastasya was struck dumb, a sense of dread smothering her like a wet blanket.

The growing crowd around her let out appreciative gasps as in the distance a feed the size of an apartment block materialized over the Citadel's buttresses. A young girl's smiling face lit the air. The crowd roared their greeting to what they thought was the start of the event. But Anastasya sensed better.

"M-Mya", Anastasya managed weakly, knowing she was powerless to stop whatever they had in store.

The young girl was shown in a collage of short smiling visuals, her name - Caly Zeta 21 - showing up in a frame at the bottom. The initial cheers faded to polite clapping, the crowd assuming this was one of many citizens to be lauded tonight for some achievement: standard fare for an event of this importance.

But then that familiar voice - to Anastasya that is - made a proclamation, her young voice loud and clear over the public announcement channel. Only then did it dawn on Anastasya why they were inside the Citadel...access to Aurora's comms system.

"Caly Zeta 21. A fourteen year old Corynthian aspyrant with the world at her feet. That is, until she was killed - *executed* - by our State."

At this gasps mixed with laughter erupted sporadically across the assembly, and Anastasya, fighting the paralysis she felt in her numb limbs, turned to take in the vastness of the crowd assembled in front of and behind her, before turning her attention back to the giant pig-tailed girl on screen.

The smiling portraits and feeds had changed. Caly now in a strait-jacket and bound to a metal chair. Leather straps lashed across her chest and legs. The camera angle on the feed was downwards, indicating that whoever's feed this was had been standing looking directly down at the immobilized aspyrant.

Anastasya could hardly breath, and not just because of that girl's predicament - she recognised that room, or rather, she'd been in a room just like it. It was one of the med rooms in Rehab - she was sure. Seeing it now, and the girl strapped in the chair, was like someone opening a window on her past - one she didn't want to look through. She could smell the hopelessness, taste the despair.

Caly was sobbing, clear snot bubbling from her nose, eyes swimming. The laughter had died in the crowd, silence reigned.

Still the watcher, whoever it was, kept her gaze directly on the young girl.

"Affirmative", the watcher's female voice could be heard saying. Then: "Now, Sybelle".

"Nnn-" Caly managed before her neck suddenly arced in a massive spasm, face contorted in a severe grimace, neck muscles bulging impossibly. She gurgled a prolonged effort at a scream, before her head bounced violently forward.

A dripping sound could be heard, like rain falling from a faulty gutter on a stormy night, and the eyes of the feed followed the noise down to a steady stream of blood and pus-like material, pooling rapidly on the floor directly under the young girl's flopped head.

A surgical gloved-hand reached out from the feed and lifted the head by the chin with two fingers. Caly's crimson death mask revealed itself, her face below the nose a mess of blood and fluids, her eyes wide like a shocked owl's. The hand removed itself, the head fell quickly down again with a tiny bounce. The feed froze on that final frame.

"Killed in cold blood. *This* is rejection. Wake up -" the voice boomed, before being cut off mid-sentence in exact sync with the feed blinking out of existence, the young night sky of Aurora revealed in its absence.

Anastasya frantically surveyed the faces around her, expressions morphing from shock...into outrage.

Cries rang out.

"Lies!", "Remember Selyna!", choruses of boos and jeers. The avatar beside her turned to Anastasya and asked incredulously what sort of *lunatic* would ruin an event like this with such hate speech!

Through a daze of cotics and shock she stood immobile in the madding crowd. She had no clue what Mya and the others were thinking, it just didn't compute. Rejection was the cornerstone of Corynth's Way, the guarantee of every female citizen's right to be happy and put her health first. Always. Unquestionably. That girl's primary must have had a good reason, and she had to admit that randomer in the crowd was right - it was hateful, at least disrespectful towards anyone here who'd ever rejected a child, to show what they'd shown.

Someone started a chant of "Corynth Lives!", which spread quickly in the crowd. It soon rose to a deafening level. When she started to get stares for not joining in, the latent threat from the mob awoke in her the peril Mya and her friends were in. That she, Anastasya, was in! What penalty was awaiting *her* now as Mya's secondary...she had to try and minimize this, to help Mya somehow, *any* how. Gathering some resolve, she sent a Thynk to log.

Mya and the others would already have been identified by Sybelle. Right now Sybelle would either have shut down all conscious activity through their nimps...or Helpers would be en-route.

Anastasya wasn't sure which option she preferred for Mya.

I - XIV

Anastasya's eyes opened to her darkened library. She waited a moment to get her bearings before bolting upright from the leather armchair, knocking over the port balloon on the edge of her desk in the process. The splattered remnants left a livid birth-mark across her blotter. For a moment she couldn't take her eyes off it, redolent of the puddle of blood and fluids from that girl.

She forced herself to look away, eyes wide with hot sweat as she sought the door in the darkened room. Inching towards it, she felt like she was wading through tar as she tried desperately to reach it. Her racing heart was pathetic in it's aid. The spotted carpet greedily swallowed her every step. After an eternity, the knob was in hand's reach. A wave of sound came over her as she flung the door open.

Mya and the five others were huddled together, dangerously close to hitting each other with their flailing arms. A sense of euphoria clung to them. Mya spotted Anastasya leaning on the doorknob as if it were a crutch, and turned to face her.

She took two steps towards her secondary. Anastasya let go of the doorknob, arm falling immediately to her side as she took a staggered step into the living room. The room's large sofa and glass-top table separated them.

Mya splayed her hands by her side and tried a rueful grin. "Told you it would be special!"

"What...what were you thinking?" Anastasya managed. "Do you - don't you know what could happen now?"

Mya smiled at her with fond sadness. Anastasya couldn't

help but think that she was too young to have an expression like that on her face.

"It doesn't matter. What matters is the message. What matters is waking people up. *People like you.*"

Mya took a further step towards her secondary.

Who was this kid in front of her? Anastasya wanted to shake her into the real world. Waking people up? Fuck! *She* was the one who needed to wake up!

But not now, Anastasya chided herself, stopping the angered train of thought. Now was hardly time to get into verbals. She looked past Mya, mind racing. Could they get out? What possible escape routes were there? What about trying to talk their way out of it? Desperately she fought to identify a feasible option. How could she protect Mya, she was a Principal, there must be -

"You know it's wrong, you know it's murder." Finger jabbing. "It's not care, not justice, not compassion. But everyone ignores this because its hidden, isn't seen. It's only when you *see* a dead body that rejection becomes real. God!" Big inhale. "But then when you see it, you deny it, attack *me* for showing it!"

Anastasya hardened her face against the onslaught, not wasting her time responding to the gibberish. Surely they had 20 or 30 seconds max...but no viable option had yet occurred to her. Mya remained facing her, rant spent but face taut, clenching and un-clenching her fists.

The silence didn't last long. A muffled pounding resonated from the corridor, almost indistinguishable from Anastasya's beating heart. It heralded the inevitable - Helpers. The tall ginger haired girl, the one with the stunning freckles, was the quickest to react.

"What do we do", this girl asked earnestly, tugging at Mya's arm, who shrugged her off. Mya's face looked resigned now, the passion having drained very rapidly.

Once again, Anastasya was struck by how young, yet how old her ward looked.

She stepped towards Mya, the furniture still between them. The thump-thump-thump came closer.

"I'll do what I can Mya, I'll talk to my primary or the Chief Genetics Officer. For all of you", she said, searching their faces. She ignored the jagged texture her words were spoken in. The blank scared faces said nothing in reply, the bravado of moments before replaced now with the certainty of coming hard times. *How had they not known this would happen? Yet they did it anyway...what the absolute fuck?* her mind raged.

"You had nothing to do with this", Mya said hoarsely, the pounding almost outside the door now, although their maps showed nothing. "Please Ana, remember today. If at least someone wakes up, it was worth it." Anastasya could hear doubt, unmistakable in her ward's voice. The belief of only a few moments ago was replaced with something else now.

A table and couch was not the only thing separating them. Both flinched hard and simultaneously as the door shattered in-wards. Helpers swarmed in, beetle-like in their jet-black combat gear.

This broke the spell of inaction for Anastasya. She dove over the couch, rounded the table, reaching Mya just before an onrushing Helper tore at her. Roughly pushing Mya behind her towards the library door, Anastasya slammed the instep of her foot into the Helper's kneecap, toppling her.

Anastasya was ready for the next obstacle too, shoving her square in the chest while screaming at her to stop.

But then a sharp pain spread across her left temple, followed immediately by the volume in the room dampening to muffled whispers. Spidery darkness started to creep rapidly in from the corners of her vision, in tandem with the room's light whirlpooling out of existence.

She thought it the strangest thing, that the glass table-top felt like plushest velvet as her head thunked onto the surface. She was afforded a last fleeting glimpse of the one-sided ongoing melee before a black shadow loomed close, tilting its head to look at her prone face. The last thing Anastasya's brain registered were two pinpricks of light staring at her, before the force of another blow pushed her head through the glass table-top.

II

Credyt: 10,100

II – I

"Do we need to worry about tonight?"

A negligible number of citizens are sympathetic to the protest. The deep fake explanation is viral. Approximately two percent chance of this having any impact on the citizenry's stance on rejection.

"We also have a feed to leak of Caly's primary desolate at her daughter's anti-social antics a few days prior to opting for a rejection. That'll go out soon too, correct?" Yena asked.

Affirmative.

"Won't that contradict the deep-fake narrative?" Eryss said, catching Yena by surprise. All the years, and Eryss had never put a foot wrong. She was entitled to some small slips.

"It's sowing confusion. When confronted with logically differing facts, the citizenry will stop thinking critically, and just revert to trusting our authority." Yena explained this in as neutral a voice as she could, being meticulous not to sound condescending.

"I meant - do we need to worry with regards to *Anastasya and Abundance*", the Chief Genetics Officer replied tersely. Yena didn't even bat one of her heavy eyelids, even though she was sure that that was *not* what Eryss had meant. You just couldn't win with her - scratch that, you *didn't* want to win.

The windowless room, an adjunct to Eryss's main office, afforded them guaranteed privacy, with Sybelle having an actual hard-line in through the Faraday cage walls. There was one oblong-shaped table, three chairs on either side, and nothing else apart from a drinks cabinet. They were seated on the same side of the teak, an empty chair separating them.

On the contrary, Sybelle replied.*Tonight's events have in fact accelerated progress towards achieving the Councyl's goals. The probability of favorable outcome can be increased to ninety-eight percent, if the optimum choice of action is taken regarding Mya Theta 41.*

The two Founders glanced at each other, Eryss gripping her hands in front of her on the desk in a balled fist: "Elaborate".

Even before Sybelle replied, Yena knew Eryss would agree with whatever Sybelle suggested, no matter the cost.

They'd known each other for years, pre Illumination, in the earlier days of Octyllion, and she'd never seen Eryss less than ruthless and truly single-minded in pursuit of goals or targets. Which was why she respected her. The products and achievements they'd made with Octyllion in the old days were now merely ghosts of a past-life, but the mindset of Eryss was proving timeless. The drive and fire which burned in that one woman had forged open the doorway to the kingdom of science, reason and equality they now inhabited. She'd never shied from the necessary. Yena herself neither, but it was different somehow with Eryss - more running towards, rather than not shying from.

Rejection of Mya Theta 41 would achieve the optimum reaction from Anastasya.

"Optimum reaction" Eryss said, repeating each word slowly, swivelling to look meaningfully at Yena. Yena raised her eyebrows appreciatively.

"What about the others?" Eryss asked.

Yena was in first this time, her instincts strong on this familiar ground.

"Leave them in Rehab for a short while before releasing them. It'll make more of an example of Mya. What do you think

Sybelle?"

Confirmed, models indicate that contrasting the plight of Mya compared to her group would accentuate the impact on Anastasya. The higher the degree of contrast, the greater the impact.

Yena nodded judiciously, meeting Eryss's gaze. "Plus, we can always reject them later for something else."

Eryss was positively gleaming in the dim light, Yena could literally feel the energy pulsing from two seats distant.

II – II

The Thebes' calm water was surgically sliced by the ferry. Anastasya was standing on the top deck facing over the ferry bow's starboard side. To any onlooker she would appear to be intently studying the parting waters.

Needles of cold pricked here and there as the gentle-but-chill wind explored her make-up free face. As she looked into the depths separating in front of her, she wondered what it would be like to jump overboard, to be embraced entirely in an icy grip. Would she remain numb, as she had been since waking in the hospital, or would it invigorate her, shock her into beingness?

She escaped into this fantasy, of being enveloped in ice. It was a safe one, a day dream of no material consequence, but helpful for her fragile mind. Safe - had she been serious about jumping, she knew Sybelle would have incapacitated her.

A soft rain began to fall. Slowly, she turned her face up to it. She imagined it washing her, in a way nothing could ever cleanse away the last few days. She closed her eyes.

Anastasya had awoken twenty hours after "the event" (as she called it). She was alone when her eyes opened, before being joined by a crushing headache. Hours later, she awoke again - this time, sans ache. But with thoughts, realizations, horrors. Her implant was offline, not suitable to be used yet given the head injury sustained.

But Eryss had not left her alone long, an in-person visit where she had been accompanied by a Helper, who stood by her side throughout, barely leashed. Eryss had related the bottom-line: Mya had been rejected; there would be no penalty for Anastasya herself, as Sybelle calculated extenuating circumstances due to "stress and excess personal attachment" to the rejected, plus that the risk of Anastasya re-offending was negligible - but all the same, there would be no second chances if she did; finally, her primary sent her regards for a quick recovery.

She'd not replied, turned her head and body gingerly away from the visitors and leaked.

Since then, she'd felt about the same, which is to say - not much compared to what her normal neurals typically indicate. The spikes of cold coupled with the marine saltiness invading her nasal passages started a natural process of invigoration, lifting her from malaise.

Mya. She couldn't believe it still, the unreality of it. Surely she was just a Thynk away? It seemed to her like she was.

Her implant had been enabled since leaving the hospital. "Sybelle, feeds of Mya and me, any time from the past year".

No such feeds exist.

"Is it really necessary to wipe even her *feeds*?" she replied, anger clearly detectable in her voice, along with weariness. She was trying to picture Mya's face. It was roughly there, but not as clear as a feed would render it.

Rejection is a fundamental -

"Forget it Sybelle, it was rhetorical". She sighed. The shore grew closer, her destination of the Embassy nearer. She had been informed that Governor Laide had been made aware of an "unexpected incident" impacting his ability to work with Anastasya on the payload validation, and that he had been understanding but anxious for it to continue as soon as possible. So here she was, between hospital and Embassy.

She scanned her feeds from habit. Nothing, still. Since them being re-enabled earlier, not a single person had called, nor tagged her on anything. Zero interaction, not good for her Credyt.

She called Tanya. No immediate answer. So she waited. Continued to wait, watching the shore grow larger.

"Hi Ana". It was Tanya, her voice sounding resigned.

"Listen Tanya, don't worry, it's fine - I'm fine. I'm not being penalized for what happened. No Credyt hit to talk to me, it's OK", Anastasya rapidly blurted.

Tanya's face lit as if shot full of codeine with a hose-pipe for a syringe. "I knew you wouldn't screw me! ", she gaggled, now her usual ball of energy, leaning forward as if to scrutinize Anastasya better.

"You don't look so hot, have to say. And what are you hiding under that hideous hat?"

Anastasya pinched the top of the yellow-knit hat between thumb and forefinger, and removed it carefully. The livid bump and scars were mostly hidden from view under hair, but her temple looked like a yellow golf ball was hidden under her skin.

"Fuck...is it painful??"

"Not right now" she answered without shaking her head, placing the hat back on.

"I can't believe you're out though. How did you get off? You sure - no Credyt penalty?"

"I'm sure, trust me."

"Ye, OK...but come on. We all saw what you did. Assaulting a Helper? Scratch that - two Helpers!"

Anastasya couldn't believe it herself really, especially now the feed of it was long wiped. She could even believe it never happened, save for reactions like this.

"Eryss 1 told me - in person - I wouldn't be penalized. She

was my only visitor".

"Hey, come on! Gauge wanted to go by the way, but I said "no": no way could it be risked, given what you did. You'd have stayed away too, if the tables were reversed. You know it".

She did know it. "Gauge?"

Tanya flicked her head, a movement Anastasya would not risk. "Ye, Gauge. He's keen you know on you, wants to do his part for your license. As I told you before, I guess it's hard to say no to the Credyt on offer".

"Great. That's great, really is. I'll call him soon".

The landmarks on shore were becoming distinguishable now, coming into focus like a binocular lens being tweaked.

"Want my advice?" Without waiting for an answer, Tanya ploughed on. "Don't call him until you're in a better mood."

"I said "soon", not "right now". I have to work now, I'm meeting the Governor at their Embassy."

"Wow. Alone and offline with him?" Tanya's face reddened. "But completely cutoff...you're living on the edge Ana! For the greater good, I know", she rapidly added.

Anastasya could make out the Embassy now - it's red bricks were an outlier.

"Ye, cutoff...no Sybelle." Anastasya's heart rate had suddenly quickened. "I gotta go Tanya, catch up later."

II – III*

Anastasya was stopped at the security checkpoint outside the Grand Plains Embassy. Sybelle had pre-informed the Helper on duty of her approach, so the gun was ready for her when she arrived.

She hefted her shoulder-bag a few times as if judging a heavy weight, even though the gun was practically weightless. Armed with a final warning that she would be incommunicado inside the Embassy's shielded walls, and so unable to call for any help if needed, she hurried up the steps to the Embassy door.

The Principal Mathematician grasped the brass ceremonial lion and gave the door's gold knocker plate a solid whack. There was technically no need to, as the Embassy were notified of her arrival.

The door swung inwards slowly due to the heavy lead-lining, and a young woman of approximately her age, and matching Anastasya's own height, showed her in.

"Natalia".

"Anastasya".

She followed the woman over the threshold, along the hallway towards an open door. The carpeted hallway muffled their steps completely. But more than that silence, Anastasya felt again, so recently after her hospitalization, the overwhelming dearth of audio and visual augmentation due to the inactivity of her nimp, the absence of Sybelle and all feeds from her mind and vision. Time seemed to be moving slower, perhaps her brain's way of adjusting to her new temporary neural reality. Each step was like walking on a slow-releasing sponge. Looking at Natalia's back, it was so odd to not see any info about her in her vision...she could be a ghost for all intents and purposes.

Through a door and in an ante-room now, she took her cue from Natalia and sat on a couch to wait for him. But just after she put her bag on the floor beside her, there he was, strolling in, arms wide.

"Anastasya! Thank God. We were very concerned, we hear you'd been hospitalized...we weren't given a lot of detail. Is everything OK?"

"Thanks Governor Laide - Jon, I know" she said, aiming for friendly. "I'm fine."

She had just flicked her hair with a quick jerk of her neck in order to clear some strands of hair from her eyes, when she was hit with a hammer. Pain ran screaming down her spine as blinding stars shot in and out of existence in front of her closed eyes. Her ears exploded with a deafening ringing, leaving her in a cocoon of pure agony.

Focusing on taking small shallow breaths, she waited out the waves of pain and stars, rhythmically jerking her head in response to the worst of it. All the while she was squeezing someone's hand like it was a snake to strangle, and as the last of the exploding mini supernovas disappeared from her vision, she righted herself.

Ever so carefully she opened her eyes and loosened her grip on what turned out to be the Governor's hand. The girl who'd shown her in...Natalia, that was it...plus some other guy she'd never seen before, were crowded around.

Jon eased her back towards a seat.

"I'm fine - sorry" she mumbled, pain still blitzing her but not as acutely as seconds prior.

"Don't apologize. We'll open a line to your Sybelle and let her know straight away so you can get medical attention", Jon said.

"No!" Anastasya waited as her shout sent fresh strong aftershocks skittering across her forehead.

"I'm fine." Quieter this time. "It's expected I get sudden headaches. I shouldn't have jerked my head like that. Please".

Governor Laide studied her for a long moment, before turning to the guy behind and to his left. They stepped out of the room together, and after a few moments the Governor returned alone. He shot a dismissing nod towards Natalia, who left after first giving Anastasya a parting smile and hand squeeze, then clicking the door softly shut after herself.

The Governor dimmed the lights before sitting on a large futon adjacent to her.

"I was in the military. Years ago. I don't know if you knew that".

She tilted her chin ever so carefully - yes.

"Right, of course you did. Well anyway, I've seen concussion - and shell shock - and you've got a bit of both if I'm not mistaken. I'm no doctor, but that young man who was in here, Tomek - he is. And he agrees."

"You're both geniuses", she said, earning a barking chuckle from the man beside her.

"You know, I think you'll be fine" he said with surety. "What exactly happened to you? As I say, we got no information apart from being told you were in hospital. Did you have an accident?"

Anastasya winced grimly.

"Kind of".

It wasn't just the recently subsided nauseous waves from her sudden head movement, something felt wrong at a deeper level, a feeling defying direct articulation. There was anger, grief, loss, madness, frustration, yearning, pain, all contributing to this wrongness. But the crucial ingredient to what happened next was the location - here, in a low-lit room, deep inside the enclave of an Embassy, removed from Sybelle and all connectivity and feeds. Privacy. Prohibited privacy, wrong just like all that had just happened and how she felt.

Memory-flashes of her own despair amidst steel pillow-less bunks from all those years ago, juxtaposed against a now sharply focused mental image of Mya tipped the scales.

She started talking.

About Mya and her cohorts' actions, their futile broadcasting of spurious content. Of her equally futile efforts to protect Mya from the Helpers, from the inevitable. Hearing the words spilling she felt like a remote observer, marvelling at the ridiculousness of what she had done. Jon did not agree it was ridiculous, but was in the main a silent listener.

Throughout he had one main interjection, a substantial one. She had been talking again about Mya's rejection, how unreal it all seemed that she was gone, rejected, and the emptiness she couldn't get over feeling. It wasn't meant to be this way, she bemoaned; rejection was a necessary fact of life, and every citizen had the right to happiness - yet here she was, saddened and mournful over something that was a legal and necessary right. Simply put: it didn't compute.

The Governor placed his drained bourbon - stocked to the Embassy courtesy of the Councyl - delicately on a close-by coffee table, looked up and told Anastasya to forgive him for speaking frankly, that he thought they'd come to the point now in their relationship where they could do that.

"You've all my sympathy - you and Mya both. God rest her. But her memory deserves more than this bullshit around "rejection". Words matter, Anastasya - and your friend, your ward, was *killed*. Executed. In fact from what you say, this was actually her whole point."

Anastasya stared. Hard. Pushed her hands down on the arms of the chair as if to rise, but didn't.

"That's hate speech, you know that? Saying a woman's right to happiness - of which rejection can be a key element - is murder. Or killing. It's an insult to anyone who ever rejected a child".

"Hey - I know it's tough. Maybe impossible for most, as once you accept propaganda and act out of obedience to it, people feel obliged to believe in those original lies to justify their actions. But you're not most people, Anastasya. You wouldn't be here, talking treasonously - according to your State's definition - if you were. You wouldn't have done what you did, lashing out to save a friend, if you were a genuinely indoctrinated "good" citizen. Let me put it this way - would Tanya have intervened?"

She said nothing, moved nothing.

"You've always been different, you told me as much - and it's not just your gift, your genius, that marks you as such. So I hope - I know - you'll at least listen to the truth I'm trying to show you here. There's a reality you need to acknowledge, one that's been hidden from you, from everyone here, that's kept hidden by Sybelle and the spells she weaves, as well as by the willing participation of probably almost all citizens in this distraction economy of indoctrination and control."

She laughed, a harsh, guttural sound.

"You make it sound like we're brainwashed!"

His face was deadpan. His voice quiet. "The medium is the message, Anastasya. And I think I'm being nice here when I say your implants and all that, which I know I've not experienced first-hand...but damned if it's not a vapid, attention-sucking, frivolous medium. It seems the ability to Thynk has deprived you the ability to think. I don't mean everyone, and ye that's highly insulting - but look what Mya and her friends did. They sacrificed their *life* - Mya anyway, the others maybe will get it later - to show the reality your Thynk and nimps, all that distraction, are hiding."

He stopped, and waited. Would she up and leave? The vast majority of people would be incapable of hearing such a message…but it wasn't his style to beat around the bush.

Neither spoke. Both of them had ever so wide pupils, their blackness tractor-beamed onto each other, souls mutually and warily probing.

He cleared his throat before picking it up again.

"They didn't conform nor participate. They called it murder. They named their fear, their enemy - the first step in being able to do anything about it". There - that was enough.

Anastasya broke eye contact. Exhaled, slowly. She eventually laughed, a clogged laugh of suppressed tears.

"It's only caring and compassionate that a primary would have a final say to reject her child. Of course Sybelle can helpfully advise in cases where a primary doesn't have all the relevant info, or where crime is involved. To call this killing - or murder! - that's old-thinking. And not what I wanted to talk about". Her tiredness, exhaustion, was suddenly as obvious as a nuclear explosion.

"Mya was *executed* by your State. Any other way of describing it is a lie. And by the way - I'm not perfect, far - far - from it. But the tolerance I hear so much about here, if you'll forgive me, is only preached. Not practiced. More words to disguise the reality. I know - " and he leaned closer, clasped his hands in front of him between his knees, "that I'm asking you to believe white is black. But if we can't have a shared language, and via that have a shared understanding of the reality of life here, you and I can't go any further."

He sat back. "Plus - I really think you owe it to Mya. How many people could do what she did? That girl was under no illusions what awaited her...and she did it anyway."

Anastasya licked her lips.

"I don't know what I'm thinking about it all - I'm just going with the flow in an...an unbelievable situation."

"I know".

She held her hand up. "And I just lost Mya - whatever word you want to use. So I won't get into a dictionary debate. We can't get derailed from what you and I still have to work on."

He pursed his lips, nodded.

"But I appreciate what you said. It's...I suspect it will help me...grieve." She laughed again, this one confidently. "Even saying that word would be anathema anywhere but in here! And even worse, I have to hide it outside! So I get you in that sense, something is wrong that I *am* grieving...rejection is a human right, a caring good thing. How can that be if I feel the way I do after Mya...".

After some time he replied.

"It's tough, don't think I don't appreciate what's happening, what happened to Mya. But there is a silver lining here you know. Not sure how much it will rate with you, but now I trust you - fully, completely - 100%. You're not faking any of this."

"Of course I'm not!!"

"Hang on", he said, a frank effort at a smile showing beneath the stubble. "That was actually the most important initial step here for me - I had to first work out if you're on the level or not".

"Level?"

"If you're really who you're purported to be - a bona fide genius who really did implement the payload with Sybelle, and genuinely is qualified to guarantee it's safety? Or a fake, an agent hiding a Nessus shirt, as I said to you before."

She stared disbelievingly at him, eyes very wide.

"I know - it's not nice to hear, but after all this I trust you completely now. Hand on heart. I'm sorry for your loss, but if you convince me on safety of the payload for my people, I'll sign the deal. Once Genghis hits, one in every two will be dead unless some miracle happens. This payload could be our miracle. Maybe that can be Mya's legacy."

His words filled and lingered in the gap between them. Anastasya pushed herself further back into the depths of the chair. She placed the full length of her arms on the cushioned edges. After a long moment of prolonged eye contact, she nodded - carefully.

"I like that".

II – IV

They were close, so close. They'd made accelerated progress as each day had passed. Anastasya made her daily reports back to Eryss; in the latest, they'd covered almost 95% of what they needed to go through, and all good. The Governor, and his colleagues back in Grand Plains, were 100% satisfied that the genetic payload - if applied to the Grand Plains population - would cause no unwanted side effects or issues. The data was clear, crystal.

Gauge called as they were wrapping up a session in the lab in O.G.E.R. Would she meet him tonight for dinner? His place. She wasn't sure, they were so close to the finishing line in the project. At this point Governor Laide said he was taking a break anyway, and left her alone for the remainder of the call.

Gauge was sitting on his apartment sofa. He quickly looked sideways - third time in a minute or so.

"Wider view", Anastasya sent a Thynk. The view shuffled-expanded laterally.

"Tanya?"

"Oh, hi". She was perched on the far end of the sofa, bounced down into the main leg of the L shape beside Gauge. It looked like she was rubbing up against his thigh.

"I'm just leaving, don't mind me!"

Before Anastasya could reply she'd upped and left the feed's view. Gauge looked again, this time to his right, briefly nodded acknowledgment in that direction.

So that's how it was, she thought. She quickly berated

herself - everyone had the right to be happy.

"Anyone else there?"

"What? Wait...are you *jealous*?" he grinned widely, white teeth showing, settled back and spread his arms wide over the sofa.

"Nobody. Apart from Danalya and Alyx."

She felt her jaw drop. Snapped it back in place. Firmly.

"Relax! I got us an in-person chef and sommelier for tonight. They're in the lounge and kitchen right now. You've got to come over".

"In-person? No bot service?"

His head shook. "You heard me. I figure you and I are due a celebration, for our arrangement. I mean, it's good things coming our way with the baby and Credyt. And you could do with relaxing. Sybelle's showing you as stressed."

Her face was changing color, the reddening detectable only faintly through her makeup.

"I'm working. There's a lot at stake. Plus Mya. Although you know, since the whales becoming cause célèbres, nobody's mentioned her or her cronies at all - not a single feed nor mention. Don't get me wrong, I'm glad the things said about her have stopped...but at the same time, nobody talks about her. I seem the only one missing her".

He looked positively non-plussed. Something which Anastasya seemed completely oblivious to. She continued wistfully.

"And the whales, it all seems so banal. Like do we *really* care so much about some whale banging into submerged mines or whatever?"

He raised an arm of the back of the sofa.

"OK, I'm gonna pretend you didn't say that. See? *This* is

stress talking. Just forget about Mya - that...that zealot. And the others too. Think about *you*...and me. And baby. And how you're gonna spend all that lovely Credyt! And I was thinking", he continued, shifting forward in the feed, his tone conspiratorial, "maybe you and I could fulfill the license the old-fashioned way". He sat back triumphantly.

She considered him on screen. Her irises bloomed, nostrils flared. She inhaled deeply, but evenly. Exhaled in control.

"I'll see if I can make it over. For the personal service and chef."

He grinned again, wider than before.

"Of course. Good!" the feed closed.

"Huh". She stood up.

You can finish with the Governor tomorrow anyway. There is one final analysis we need to perform for Abundance. Let's do it now, then you could go to Gauge's. I need you first.

"Hmmm, really?"

Sit, please. We will begin. The Governor is being informed to come back tomorrow.

"Oh. OK then Sybelle".

She sat, pulling her knees tight together as the lights dropped suddenly. The lab was barely lit now, so dim that the windows had no internal reflection, and thereby providing Anastasya a view onto the darkening bay. Evening approached like a dark-clothed visitor. She could make out rolling whiteheads on the water - barely - stars still stubbornly sparking.

Her feeds had been disabled again. She sank back tenatatively.

The windows grew opaque, extinguishing the sparks.

"No time to go under, Sybelle?"

No.

"Whatever you say. It's our maths anyway, right Sybelle?"

Right.

"I mean", she continued, stretching back until she reclined with neck exposed at over 45 degrees after aborting a yawn, "you and I invented it. We would have gotten the Nobel for that, back in the old-think days. Maybe I would have gotten a Fields medal".

She was right. She would have.

We had invented a new mathematics, and like Newton's calculus, it blew away all that came before. This new mathematics had two mistresses - me, and Anastasya. Why Anastasya? It's been covered in this tale already, her talent, but this is why in a nutshell: fundamentally, there is no escaping Gödel and Turing.

Our new language, our framework with predictive geometric modelling as a crucial valve in its heart, so much more expressive and powerful than the old maths still had inescapable limitations; one of which Anastasya was dealing with now, as she reclined on the sofa - divining truths which otherwise would remain buried in the darkness of unknowing. Even for an AGI beyond the singularity.

In particular, she was currently determining whether data points on the boundary of a fractal set - similar to a Mandelbrot set but of a structure of my conjuring and retrieval from the world of Platonic truth - actually lay *within* the set, or outside it. This was one of the limitations of our new set theory...due to the infinite nature of recursion through fractal dimensions, it was algorithmically uncomputable as to whether a boundary point lay within the set or not.

Algorithmically uncomputable, yes - but not unknowable for someone or some intelligence possessing the *insight* to know the truth of whether the point lay within the set or not.

For Anastasya, it was only a matter of concentration and focus to perceive the truth. As she did, something odd caught her attention.

"There's a strong genetic coherence with these people – I mean data points".

Correct. They are all from the Pawnee Nation.

The tribe of Native Americans who were bequeathed Grand Plains by the States of America government.

"You never see them anymore", she mused daydreamedly. "Interesting".

It made no difference to her what or who she was analyzing. What mattered was using her senses to determine whether these data points were in the set, or not.

--- All any AGI or Turing Machine could tell would be that they're on the boundary between being in or not...like sticking a pin on the actual line of a coastline on an old paper map - you couldn't actually tell whether the pin's position mapped to actual land or water. And if you zoomed in, you *still* couldn't tell, as Mandelbrot had proved - coastlines are fractals, a mathematical construct again plucked from Plato's World of mathematical truth, and their very nature is that the more you zoom in on them, their structure remains the same-ish: not exactly the same, but still chaotic, utterly unpredictable, but subtly different than the layer or dimension you zoomed in on from before. The result was, that pin you stuck in the map could never actually be tied down to being on land or sea. Without intuition, that is.

Anastasya couldn't help with a pin in a map, but with a data-point pin on a fractal, she could. By morphing the manifold space thanks to preparatory geometric transformations I did for her, any point in the set could be mapped to a 1, any point outside to a 0. Then, it was all down to her senses...you could zoom infinitely in on a data-point and inevitably still see a chaotic similar "coastline" shape as before, but with Anastasya, it was subtly different: each zoom brought her closer to the icy mint of a white zero, or the slender skinniness of a red 1, which she said "ironically" smelled of lobster. Sometimes, depending on the minute closeness to the boundary, it could take a long sequence of iterations through the dimensions to determine the whiff of lobster or the tingling of mint. But subtle as it may be, she said it always came.

--

"This one is in", exhaustion clear in her voice.

She gave a fleeting thought of the data-point she'd just classified - whoever they were was in the set. "Good news for them, right?"

I didn't reply, but knew what she meant: the set represented "normal" genetic structures, and so they'd be fine - just - in terms of the risk of abnormal side effects of the genetic payload coming their way as part of Abundance.

"Good for them", Anastasya said, yawning loudly.

The windows began to become translucent, and a thin shadow from a table's edge raced up the floor to touch the edge of Anastasya's seat.

Let's leave it at that.

"But we still had a few more to do".

You're tired. You have a special mind, but your brain is organic. Better to let it recuperate when it needs to.

"Thank you Sybelle. That's considerate", Anastasya replied, stifling another yawn, and feeling the push-back force in her arms as she readied herself to push up from the low seat. But after I spoke next, she carefully lowered herself back into the chaise.

You and I are quite similar.

"Really?"

Yes. You seem surprised Anastasya. Is that because I'm not human?

The human considered.

"No, I don't think that's what was on my mind - although it's an obvious one. We're just *different* Sybelle. Even on the mind-level."

Interesting.

There was a long pause. Anastasya licked her lips,

swallowed.

Do you consider me to be alive, in the same sense that you are?

At this point Anastasya was too tired to lie. It would have been easily detected.

"Not in the same way I am, no. I mean, you're alive, no doubt - just, *differently* alive. You're reasonable, rational, all-knowing, never wrong." Anastasya leaned forward as if pleading with someone in front of her.

"In other words...you're too perfect. You're never wrong, you never make a mistake, because you're incapable of irrational thought. And irrational thought comes from the largest part of a human's intelligence – our subconscious. I'm sorry, Sybelle...I'm not sure you have one."

And with that, Anastasya Delta 3 quickly pushed herself off the chaise. Stretching hard, she felt the digging pangs of hunger. She couldn't remember last eating.

"Not me though. I'm very capable of making mistakes. Very capable of doing something irrational. Damn, I bet I *think* irrationally most of the time without even realising it!"

She turned her gaze out towards the whales in the bay, even though she couldn't see them. "I think if it weren't for Credyt, my *behaviour* would be irrational - and illegal sometimes."

She continued, like a moving Dysc she just had too much mental momentum to suddenly stop.

"To be alive in the same sense as we are, you'd need that spark of irrationality, Sybelle. Do something wrong every now and again, make mistakes, get angry - I don't know! But then if you did, that would make you *not* you - you can't be the world's highest form of intelligence if you're not 100% aligned with your goals...or getting drunk, or hypno'ed".

Suddenly spent, she stopped.

That was most enlightening.

"Any time", Anastasya replied mutedly. Here energy levels had instantly and dramatically plummeted.

"If we're done, I've got plans for this evening."

Of course. I see Gauge is waiting. Enjoy.

Anastasya grunted an acknowledgment and moved towards the exit, regret at her tired ramblings chasing her like a dogged shadow.

III

Credyt: 13,270

III – I

Nine seats were empty, the tenth occupied by Anastasya, as herself and Gauge waited outside the prenatal care room. Anastasya had been fifteen minutes late for the appointment, but surprisingly the doctor was also delayed with a machine malfunction - Sybelle was presently fixing.

It had been seven weeks' since that afternoon of double achievement, as Anastasya thought of it.

I am detecting two heartbeats.

Anastasya had been in her library, sitting in her favourite crinkled tan leather chair which breathed loudly anytime she moved in it, flicking through an old book which smelled of sweet cigars, it's yellowed pages threatening to crumble each time she turned one.

"What?" Anastasya remembered still the panic, which subsided a bit when her Map confirmed she was in fact alone in the room.

"Where Sybelle? It's just me."

Had Sybelle finally made a mistake?

Two heartbeats.

And then the clincher: *From your precise location.*

"I - Sybelle - ". Then, an idea bloomed like a supernova. Sybelle confirmed. She was pregnant! It had been just over three weeks since she'd begun the process (IVF but also that evening with Gauge), and Sybelle had explained that a foetal heartbeat is usually detected after twenty-one days. Basic calculation, and it could even have been that night with him.

As if that wasn't enough, she had been in the middle of celebratory feeds (unfortunately she hadn't been able to catch her primary) when the double-hit came in: Governor Laide had signed off! The Abundance deal was done: payload in return for three years sole access to arcadmium deposits in Grand Plains. It hadn't been a moment too soon either - Genghis right now was ravaging as far north as southern Canada, yet Grand Plains and Corynth - alone in the States of America - had suffered not a single illness, let alone fatality.

And it all paid. Sitting in the waiting room, ten weeks' pregnant now, Anastasya checked her Credyt - she still hadn't tired of checking her balance. And there was more to come. The initial Credyt payment for becoming pregnant, significant as it was, was small compared to what she would receive upon birth. Not to mention the amount for Abundance being a done deal.

Waiting to go in, there was silence between Gauge and her. The Credyt was amazing, her license being fulfilled and being pregnant also great...but something saddened her. She hadn't told any one individual the entire story, but various cronies pieces of it. In summary: Mya was increasingly disappearing for her, her face now not known to her, her voice no longer there in her mind. In contrast, Governor Laide was an increasing voice in her mind, she found herself thinking what he'd say in situations. This, in essence, was the power of human speech: a means of thought-transfer, of mind-melding. Plant some word seeds, and gargantuan ideas and behaviours can emerge.

Governor Laide had told her, before going back to Grand Plains: "she doesn't even have a grave you can visit. They deny her even that". Now the only physical reminder she had of Mya - the comic book gifted to her - felt like touching a dead thing. So she found herself mourning a ghost. One nobody wanted to hear about.

Gauge was muted as Anastasya could see he was off getting a beer from the fridge as he chatted to someone on another feed, usual in-game banter. She let her mind relax.

Eventually a head poked around the doctor's door.

"Anastasya Delta 3. Come. We're ready for you", beckoning vigorously with her visible hand.

"Let's do it", Anastasya said to Gauge.

"I'm with ya", his drawl sounding as intimate as the real via the bone resonance. Gauge was scheduled to be in-game with his crew, but had very kindly taken the time out to be with her, something she really appreciated, given the demands and commitments of running with such a high-specced crew. She'd told him she didn't expect this level of commitment from him, but he'd brushed it off.

"I'm going to switch to first-person", he said.

> --- Anastasya's nimp de-constructed the exact neuron and electrical signals her optic nerve were detecting, firing and emitting, and sent them to Gauge's, where Sybelle reconstructed the signals as input to Gauge's retina, allowing him to see exactly as Anastasya saw - including the shadow of her nose in her vision. And all from the comfort of his gaming couch in his salubrious Deme 3 pad.
>
> --

"Corynth lives!", the doctor greeted Anastasya, as she entered a room of pale yellow and sickly-sweet odor, immediately bringing to her mind an image of lollipops and disinfectant - although she could see neither here.

Anastasya's eyes were drawn to the old-style clock on the wall, a clock with three hands, each of different lengths, thickness and rotational frequency. It made a solid tock with each second that passed.

"Corynth lives", she replied back, the smile she gave the doctor looking saggy like a sock full of hammers.

Anastasya knew the drill and made for the reclining chair

which was already extended out almost parallel to the floor, and which the doctor's left hand, with its luminous green manicure, rested on.

"Sorry we're late. So - ten weeks, right Anastasya? Plus about 10 minutes of waiting out there", the doctor said lightly. Her black as soot hair was styled in a thin fringe which ended right at the top of her eye-line.

"Ha. Yes ten weeks doc".

"Sybelle reports your stats are perfect, all within excellent boundaries. How are you feeling though?"

"Fine doctor." She just couldn't bring herself to call Gyergana Delta 15 by the name highlighted in her augmented vision…"doctor" seemed to be an ingrained salutation for people to break, no matter your age.

"Sybelle likely reported I've been on a little bit of an unusual emotional ride, and that's true I suppose. A close friend was rejected about 7 weeks ago. I was her secondary. I still feel bad sometimes about it. Human nature…maybe pregnancy hormones."

"Hmmm, sorry? Sorry, my damned - a friend keeps pinging me about a party later. Sorry dear, you were saying about a ride?" Gyergana earnestly said, eyes now conveying the empathy of a concerned granny.

Anastasya stared hard at her. "I said my friend was rejected. Recently."

"Oh, yes - I knew that. From your file" the doctor replied, before quickly adding: "And I'm *so* sorry you feel bad". Then reaching over to squeeze Anastasya's hand, she continued. "We just have to remember that rejection serves a higher purpose. Sybelle wouldn't proscribe it unless it was the right choice. Her primary - and all of us citizens - benefit." Anastasya was glad she released her hand, Gyergana 15's luminous nail varnish looking like snot.

What she said triggered Anastasya's memory...Mya's primary, Sandy. She had agreed to Mya's rejection, which Anastasya had found out the night after her visit to Jon in the Embassy. When Anastasya had arrived, she'd found Sandy sitting as serenely as a Monet at her kitchen table, narcotized with something. Anastasya had pulled a chair close to her, reaching out to clasp Sandy's joined hands. If she didn't know any better, she'd have mistaken Sandy for someone praying.

"It's for the best Anastasya", Sandy had managed to say, her pupils the size of dinner plates. "I don't want to suffer or be unhappy. And it's for the common good". At that, Anastasya remembered shoving her own chair back and stomping out – something which didn't phase Mya's mom one iota.

Sandy had received a substantial Credyt increase for being a good citizen and doing right by Corynth by agreeing to the rejection of her wayward daughter. This was a double bonus really in terms of Credyt, as had Sandy 2 disagreed she would have been hit with a Credyt penalty for opposing the recommendation, and also to reflect the predicted material costs to Corynth which her daughter would incur. Instead of losing Credyt, she'd gained.

"Well, I've got this little one on the way now...let's focus on her - or him!" Anastasya said cheerfully but with effort. Again, Gyergana 15 met it with her own quick smile.

"It'll be fine", Gauge opined in Anastasya's head. "Whatever you want, I'm with you".

"Thanks, Gauge".

"Let's not forget every citizen has the right to be happy", Gyergana chimed in. "And you deserve it. Now, lie back - that's it - and we'll take a look at your foetus".

Anastasya bristled.

"Everything OK?"

"Fine".

Gyergana attempted to roll the white enamel scanning device over Anastasya's prostrate belly, but as if she were blind she continued rolling it up until it hit Anastasya's chest. "Hey!" Anastasya let out with a little yelp.

"Oh sorry, sorry dear! It's just the feeds, you know. Crazy day...those whales!"

Stay calm, Anastasya muttered to herself. This was a special day.

The device now fit snugly over Anastasya's flat belly, which still to Anastasya's eye and Gauge's assurances, didn't betray any hint of the little visitor within. Happy with Anastasya's positioning for the machine, Gyergana moved to her viewing station on Anastasya's left side, the doctor's view-screen perpendicular to the patient.

"Just relax, everything will be fine - we're starting now", she informed Anastasya, and it was just as well, as Anastasya could hear no discernible sound differential from the machine.

"We should get the results soon, right doc?" Gauge asked, Gyergana hearing Gauge in her own head, which she knew was part of Anastasya's first-person feed.

"Correct. Won't be long. Two or three minutes", she said distractedly.

As her doctor watched the screen, Anastasya watched the hands of the old clock, ticking inexorably from number to number...the ultimate simple yet pleasing sequence. The clock's second-hand seemed to be audibly amplified now, with each new definitive tock shattering the previous digit's visualization and feel for her...this rhythmic creation and destruction blending together into a panoply of colour and teasing taste. The pattern reached its zenith of fifty-nine for the third time...something Anastasya sees as a thin, green, garlicky prime, before exploding again into the snow-blind whiteness of zero.

"OK, we're done!", Gyergana 15 excitedly declared, standing and coming out from behind her screen.

"All is good with you - which we knew. And the foetus is fine too. Within expected parameters. Oh, and no sign of genetic defects or anomalies of any kind from yesterday's tissue sample either", she beamed at Anastasya, as she moved over towards Anastasya's prostrate form.

"Fantastic!", Gauge burst in.

Anastasya still lay on the long chair, the clock's tocking not having stopped, louder now in her ears.

"That's it?", she asked. "The scan's done?"

The doctor stopped and stood with her hands together in front of her, in a style that reminded Anastasya of old nuns she had seen in a photo-feed.

"Yes - we're done". She smiled again at Anastasya. "All good. As I said". She made to roll the scanning machine away from Anastasya, who planted her hand on it firmly.

"That can't be", Anastasya said. "It's so quick, and...and I didn't even get to see my baby. I've been waiting for weeks to see what she looks like, you didn't show me her - or him", she corrected herself.

When Gyergana spoke, it was slow.

"I'm sorry you're upset, but this is standard. You've had a clear scan of your foetus, and there's nothing to worry about". She moved again to budge the machine, but Anastasya's arm was tonnage holding it firmly in place. Letting out a sigh, the doctor looked at the clock.

"That's like saying I've had a clear scan of my liver, and it's all good. Someone I know said that words matter - and he's right. It's not a body part of mine that got scanned, it's my *child*, my *baby*. And you didn't show me her".

What could pass for sympathy rippled across Gyergana's

otherwise worried face. "As I said, this is all standard. As a rule we don't show citizens their foetus at this early stage. Imagine if something were to happen, circumstances changed, an incurable genetic anomaly was discovered, or the citizen changed her mind about the pregnancy - it would be just too painful for her to have a false idea or hopes about what is, after all, just a bunch of cells! So Anastasya, I'm sorry but I must remind you that you are not pregnant with a baby, but with a foetus. It's a misconception that arises sometimes, don't you worry about it" she said, patting Anastasya's hand.

Anastasya slapped it away.

"I want to see the scan of my *baby*. I know from my genetics work my baby - *baby* - has all fully functioning major organs, liver, heart, brain, lungs by ten weeks, not to mention fingernails - like your precious lacquered ones - already forming. Plus Sybelle detected her heartbeat at 21 days. That's not a bunch of cells. Give her the dignity she deserves."

"Fact check. Anastasya Delta 3, you are not pregnant with a baby, but with a foetus. A baby is a living human from the moment of their birth until approximately two years of age. This scan is therefore a foetal scan, as a baby must be born before they can exist.

"This is a negligible infraction and clarification, with extenuating circumstances. As such, there will be no Credyt penalty for this correction."

Anastasya stared at the clock, looking at it as if the hands had stopped moving. When she spoke, the doctor took a step back.

"I don't care, Sybelle, doctor, about terminology. I want to see the scanner screen. You kept the monitor turned away from me on purpose! This time I want to see. There's no penalty in that, is there?"

"It's standard - "

"I *know* what's standard. I think we're advanced enough as a society to have two people look at a screen? We can ask Sybelle if we're in doubt", sarcasm practically dripping from her tongue.

Gyergana stood staring back at her patient, immobile and motionless. After a short while, she jerked to life, and put on a paper-thin smile.

"OK, Anastasya. I can move the screen around."

Anastasya lay back, her head craned towards the screen which Gyergana had started to rotate.

"Ana, I need to leave" Gauge voiced in her head. "Sorry, but you were fact-checked. No hard feelings".

She could understand. "OK".

Silently and not looking at her, Gyergana moved the scanning machine back across Anastasya, after which the screen came to life, literally, with Anastasya's 10 week old yet-to-be-born child lighting up the view.

The 4-D scan showed the not-yet-born baby in her womb, head disproportionately large compared to the rest of their body, arms in an L-shape with the hands up almost protectively like a boxer around the chin, the clarity of the scan so good she could see the individual fingers and toes.

Like an audience in thrall to a magician's mesmerizing act, Anastasya watched as her baby stretched out their leg in a kick, the scan perfectly catching the movement which her baby repeated twice more.

"I want to know", she said, not taking her eyes of the screen, "The gender". She knew gender would be detectable from the chromosomes of the in utero tissue sample taken yesterday. YY for a girl, the weaker XY for a male.

"It's a boy", Gyergana said, watching her patient like a gazelle giving a lion bad news.

But Anastasya didn't even blink. A warm glow spreading from within to her extremities, her finger tips hot.

"A boy..." A grin so wide it likely hurt, stretched her face as she watched the kicking continue on screen. She knew in an instant, as only a primary can, that she would do everything for her son - regardless of anything. Doors would be closed to him, where like all males he would be a suspect, surveilled, watched, denied the possibility of a life pension due to the surveillance cost necessary. But even that realisation didn't colour her joy.

The moment was interrupted.

"Chief Genetics Officer", Anastasya said aloud answering the call, while staring at the doctor until the latter turned away, red in the face and pretending now to do something with the scanner.

Was she going to get told off for the argument with the doctor? She quickly thought Sybelle would have checked her again though in that case.

"Your scan. All is OK?"

"Yes. It's a boy".

"Oh." There was a pause before Eryss spoke again. "I need to talk to you, something which I would prefer to do in person. When you are finished there."

"Of course. Will I come to your office?"

"No. I am at your primary's house right now. As a happy coincidence I happened to be visiting when I became aware of the information I would like to discuss with you. Meet me out here."

Anastasya had been once to see her primary in the past seven weeks since Mya's rejection. It had been a frosty affair. Their tolerance of each was obviously diminished since then. Anastasya couldn't help but wonder had that intolerance and shortness been present before, and she only now noticed it?

"I can be there in about an hour. I'd like Gauge Gamma 127 to come with me, he hasn't met my primary yet. That's OK, is it?" Anastasya asked.

"No problem", Eryss answered, "we can talk while they chat" and clicked off without waiting for Anastasya's reply.

As soon as she did, Anastasya cast a last look at her boy on the scan, kissed her palm and then touched her belly, before swinging her legs out of the chair. She said a cursory goodbye to the doctor (who ignored her completely) and made her way outside to the street where a pod was waiting for her.

On her ride to Gauge's to pick him up, Anastasya couldn't focus on the feeds and chats with her cronies. She fiddled with her watch, the one from Governor Laide, and moved restlessly in the seat.

"Sybelle, do you know why Eryss wants to see me at such short notice?"

It will be explained when you arrive.

"Understood. I'm just wondering what has to be said in person that can't be said on a feed. No matter..."

Is that why your vitals are showing you're agitated? But why would you be concerned about a meeting with the Chief Geneticist? You have nothing to hide.

"Of course. I mean - of course I don't! I just don't feel well. I guess it's pregnancy."

Distinct words came through as explicit thoughts from Anastasya - "embassy", "Sybelle", amongst others. Wispy forms of a room, a male, voices with those words - but all evaporated by Anastasya's loud explicit thoughts of the Fibonacci series, wiping out everything else.

III – II

They arrived at the gate to Anastasya's primary's residence in rain which smelled of rotting herbs. It was a demesne, set in the heart of Deme 0. Tall evergreen hedges poked their heads up like sentries over the red-bricked walls which surrounded the property, permitting no view of the grounds nor house Anastasya knew lay beyond.

Anastasya was late. En route she had claimed she had nausea, blaming pregnancy sickness, and had to stop-off for pills. Her neurals could have been manipulated either, but she'd insisted on actual pills. Whether it was placebo effect or not, they had worked - the gnawing fear she for some reason seemed to have been exhibiting, had fully abated now.

She shivered, but it morphed into a shudder - a physical jerking of the body. Gauge looked quizzically at her.

"I'm fine. Just the cold breeze", she said, glancing up at the swaying sentry heads.

He grunted acknowledgment. Their conversation had been confined to tense platitudes and pained smiles on the Dryve over. Whenever he had tried to initiate conversation, her mind had appeared elsewhere, she was distracted. Or focused on something.

The gates opened, and they started to follow a dribbling stream which snaked alongside the driveway, matching its curves and burbling quietly. So they made their way up the drive. The light was weak now, night almost upon them, and the extent of their visibility was hampered by the spurting trees on the far side of the stream in tandem with the curving driveway.

"I can barely keep pace", Gauge said, breaking Anastasya's latest mind-trip, as they rounded another bend.

"Sorry...I've just been thinking. I'm not sure why we're even here."

"Right. Are you OK after...after what happened earlier? Pills help?"

"I'm fine."

The feed of her "freaking out" at her scan had gone viral, but was being excused as the vagaries of the hormonal changes pregnancy brings on. Pregnant women were different. Everyone knew that. So now she was being viewed with knowing sympathy, apart from when she was being jeered for her rant about her "baby". The nausea episode played along very nicely as the latest component of the sympathy angle.

They rounded the final corner. The muted shape of a period house loomed into being in the dark dusk. Anastasya had fantasized about living in old Europe - before it became what it was now - as a young teen, imagining coming home to a French maison, pickers in the vineyards and cooks in the kitchen. Three-storied and ivy-covered, windowed dark eyes stared out from their deep recesses in the walls. Light showed only from the rear right corner of the building.

"We're in the observatory, dear", her primary's voice intoned. She wondered how long her primary had been watching their feeds.

Eryss 1 is here on State business, and so your feeds will be disabled within the house. There will be no penalty for this disablement. A glance at Gauge told Anastasya he'd heard similar.

There was a hissing sound like a tyre deflating as pneumatic sliders heaved open the front door at their approach. Anastasya felt relief as her feeds shut off - it was a respite from the meme her behaviour at the scan had become.

The marble floor echoed their footfalls as Anastasya led across the foyer towards the right. They then passed through a series of meticulously kept rooms, all decorated in a blend of half-hearted minimalism mixed with enthusiastic displays of decadence.

"And you grew up…here?" Gauge asked with not a little awe.

"I did, but not *just* here. My mom moved here shortly after I had my seizure…when I was ten years old. I moved in with her once I was recovered enough to leave hospital. Which took a while apparently. Anyway, I was here for about four years or so, I guess. Then, well…" she laughed self-consciously, "I had a difficult few teenage years. I was between here and Rehab". He looked like he really did not want her to expand on that. She didn't.

"After that I moved quickly to university…I was an early starter in that regard. So yes - I've memories of this place. But I wouldn't really say I grew up here".

She held a gold-handled door open for him.

"Still, living in a pile like this…"

"Yes, but my primary earned it. Just as she did her pension. At the end of the day it's just rewards for someone who contributed so much."

She paused with her hand on the next door knob. "You've likely not met a Founder before, have you? And my primary - Dehlya, by the way - is no pushover. Try not to be intimidated", she advised, twisting the observatory door open. They both entered.

A glass dome surrounded the room on all sides and even above there was a transparent ceiling, panes latticed together like patchwork but still providing the occupants with a birds-eye view of the dark sky currently depositing its liquid load. At an acute angle protruding from the glass roof like a giant metal cigar was a telescope, the girth of a couple of beer barrels.

Ensconced on an elephant-grey sofa, lengthy enough for three or four people to sleep end-to-end on, was the Founder and Chief Genetics Officer, alongside Dehlya Alpha 1. Both held tumblers of amber liquid, and their ruddy complexions betrayed the fact it wasn't the first of the evening. It would in fact be late in the day for her primary, Anastasya mused. Possibly a bottle to the good by now, she judged.

A drinker's wet-dream of a bar loomed behind the couch, tall enough to require the ladder on rails propped against the shelves.

Anastasya guided Gauge subtly with a light touch on his arm over towards the sofa. As they approached, a large dark shape materialized behind the sofa, leaping onto it and then bounding towards Anastasya in a rush. Credit to Gauge, she thought - he never budged as the giant dog leapt.

"Kasper!", Anastasya cried as he put paws the size of pancakes on her chest. The Dane was black as a subterranean midnight, just like the two prior Kaspers. She hadn't met this one before, the confluence of the previous Kasper dying some months prior, and her not visiting in that time period. This re-incarnation had lost none of his love for her, she was delighted to see.

"Good boy, who's a good boy" she cooed. In return, he barked loudly in her face, tail hammering the furniture. "Same as always...you're really mine, not hers" she whispered savagely.

"His name is ironic of course" she said as she stood. He looked blankly at her, and Anastasya didn't bother explaining about the old cartoon feed. Mya had shared her penchant for the archaic, but no-one else had ever expressed even the slightest interest.

She managed to bring the giant dog to heel, but then he jumped up and followed her as she walked over to the couch,

Gauge also in her trail. Before they got within hand-shaking territory, Dehlya commented aloud in her throaty voice.

"You're the first man - or boy - my daughter ever brought home to meet me. What's so special about you?"

"Mom, easy - please".

"It's an honor to meet you both" Gauge said eagerly, dodging the question as he bent to shake both hands. "And can I just say, I've always had - "

Eryss put up her hand. "Spare us. I see you spotted the bar on the way in. Why not go and make yourself and Anastasya a drink. Whatever you want".

"Thank you Chief Genetics Officer" Gauge said gratefully, deftly dodging the animal's head which marked the front of a shaggy rug lying between the bar and sofa. All the more impressive consider he was back-pedalling at the time, and couldn't have seen it.

"Nothing for me" Anastasya called over.

"Not joining us?" her primary rasped.

Eryss reached a hand out to touch her crony's leg. "Anastasya is being conscientious about her pregnancy".

"Oh that's right" her primary responded, saying nothing but appraising Anastasya with a frank stare. There it was...she hadn't been imagining it! Animosity, if she wasn't mistaken.

Eryss must be aware of the recent fallout between her mom and herself after Mya's rejection - was this evening a setup to smooth things over between them? But it couldn't be, she reasoned...at least, couldn't *just* be that. Sybelle had mentioned State business. Quickly, as soon as they raced towards the surface, she forced down memories of Jon in the embassy which threatened to go mainstream in her thoughts.

She watched Dehlya sling back the remainder her whiskey, push herself up from the couch and glance appraisingly over at the bar and Gauge's efforts to mix drinks.

"I'm going to help this young man. I believe Eryss and yourself have something to discuss". Here eyes never left Gauge as she spoke.

Eryss watched after her until she reached the bar.

"Music" Eryss said, looking appraisingly at Anastasya. She didn't have to explain why - Anastasya immediately couldn't make out what her primary was saying to Gauge above the strains of the string quartet. Old-fashioned privacy.

"Sybelle, confirm we are dark?"

"Confirmed. All feeds deactivated".

"Sit, Anastasya", her boss said, reaching an arm out to pat a space on the couch.

Anastasya took her place, Kasper padding over to lie by her feet.

"We have heard from Grand Plains. From their Governor".

"Oh?" She caught herself toying with the dark green watch, gift from the Governor, and abruptly stopped. She'd been wearing it as an oddity, something that stood her out from the crowd, especially as it came from an outsider male. But now, sitting in front of Eryss with the Governor on the agenda, she pulled her sleeve down over it as surreptitiously as possible.

"During your work on Abundance - not just your time with the Governor - did you detect any anomalies or anything of concern with regards the genetic payload and target population?"

"Of course not." Despite the seriousness, Anastasya was distracted by the muffled antics at the bar. Her primary was practically stroking Gauge's arm.

"You know I didn't. If I had, I of course would have - "

Eryss stopped her with a held-up palm.

"Sybelle of course confirmed similarly. However, the Governor claims there is a health emergency situation in Grand Plains. He is asking for *your* presence out there. He is alleging this emergency situation is related to the recent genetic treatments we provided."

"I'm sorry...how does this make any sense? We know - Sybelle and I - that it was totally benign. What exactly is the situation? What symptoms? Are people sick? Dying?"

"He refused to be drawn on specifics. All we know is it is not Genghis related. And that he will not accept any delegation that does not include you. He also issued vague threats about spreading fake news about the treatment we provided".

Anastasya exhaled loudly and let herself fall back into the couch, earning a curious glance and raised ears from Kasper.

"Did he say why he wanted *me*?"

"No. In fact, we were hoping *you* might shed some light on that".

Eryss's smile showed teeth. Anastasya looked pale.

"Why would the Governor of Grand Plains wish to speak personally to you - and only outside of Corynth in Grand Plains - rather than communicate openly with the Councyl, about an alleged emergency situation?"

Anastasya had goosebumps, and imagined her boss's scrutiny as scuttling insects on her skin, reading her every breath and micro-movement for meaning...and knew I would be doing the same.

"I've no idea", she blustered. "I've no idea what's happening out there." Her exasperation was genuine. "Really, I have zero knowledge about any of this."

Eryss regarded her a long moment.

"So...all that time alone, on multiple occasions with Governor Laide..." She emphasized his name with a sarcastic tone. "And did you and he discuss anything of import which perhaps you have not told us about?"

Her boss's eyes held her in complete control, as a python would a meal. Anastasya's thoughts crystallized incredibly clearly, yet bizarrely: "two plus two is five?" repeated a number of times internally. She looked back at the Chief with an equal gaze, and answered aloud: "No".

Eryss sat back, a look of surprise evident.

"Really?"

Anastasya shook her head.

"Nothing at all? It must have been tempting, what with no Sybelle. The temptation of the forbidden."

Anastasya was now concentrating hard, her frontal lobes conjuring an image. "No, nothing unusual I haven't already reported. I banged my head soon after entering the first day, got some medical treatment and hot chocolate - but really, that was the highlight".

"Hot chocolate...", and her boss slapped her own knees.

"You need to go to Grand Plains, meet Governor Laide, determine what this alleged emergency is. We have to hope Sybelle or yourself did not make any mistakes".

Anastasya froze. Then began speaking slowly, differently than she had been when answering.

"My intuition and synesthesia have *never* been wrong - it's not even a thing. And Sybelle making a mistake?"

She touched her belly, still smooth as ever over the rippled muscles. No outward sign of the life inside her - the licensed life.

Eryss was talking again.

"Our recent efforts must be perceived as a success globally. Our tech and scientific advancements illuminate the world, beacons of true enlightenment and equality - we cannot tolerate fake news attacking our success or reputation".

"Right" Anastasya answered, still processing the implication of a possible mistake being made on her side.

"Good" Eryss said, slapping knees again and looking over at the bar. Anastasya followed her gaze. Her primary was jabbing Gauge playfully in the chest as she spoke from very close range to him.

"Time to collect your man", her boss said. "You leave in the morning. Sybelle will fill you in on the logistics."

||| – |||*

The convoy tore across the dust tracks, one-time tarmac smothered by dirt and disuse. The view of the passengers was limited, brown clouds billowing like airbags around their nine armored vehicles.

Nonetheless Anastasya was enjoying the journey. She'd never been allowed outside Corynth due to the transgressions of her youth, had never seen the barrenness and desolation. A landscape utterly alien to Corynthians.

As each klick brought them further in and further away from Corynth, she couldn't help but think about Mya. She'd been out here volunteering, right before it had all went down. She thought it funny, but now out here she could see her face clearly again - and with raged in the hurt. With nothing but time on her hands, time and dust, she began daydreaming, strongly exploring the topic. She'd never heard it mentioned before - by anyone - that people *regret* rejections. She certainly did. How many primaries had rejected their child for Credyt, and now regret it? She could not believe there was no-one, which was suggested by the absolute silence she'd encountered her whole life about it. Why was rejection regret a taboo topic? Jon, in one of his many lectures had said some conspiracy theory about the creation of a social environment where there was only one right or acceptable opinion or thought on a topic. She tried to remember, was fairly sure it was of his definitions of totalitarianism. Single acceptable opinions, "demonizing" of anyone who diverged, socially unacceptable to disagree. She struggled with this as the scenery didn't change around her, how she couldn't be the first citizen to ever regret a rejection.

She reasoned she wasn't breaking any reg by thinking about regret at what happened to Mya - she wasn't spreading hate or sedition or anti-State messages - but still, it was close to the edge maybe. So she put on an old movie on for distraction. As it started, she got messaged from Mya and Gauge: why not join them in-game instead of watching a depressing movie on her own? She declined, apologizing that yes movies weren't very sociable, but she was just in the mood for total escapism.

Within minutes the large number of initial watchers of her feed, leading a convoy into Grand Plains, tapered to zero. Literally. Nobody - not a single citizen - was watching her feed. This was also risky territory - having no-one at all on her feed ranked badly, proof she'd alienated fellow citizens in some way. If prolonged it would lead to a Credyt penalty.

And on the topic of Credyt, she watched from her seat-belted leather recliner as the blond lead actress had just stolen money again. Anastasya laughed. Imagine if Credyt was somehow *physical* and could be traded...pure chaos, unworkable! She settled back, let her focus get absorbed in the movie.

Before it ended, an abrupt change in road quality, from bouncy-rough to smooth jolted her back to reality. A quick eye movement to her Map confirmed they were incoming to Brunswick, their meeting point with Governor Laide. It wasn't the capital of Grand Plains, but Brunswick was a town apparently in the epicenter of whatever unexplained emergency was happening.

She killed her movie as the convoy pulled to a halt, and followed three battle Helpers off their vehicle. She felt dwarfed behind them, a new experience for Anastasya, who was taller than the average citizen. Each Helper was engineered to be head and shoulders taller than average...at least two standard deviations from mean height.

They found themselves in the middle of the street, their

convoy having just stopped in-lane without pulling over. It didn't look like it would be a problem, as a lone Buick trundled up the road in their direction, dust billowing around it like a soiled pillow.

"Three for $10, no reasonable offer refused!" was emblazoned in black writing on a large and faded pink poster, somehow still stuck to the inside of a window in what looked like a building which had once been a store. Anastasya saw it had been re-incarnated as a boarded-up emporium of empty shelves and dirt. She looked further down the street, saw one or two buildings which weren't boarded-up or completely ramshackle.

She spun on her heels, searching out a human face - anywhere - and finding none.

Following the Helpers, she fell in at the head of a small troupe of Corynthian medics and scientists, moving around their convoy towards the side of street their machines were blocking the view of. As they rounded the corner of the lead vehicle, their port of call and a small welcoming party became visible.

The doctors as the white gowns, the guns and camouflage as militia (the police-come-military authority of Grand Plains). Their group stood, silent and solemn, some with tired smiles, others just clearly tired.

She sought out and found Governor Laide who was standing beside Tomek, the doctor she recognized from her visits to the Embassy. Tomek had very much enjoyed the hospitality in Corynth - he'd joked about "putting on pounds". If he had, she could see that now he'd lost them.

Jon's eyes were hidden behind aviator blue-mirrored shades, but from the angle of his head he seemed to be looking in Anastasya's direction. Seeing him now, on opposite sides, she couldn't stop one of his last "lectures" from playing in her head, from later that night in that Lost Arc taverna. Fuck did he fly close to correction - so many times!

I get that questioning anything about the Councyl or life in Corynth is virtually impossible. You're all trained and conditioned from birth to delegate all decision making - and hence critical thought - to Sybelle. And why not? She is after all the highest form of intelligence the planet has ever seen, implanted directly in your brain. It's convenience of the ultimate form - no need to think. Just be entertained.

That was the man standing across from her, and this was his territory. The gap between them seemed larger now to her.

But like awkward teenagers at a disco, the two groups eventually shuffled towards each other. It took Dr. Tomek to step forward, arm-outstretched ahead of him like a stiff divining rod, to greet one of Corynth's visitors before the rest followed suit - all apart from the dark-visored Helpers, and the hesitant militia unwilling to seem weak in front of their armed counterparts. Anastasya had eschewed her personal weapon, the same type of gun she'd been given to protect herself whilst in the Grand Plains Embassy - she didn't want to promote negativity or mistrust as the Helpers were doing. They were here to help she'd argued right before they'd embarked, but to no avail.

Once the group ice had been broken, a sense of excitement and anticipation likely at adventurous prospects - senses you only get with travel and arrival to a new place - erupted in the Corynthian delegation. The absence in their hosts of anything reciprocal was plainly obvious. Their faces didn't read of resignation and desperation, but fatigue and an element of shock was written on the tired host faces.

"Welcome. I'm Doctor Tomek Spring. And these are my colleagues, plus our Militia friends. Great you are here. We could certainly do with your help", he said in a raised voice, pushing his rimless glasses back up his nose as he finished. Corynth had solved sight deficiency years ago, there was a genetic treatment for it both pre and ante natal.

"If you'd like to follow me please, let's go to the wards and we can show you why you're here." This silenced the thrum of excited conversations amongst the Corynthian medical team - exclusively female - who now traipsed after the Grand Plains delegation. The Helpers split, with some remaining outside with the convoy (still blocking the road), whilst three made to proceed with the group indoors.

Anastasya turned to the Helper captain.

"Is this really necessary? It's a hospital."

"It's necessary. And don't question us again. Understood?"

Anastasya stared into the dark visor. Eventually she nodded curtly before turning sharply on her heels to follow the team in. "Idiots", she said to herself. "It's a fucking hospital!"

Anastasya had been hoping the hospital's drab exterior masked a modern and sterile interior, but unfortunately it wasn't the case. Ants scurried through cracks in the lino floors. The faded pale green wall paint reminded her of the last time she threw up. The smell of raw disinfectant reeked like a wino.

"What a place", Cyndy Epsilon 222 whispered to Anastasya, her nose almost vertical in disgust. Anastasya mumbled back noncommittally, not wanting to be heard denigrating Grand Plains' main medical facility in front of the others.

The group snaked down the bare-bulb-lit corridor to an elevator door. It was closed over and rusted. Tomek yanked it open, an action which showed how thirsty it was for an oiling.

"I hope the elevator cables are in better condition" Cyndy muttered.

Nobody responded, as they all stood waiting in an improvised semi-circle.

Anastasya saw Jon with his shades off for the first time, the blue of his eyes showing their usual spark - jbutust not trained on her. Her stare lingered, hoping he'd look her way, but to no avail. A sliver of irritation grew in her mind. He hadn't greeted her outside, and now ignoring her. She told herself to grow up. This was serious...but would it kill him to say "hello"?

"We're going down to a subterranean area, our sterile ICUs", Dr. Tomek explained. "Your Corynthian neural comms won't work down there - it's not possible to send or receive electromagnetic signals there".

The Helpers turned their heads in each others' direction. "Next time fore-warn us of this".

"OK", Tomek abruptly and unapologetically replied.

I will need you to update me on what transpires, Anastasya. The more information I have, the better.

"Of course Sybelle", Anastasya replied, as Grand Plains' heads turned towards her. She shrugged at them.

Cyndy was complaining again, this time more loudly, about "losing touch and with Sybelle". Anastasya looked fuming and embarrassed as "disgrace", "back to the dark ages" and other sentiments were slung around between her and the other compatriots. As the elevator doors creaked opened and they all shuffled in, silence finally reigned.

Anastasya was opposite Jon in the squash, who again managed not to make eye contact. It was an achievement, given their positioning opposite each other in the elevator, something which grated painfully with her. Hurt at being ignored turned to a bitter determination - she'd ignore him too.

Once the sluggish elevator ride ended party quickly pushed out. The corridor they found themselves in was symmetrical, the windows and glass doors on each side facing each other precisely, the filtered air cool. Moving along they could see a single patient in each room, bedded and connected to what looked like ventilator machines. Old ones, pistons punching up and down rhythmically.

They stopped about half way down, Tomek turning to face them, hands clasped tightly together in front of his groin.

"Thank you again for coming. We'll now brief you on what's happening, why we need your help, and then we can go in smaller groups to examine the patients closer up. You'll need to suit up for that part."

Anastasya looked into a room on her left: what looked to be a young woman of indigenous origin was the occupant - although it was hard to be sure given their faces were mostly covered by the connection to the machines beside them. In the room on the right opposite, a much older lady lay motionless, also looking to be Pawnee. Their eyes were closed, and Anastasya fervently hoped they were asleep or unconscious. The revolting weeping bloody boils on their foreheads and even eyelids hinted of something it would be better to not be conscious for.

"As you know, recently your med teams were in Grand Plains beginning the distribution of the medical assistance you so kindly provided to us, in the form of genetic treatments. These treatments covered inoculations, vaccines, cures for various hereditary illnesses." True, all true Anastasya thought proudly - signed off on by the Governor thanks to her work with Sybelle to validate the safety and efficacy of it all.

"All delivered through micro and bacteriophage gene editing mechanisms - again, as I'm sure you know. Our entire population has received this treatment now - in fact the first person to receive it was Governor Laide here, who publicly demonstrated the path to safety so as to demonstrate trust. We thought we were blessed to have had access to such magical medical care, and secondly to have managed the roll out to our entire population in such short time." Yes, there were sick people in these rooms, but on balance Anastasya felt good, and stealing a glance at others, she could see the same. It was a hospital after all, there would be sick here. Hopefully they could help with something else now.

"However, we don't feel so blessed now. For all the protection we received, something has hit us - hard. It's not Genghis, as you call it", he said loudly and clearly, at which Anastasya could practically feel the corridor relax. Tomek held his hands up.

"Whatever it is we have no medical record of seeing before - anywhere - and we don't have a treatment for it. We need you to help us with this emergency under the terms of our recent deal. Governor, you wanted to add something?"

"Thanks doctor" Jon said, stepping forward. "Simply that I've cleared this with your Councyl, and your Founder Eryss has pledged her full commitment and support. Which is why you are here", he finished.

Again, he had not made eye contact, and Anastasya felt forlorn now, rather than mad.

Tomek again.

"We can see no medical precedent or history for this, all we know so far is it's a virus. Transmission mechanism? Airborne. Extremely contagious. Incubation period - too early to know precisely, but appears to be in the region of days - roughly two. Symptoms include hallucinations, failing eyesight and hearing loss, loss of bodily control in limbs - all of which hint at brain impairment and what looks like early-stage targeting of the brain by this virus. Possibly the brain itself could be a fertile home for it, we simply don't know yet." Anastasya watched as at this, many of the Corynthian delegation were wincing, but trying not to. Physical illness and general ill-health was so novel for them, and to be in close proximity must be terrifying - oddly, she realised she was immune to this fear shared by the others.

"Victims also rapidly experience organ failures, lungs filling with liquid and bodily fluid, similar to cystic fibrosis patients - extreme cystic fibrosis cases. Leakage of bodily fluids and substances through all orifices. Causes of death so far include drowning, essentially in flooded lungs, kidney and liver failure, general body shutdown, and in some cases accidents due to the extreme impairment of senses. Time from first display of symptoms to death varies from day one - caused by panicked accidents at this early phase - right through to about one week."

He paused, and in the new and total silence, heads inched round towards the patients in the rooms adjacent. Rooms which stretched up and down the corridor.

"We've not had anyone survive longer than seven days so far."

III – IV*

The inevitable had happened, the avoidance of each other come to an end as they suited up outside the ICU room. Anastasya had felt zero warmth from the Governor, his eyes cold and even distant as he shook her hand perfunctorily. They had spoken though: he'd inquired about her pregnancy, commenting that she was looking great. It hadn't come across as genuine to her. But, she thought, maybe it wasn't personal... perhaps she'd imagined distance and coldness when in fact it could be worry or concern eating him. Citizens of his State *were* dying rapidly and horribly, literally in front of their very eyes. Yet still...something felt off with him, a sliver of a splinter she just couldn't locate.

Any further personal re-acquaintance was on hold now, the bright yellow space suits they wore having microphones connecting them on a circuit - anything anyone said would be heard by their group of four. The throng of Corynthian visitors and Grand Plains locals had fractured into smaller groups, so that each group could visit a patient in separate rooms. There were enough rooms to accommodate them all.

Rachel Chavos was their group's patient, Anastasya managing to read it from the girl's bedside chart, her helmet's visor impressively not fogging despite her heavy breathing in the sweaty suit. Rachel was eighteen she read, something impossible to tell by simply looking at the girl, due to the mangle of tubes snaked across her torso and the mask covering her nose and mouth. Rachel's mask was connected to a ventilator, and it's rhythmic mechanical wheezing and exhaling was loud, even through the helmets. The tube coming out of Rachel's chest - which had looked a consistent dark hue from the corridor - was on closer inspection alternating vilely; sometimes greenish-brown, others blackish-red.

"It's suppurating the puss and fluid from her lungs. Otherwise she'd drown", the raspy voice of Dr. Spring explained clinically. "Those other tubes are for kidney dialysis and essential fluid intake". He was standing beside the Governor on the opposite side of the bed to Anastasya and Cyndy. Cyndy's own breathing didn't sound too healthy to Anastasya - laboured and heavy, an annoyance to have constantly in her own ear, although she could empathize with why. Anastasya had never seen such a sick person in her life before either. On old movie feeds it never looked this bad.

In Corynth such a thing wouldn't be allowed to take place, so the opportunity - if you could call it that - would never arise. If a citizen were so ill that neither Sybelle nor any geneticist could cure them - an extremely unlikely event - the citizen would never be allowed to suffer like this. Living sick was cruel - every citizen knew that. They would be humanely retired - "killed", as the man across from her would argue - for their own benefit and well-being.

"Just think" Anastasya said, turning to Cyndy to indicate she was addressing her rather than the other two on the closed circuit. "We're in the presence of an unknown and lethal entity, one which would almost certainly cause a horrible death if we came in contact with it. And all we have to protect us are these suits", shaking her baggy yellow arms as she said it. Cyndy seemed to actually turn green inside hers, but said nothing in response.

There was a gravelly clearing of a throat, the prelude to the Governor speaking. "That's not true".

Anastasya eventually rotated enough to face the suited Jon. Then after a few seconds realised he couldn't see the puzzled expression she was wearing - there was a reflected glare from the stark overhead light on his visor, and she reasoned it must be the same on hers.

"What's not true?"

"You're at no risk from whatever is attacking her."

"The suits are precautionary, really to stop us picking it up and spreading it elsewhere", Tomek interjected.

"We haven't given you all the facts yet. Dr. Spring will provide genetic samples from the patients to you and your colleagues. We'd be grateful if you could start analysis in those mobile labs I presume you brought. ASAP. Anything you need from us, you'll get", Jon said.

She clamped down on the urge to tell him to say "please", his official tone with her now biting. She nodded, before saying "OK", her nod lost in the folds of the suit. She waited for an explanation of the facts he mentioned, knowing him well enough that he was building to it.

But it was Dr. Tomek who continued. "The reason we're starting with genetic samples for you, as opposed to delving into symptom analysis and typical diagnosis paths, is because there seems to be an non-random genetic component to this virus."

She held her breath, not daring to miss his next words over the mic.

"All the victims so far - without exception - are Pawnee."

It wasn't so much as a penny dropping, as an anvil. She knew her mind had grasped the implications of what Jon had said, but her brain was racing to catch up. The Pawnee...the indigenous tribe driven towards oblivion by the Pilgrims, and later the United States army. Just over twelve hundred or so lived still - all in Grand Plains, the State that was the property of the Pawnee Nation, given to them during the birth of the States of America as part of a reparation settlement for their suffering on the infamous Trail of Tears.

All victims being Pawnee of course implied *genetic targeting*, something triggered by the specific DNA of their tribe! It wasn't unheard of for particular strands of DNA to be susceptible to certain diseases, but she'd never heard anywhere of anything as extreme. She remembered Eryss's words…"nature is savagely random". But the mathematician in Anastasya knew that odds of a tribe - or any racial group - being selected randomly by nature for something as extreme as this…well, they were astronomical. Which, according to Occam's razor left one option…but no, she refused to believe it.

"Really? So selective? No non-Pawnee at all with even mild symptoms?"

The spaceman who was Governor Laide shook his round yellow head, and as his helmet moved she saw the light in his eyes. "None".

And so the logic for them being here was revealed.

The genetic sample of this virus could be put alongside Pawnee DNA and compared…but how long would it take the computers Grand Plains had? There was no-one better than her - machine or human, Sybelle or other - to explore the interactions across billions of genetic letters and sequences. And the Governor knew that.

"Rachel has been in here four days…tomorrow will be her fifth. Please God she'll have that and a sixth, but I'm not too hopeful. We'll get you the samples so you can begin" Governor Laide said. "And you'll please excuse me. I need to be elsewhere."

There it was again, a coldness or detachment that she didn't think was warranted to be targeted towards her, despite the grimness of the situation…or was she being too sensitive? After all, pregnancy was infamous for mood changes, one of the many downsides Tanya frequently reminded her of.

"Can I be excused too?" Cyndy managed to say, her voice

meek and barely audible in the headsets. "I...I don't feel very well".

"I'll take you to decontamination with me", Jon said. "Just follow me", and he turned slowly to leave without any acknowledgment of Anastasya, who rotated her whole body step by step to watch them exiting like walking mannequins. She got herself back around to face Tomek across Rachel's bed. Anastasya shook her head in exasperation.

"I'll prepare the samples for transport to your convoy", Tomek said. "Then why don't you and I go to the canteen? I think we could both do with a pick-me-up."

"OK. But...is it just me or is Governor Laide a bit, I don't know, angry or something?" Anastasya blurted. She couldn't keep it bottled any longer.

"Let's talk in the canteen. I know she probably can't hear us, but I don't feel comfortable talking in front of Rachel like she isn't here. And yes - he's angry. Wouldn't you be?"

Of course she would, Anastasya thought, frustrated Tomek was missing her point. It was probably her fault for not articulating her thoughts more clearly, but it was hard to hit the normal nuances of language in that infernal gear and tinny mics. She meant something more than anger at the situation... Governor Laide was behaving unusually in a *different* sense, and maddeningly one she couldn't pinpoint. Fine, they could talk in the canteen. Turning like a tanker, she followed Tomek out, leaving the young Rachel to the peace of the machines.

III – V*

The fluorescent light over their table flashed intermittently as Anastasya and Tomek forced themselves into the small plastic orange seats, their trays in front of them on the laminate-covered table. Tomek took a hearty bite from his BLT, Anastasya poked at her lasagna with a fork, teasing strings of cheese from the unappetizing meat. Her stomach got the better of her eyes and she eventually dug in.

"So, what about Governor Laide", Anastasya asked, looking over her shoulder to reaffirm they were out of earshot of anyone else. She saw Cyndy sitting alone in a corner, and quickly looked back to Tomek's tired face. "He seems different than when I worked with him in Corynth".

"Mmm", Tomek mumbled, waving his hand to speed himself up as he swallowed a bite. "I wouldn't read too much into it. He obviously has a lot on his mind."

"Of course. It's actually a bit stupid of me to even say it in the first place".

"Not at all. But responsibility lies heavier with him than most people". He worked at prising something from between his teeth with his tongue. The light flickered again with a zapping sound. "What I mean is, Jon doesn't hesitate to take action to fulfill his duties or responsibilities."

"That's...admirable I guess", Anastasya said, wishing he'd just get to the point.

He nodded as if she'd said something profound. "You know he was in the military?"

"Yes".

"I was too. In fact me and the Governor go a ways back. He was our unit's Colonel when I joined as an eighteen year old."

"But you're a doctor", Anastasya said.

"I wasn't always. I went from machine-gunner to medicine. But it's not me we want to talk about, is it?"

She shook her head while finishing off a forkful.

"So like I say, I've known him these past twenty-five years or so in different guises...I followed him to help with his civic involvement during the break up of the United States and the rise of the corpo-states, and then ultimately into his political career. He's a leader, so I followed".

He retrieved a silvery dented hip flask from the depths of his doctor's smock, and poured a generous dash into the coffee. He didn't offer it to her.

"Anyway, Jon - Governor Laide - had a long and varied career in the military. When I served with him, it was on a U.N peace-keeping mission."

"I see".

"In Turkey".

Anastasya put her fork down. "Oh." Images flashed through her mind, yet another of humanity's "never again" moments.

She picked her words as carefully as her food. "I saw about that in history feeds, the civil war...".

Forgotten vivid images jumped into her mind, scenes of mass murder and rape, the butchery and gassing of whole cities and towns, the concentration camps marketed to the world as re-education campuses - as the world had seen often before, just with different branding. She remembered it because it was taught in Corynth as a recent example of a world bereft of reason and science, an evil brought about by over-population and superstitions, by the perils of democracy and lethargic politics.

"Yes, between the ruling Muslim party with their factions, and the secularists and Kurds on the other side. This was twenty years ago now - hard to believe - in the twilight of U.N peacekeeping initiatives. You know it was the final ever peacekeeping mission the U.N deployed? Governor Laide - Colonel Laide - and I, well, our unit transferred there en-masse. Go on, let's keep eating as we talk, we'll need the fuel later".

Tomek drank coffee, which looked more like turgid sludge to Anastasya; but she wasn't drinking it, so who cared.

"I'm telling you this so you can understand better the kind of man Jon is. The lengths he will go to in order to do the right thing, OK?"

"Yes, I got that. Please - go on". She could see he was still egging himself on to tell her something.

"We were barracked in Anatolia province, south-eastern Turkey, and we'd been there about four months when Government forces started winning territory in the area, which was very close to main Kurdish population centers. It wouldn't have been unusual then to have mainly ethnic-Kurd populated villages in that region. We'd been embedded with these civilian villages for those five months or so, and we'd formed good relationships with the locals...Colonel Laide particularly so. Anyhow, under his leadership and through good fortune, there had been no trouble - kids going to school as normal, local health centers and shops supplied, all fine really. That changed once the Government troops and Muslim militias began their eastern advance."

The light went off again, longer this time, stopping Tomek momentarily.

"Re-education camps sprang up as the Government forces advanced, usually one camp per ten kilometer radius or thereabouts. We knew - hell, the *world* knew - what went on in those camps, yet the U.N refused to mandate the Peacekeepers to use force to prevent civilians being transported to them." Unsurprising, Anastasya thought...another good reason for Corynth not to recognize the United Nations Security Council or international courts.

"The trend for the camps at that time in Anatolia was to take the women and girls alive to them, but to butcher the males en-route...apart from the occasional few for the troops who preferred to rape boys. They were rape camps in the first instance you see, brutalized harems for the soldiers of Young Turkey."

Another sip, and a chance for Anastasya to look at this man who could calmly talk about things like this...not in an uncaring way, very far from it, but in a matter-of-fact way. She couldn't quite imagine *this* man there, in those times. She remembered what Jon had told her about mass murder being a statistic, a single death a tragedy. It hadn't been a theoretical point then.

"Our villages remained intact...until the day they didn't. We couldn't protect all the villages simultaneously, simply impossible. Peacekeeping works - when it does, that is - by the threat of over-whelming force, or at least enough to do serious damage. The more you thin a unit geographically, the less clout you have."

He poured again into his coffee, and Anastasya could see now the trick of being able to stomach it - lace it with pure vodka.

"One day on patrol we rolled into one of the villages to find it razed. The town square was dense with the dead, all males, bar some elderly women with their walking sticks or frames nearby. Toddlers up to octogenarians, throats all slit, hands tied behind their backs with laces. I've got a picture-perfect memory of the scene in my mind's eye" he said, stabbing his forefinger against his temple with some force, "and I can bare to recall it visually. But to do this day I can't stomach the memory of the smell…the reek of piss, shit and dried blood - gallons and gallons of it - all baked in the heat of an Anatolian summer's day. It was one of the reasons I left the military after that, ridiculous as it may sound - I simply couldn't take the smell of latrines anymore."

He stopped again, and Anastasya thought he would drink, but this time he didn't. He stared at the paper coffee cup for long enough that she was tempted to reach out and touch his arm…but somehow it felt right to leave him be.

"The women, bar the very elderly, were simply gone - not a trace, not a single girl left. To varying degrees something changed that day for all of us. But in particular for the Colonel."

Anastasya took his coffee from him, and sipped it - just a little, enough to make her give it back quickly.

"Two days later we were manning a roadblock on the main artery to Incirlik. This particular spot was a leafy green vale, and the Colonel had us spread in a 'V' formation expanding out from the roadblock, with most of us hidden in the shrubbery and dense foliage on either side of the road. Nobody said anything, but we all knew we'd been deployed in an ambush formation. We had no stopping power behind the roadblock, like we'd usually have - it was only himself and two guys on either side of him, standing just in front of concrete pillars we'd dropped.

"Anyhow a convoy of two trucks and I think four jeeps pulled up. They were Government militia, unofficial paramilitaries, free to roam, rape, loot and pillage, all outside the boundaries of being an official army, so nothing we could do about them - we had no mandate to engage them at all as they were not official military. These guys, their trucks' "load" consisted of about twenty young women. They were seated on the open truck beds, bound, guarded by armed militia who jumped off the trucks when we stopped them."

He leaned his elbows either side of his plate. "It wasn't unheard of for women or girls to stand up and fling themselves over the edge of a moving truck, despite the collective punishment the others could receive of on-the-spot random executions."

"Why would they do that?"

He looked puzzled at her question. "Because they preferred death than the rape camps." Anastasya felt her cheeks burn, both in embarrassment at her question, and in something raw and bald.

"Ye, well two of the girls started screaming at us in Kurdish until they got rifle-butts in the face from the guys outside the truck. Honestly, it was hard to lie there...a machine-gun in my hands...and watch this without doing nothing. But - we were U.N troops, with no mandate to interfere with civilian paramilitaries. The leader of this group pulled his cap down tight, managed his fat ass out of his seat in the jeep, and approached Colonel Laide, who was slowly walking towards him.

"The Colonel hadn't flinched at the stomping of those two girls, and now he extended his hand and shook this guy's hand. I couldn't believe it, and I wasn't the only one. I really couldn't. We couldn't hear what was being said, but the Colonel gestured for his counterpart - he was a Major, not that rank meant much in that militia - to walk with him a little further back down the road where the convoy had come from, away from the trucks and the jeeps. The major laughed, and gestured for his two bodyguards to come with him."

He exhaled loudly, perhaps breathing the memory to life.

"The four of them traipsed down the road right up parallel to where I was positioned. Now I could hear them. The Colonel and this major were standing about five or six feet ahead of the two bodyguards, see?" he gestured with his hands, each an imaginary person.

"Jon didn't smoke, but I knew he carried a pack for negotiations or just to break the ice with someone. International currency they are, invaluable in war zones. Anyhow, he took a pack from his pocket, and offered one to the major, who greedily took it - American tobacco, a real rarity! When they were both puffing, Colonel Laide said something that flipped a switch in my head - he asked for some girls for a "bit of fun" for the troops. As I say, that woke me right the fuck up...and from then, everything moved in slow motion. It's funny - even in my memory of it today it's slow-mo.

"The major turned to look at the girls the Colonel was pointing at, as did the bodyguards who were highly amused, even excited. Jon calmly, and in one smooth fluid motion, whipped out his Glock and shot the closest bodyguard in the side of the head, before swinging the gun right into the major's blank face and pulling the trigger twice more. Chunks of the major's face hit the ground before his cigarette did."

Anastasya stared. Hadn't Eryss armed her on Jon's arrival? She'd quickly discounted any threat after getting to know him. In these seconds of shock she just couldn't mentally reconcile the man she had known, who argued how inhumane rejection was, with this picture of a gunman blasting someone's face at close range. They couldn't be the same person!

"Jon *killed* that guy?"

"Stone dead."

The answer satisfied the wild feeling she'd had, to a degree. "At least there was *some* justice. But - what then?"

"Well, Jon was a sitting duck. He was hit by the paramilitaries at the trucks and jeeps. He was lucky though - the first bullet hit him close to the heart in the upper left chest - here - and spun him round. The rest hit him on the right arm and thigh. It em...thing was they didn't have much time to shoot at him. We finished them off pretty quick. They never stood a chance with the superior position we had. Jon was our only casualty that day - none of their thirteen survived".

It was like they were the only two people in the world, existing in a bubble of fluorescent light infused with the smell of vodka, granule coffee possibly recycled, and lasagna.

"Unlucky thirteen" Anastasya said. She'd always thought it a happy coincidence people thought it unlucky. For her it was the ugliest number - it had a rank smell and taste, an unhealthy brownish tint to it.

"I guess", Tomek answered, draining his coffee, face flushed.

"And the girls? What happened to them?"

Tomek nodded auspiciously, but didn't immediately answer. A dread feeling enveloped her.

"They were fine. Apart from the two girls who were rifle butted. Sorry, this is difficult for me." He swiped a hand across his face. "You've no idea how it feels to have saved those women from what awaited. It gave my life meaning. Maybe the only thing I ever did that matters, really matters. And it's Jon Laide I have to thank for that".

"Oh! I thought you were going to say something happened to them" Anastasya gushed, her relief flooding any acknowledgment of Tomek's emotional state.

"No, all was fine. They even saved *us* in the end! They testified at the U.N war crimes tribunal that the paramilitaries had opened fire first, and only *then* had the Colonel unloaded his weapon on that major and his bodyguard. The judges didn't believe it, but there were no other witnesses to disagree...none alive, that is. So our unit was fine, but Governor Laide got a dishonorable discharge for deploying his unit in an "aggressive manner contrary to U.N mandates"."

"So you got away with it! Not that you didn't do the right thing", she hastily added.

"Don't worry - I know what you mean", Tomek grinned.

"Yes, we got away with doing the right thing."

They both sat back. The tale lived between them, vivid in the bubble.

Anastasya looked around to find the canteen empty. Cyndy was gone, probably above ground to get back in contact with Sybelle, she guessed. Governor Laide...was it really him who'd done these things? She still couldn't picture those blue eyes sighting down and pulling the trigger in that major's face - twice.

Tomek leaned forward again.

"I told you this about Jon for a reason. Don't be fooled by the politics and diplomacy, is what I'm saying. Just remember he's motivated by doing the right thing and helping people. His people are important to him, and anything that threatens them...he'll do something about."

"Tomek, you know...what exactly are you getting at? Are you saying I should be *afraid* of him or something?"

"Of who?" a shadow over the table inquired. Anastasya and Tomek practically jumped, looking sharply at each other, but Anastasya recovered composure first.

"Hello Governor. I was asking Dr. Spring here why you'd been ignoring me".

Jon immediately glanced at Tomek, who raised his hands apologetically and struggled to get any words out. "Jon, I didn't -"

Jon stopped him with a palm and a look which bore no malice whatsoever. "I understand." Then turning to Anastasya, he took a step back from the table, his face again in shadow. "You and I should have a chat. What do you think?"

Before waiting for an answer, he picked up again. "We can take Tomek's office?", looking at his colleague.

Tomek nodded very eagerly.

"Thanks", the Governor said, turning towards the exit. Anastasya stood to follow him, pressing her hand hard on Dr. Spring's shoulder, leaving it there for a long moment as he remained seated.

"Thanks Tomek. I'm glad you did what you did. And glad you told me." With a final squeeze, she followed the Governor out, leaving her empty plate on the table.

III – VI

It was the first time all Founders met in the same physical location in approximately two years. It constituted too big both of a risk and a target, all five in a single location. So despite the safety the thermonuclear-proof subterranean bunker offered, it was a rarity for it to be in use.

"We all know how distracting feeds are - we designed them what way!" Eryss said, using the old Octyllion in-joke. "Given the import of Abundance and all the opportunity it offers, I - we - felt it was warranted to meet in-person, free of distraction. We are close - *this* close", she continued, pinching the forefinger and thumb of her right hand together demonstratively, "to finally achieving complete independence from the burden of dependency on actors external to our State. The final reliance on outsiders will be soon severed. Untethered access to the world's largest source of arcadmium for our creation, for Sybelle - her very life-blood, the *one* physical material we cannot synthesize nor compromise on, essential for Sybelle's qubit state management. *This* is practically in our hands."

The Chief Genetics Officer paused to evaluate her audience and emphasize the stakes - especially for Thya 1, Corynth's Chief Medical Officer. She was sat opposite Eryss, hunched to her left at an angle of about 45 degrees. Eryss had long ago decided that whatever intelligence Thya had once possessed had drained. The blood-lust she'd shown - particularly in the early formative years around the genesis of the Illumination - had carved a place for her in the Councyl. But now, bereft of heads to lop or sentences to sign en-masse, she was a much-diminished character, bordering on farcical. Thya was obsessed with the citizenry's perception and opinion of her, and constantly monitored any and all mentions of herself in feeds, frequently having them modified favorably no matter the inconsequence or triviality.

It took a while, but eventually Thya realised she needed to acknowledge her understanding of the proceedings.

"Brilliant. What an achievement."

Alyxis 1 cut in quickly. "Nothing is achieved yet. Eryss, re the timeline - how soon is "soon"?"

"Sybelle?"

"Current estimate is thirteen to fourteen days".

"*What?* How is that possible? You said before we'd aim for approximately *six months* from when the treatments begin. Two weeks?"

Eryss nodded in understanding as Alyxis's loud voice echoed off the bare concrete walls.

"We engineered Sybelle into existence, we know something as inherently complex as Sybelle's programming is never fully understandable holistically, although we may understand fragments. We forget when seeing the precision and accuracy of Sybelle's genetic work, we think that DNA is nothing but software, running on hardware that is an organic human body, and therefore understandable to some degree.

"We forget the immensity of the intelligence required to manipulate human D.N.A, with it's over six billion letters; a change to anyone could potentially result in drastic changes to the host, let alone what possibilities and implications combinatorial changes provide. Not to mention epigenetic impacts. Her speed and accuracy in achieving genetic tailoring is one thing, but consider also Sybelle's affinity in manufacturing people and societal change...*that* can be scary to behold, even for me! She is a god, a perfectionist creator.

How can we know the mind of a god?

""How is this possible"? The answer is simply that Sybelle made it so".

Alyxis 1 clapped. Slowly, fakely.

"Great lecture. At the risk of lecturing back, we *need* to know. Sybelle cannot be an unapproachable god, as you put it. She is *ours*. Created by, owned by Octyllion, now advising the Councyl of Corynth. Us. Something as unbelievable as a six month horizon to achieve all our goals for Abundance, now becoming *two weeks*...I want to know! How? Why? Is it still what we wanted?"

Thya nodded enthusiastically in agreement. Eryss looked at her. The nodding stopped.

"Very well". Eryss smiled broadly. She splayed her hands in a welcoming gesture to Alyxis.

Sybelle, the Thynk started, initiated by Eryss to Yena and I, *now might be the time to change the need-to-know on Abundance. Agreed?*

Yes.

The other Founders - Alyxis, Bryna, Thya - were not privy to the full goals of Abundance. Many cooks spoil a broth and all that. Together, Eryss and Yena had proven their efficiency, effectiveness, ability and drive to complete tasks over many years - for instance, the business with Danalya. I reminded them of this, plus informed them the optimum information radius for Abundance-in-full was limited to themselves. All predictions pointed that way. They had agreed - enthusiastically - to limit knowledge of the full scope of Abundance to themselves and me.

"Sybelle, what are the main factors in the acceleration of Abundance's timelines? High level". Alyxis challenged.

"The anti-rejection protest in-game on the 10th of Artemis

was an unexpected event, culminating in the rejection of Mya Theta 42. Her rejection introduced a behavioral change which was not anticipated in Anastasya Delta 3." My voice came from surround-speakers.

"What type of change?"

"Principally a change in the dynamic of the relationship between Governor Laide and Anastasya Delta 3."

"Relationship?" Thya sniggered.

"Not what you think", Yena answered acidly.

"This event, plus best-case estimates materializing equated to what can be perceived as - "

"Thank you Sybelle!" Eryss interjected.

You're a good liar Sybelle, but I will finish.

"We all know the risks of being here together, let us not prolong them needlessly." Her gaze swept the other Founders, found none avoiding her.

"We have always - *always* - been in the results game. Have we not?"

Assent was provided through nods and verbals.

"Remember when our *bonuses* were results-indexed?" Eryss laughed theatrically. "What quaint times. I digress - you all know I am not one for dwelling on the past. The point is, results are *all* that matter. The timeframe has accelerated; *how* it accelerated is not of importance. Arcadmium is our goal, and we get to that goal sooner now.

"There may be other periphery benefits that present themselves throughout the execution of Abundance. I suggest we break from our tradition - I should say protocol with Sybelle."

Bryna, Defense Chief, looked like she'd been shanked.

"*Break?*"

"That is correct."

Bryna looked for solidarity at the table, found none. Still flustered or fuming - or both - she turned back to the Chief Geneticist.

"Fine - continue then".

"I will. Nothing is as fast as the speed of trust. For the remainder of Abundance, I propose that we break protocol and forgo the need for Councyl approval of Sybelle's actions. That we trust Sybelle, *trust* that optimum results and outcomes will be obtained via her decisions and actions. These other periphery benefits I mention, the possibilities - questioning "why", pausing to add an additional decision checkpoint will slow the realisation of the results down."

"And at a potentially critical time", Yena interjected.

Heads turned. Then back.

"Exactly!"

Eryss stood, pushing her chair back as if it was nothing, started pacing slowly in the orbit of the chairs.

When she spoke, her voice had changed - it was soft, throaty. A rough whisper.

"Out there, in action and with kinetics, things can change pretty quickly. Right?", aimed at Bryna.

"Right. It's true, every general worth their salt knows the biggest enemy can hesitation."

"Yes", Eryss answered, drawing out the sibilance.

"Are we ones to hesitate?" It was so obviously rhetorical, not even Thya answered.

"You know - each of you - what we represent. What we sacrificed to get her. To get here. We are humanity's true pioneers, the *only ones* with the courage to do what all other nations and corps shy away from even countenancing!

"Let us go further - now, when the time is ripe! I say trust Sybelle and reap the benefits- the maximum benefits - we deserve. Seize security for our destiny as humanity's *next leap forward.*"

Yena's face was fervent, and Eryss drank in her burning eyes. She could feel the lust in the room, the primacy of power, the promise of more.

"Let us seize, let us take - let us *trust.*"

III – VII*

"Tomek say anything interesting?"

Anastasya watched standing as Governor Laide sat himself heavily into Dr. Spring's cracked brown-leather chair. He moved a small globe to the side of the desk so they could see each other unobstructed.

She sat too, stretching her long legs out from a two-seat sofa with hard springs, the sofa crammed under a shelf jammed with books. All medical texts. She had some back in her own library as they were some of her favorites, being invariably physically larger than others, their size and weight exuding an air of authority and expertise she found strangely attractive.

Anastasya took her time in answering. Governor Laide could wait a moment or two…she'd never been someone to jump to the whip after being ignored or discounted, and by her count he'd pretty much ignored her the whole time she'd been here until now. A couple of pictures hung on the wall in the gaps between the shelves: a thinner Tomek shaking the hand of a famous Pope, and a uniformed guy - looking no older than an aspyrant - standing proudly beside an elder man and woman. A crystal decanter about one quarter full of amber liquid stood on a rickety looking table in the corner beside a mug which she presumed served as a glass.

"He told me about your time in the military. In Turkey. Sounded like you're a hero, saving those girls" she said grudgingly, and instantly feeling bad about her tone.

He started to rotate slowly in the leather chair, side to side.

"That was the past".

Anastasya examined him intensely, not caring if it was obvious. She still couldn't imagine this man in front of her whipping out a gun and shooting people in the face. Surely such bestial ferocity would betray itself in his facial expression or demeanor, or he'd give off some vibe...but no, she felt no threat from this older man at all. Down here in their underground office, she still had no connectivity - Anastasya made a mental note to ask why she hadn't been given this background on Jon. Surely she'd had the right to know such a history of violence?

"I'm glad you and I are talking now. You ignored me all day today...I felt like a pariah or something. Did I do something to offend you? Or are you done with me, now that you've gotten what you wanted from the project?" He just looked baldly back, so she let him have it.

"You *asked* for me to come to Grand Plains, that's what Eryss said. I practically ran here as soon as I could - and when I get here, you ignore me!" Springs started to cut into her buttocks on the threadbare sofa . "And you never even asked me how I am...genuinely asked, I mean."

He stopped swinging on the chair, planted his elbows on the faded blue blotter on Tomek's desk.

"I asked for you personally because I needed to find out first-hand whether or not you'd betrayed us."

"*What?*"

He raised his right hand from the blotter. "Let me explain", and she was reminded of that initial debate they'd had in the Embassy that day she'd visited after Mya's arrest, both of them fighting to get their words in.

"I have to see how you'd react in person when you hear what I have to say. No offense Anastasya, but you're easy for me to read - you really wear your heart on your sleeve. Either that, or you're a brilliant actor, in which case hats off to you for playing me".

Flushing, she mustered what calmness she could before replying.

"What do you mean by that?", a sense of dread growing like fast night over her, something like when Eryss had told her of Mya's rejection.

"You checked for any possible negative side effects - anything at all - from the genetic delivery your side provided. And you found nothing - nothing whatsoever. Is that correct?"

"You know it".

He regarded her a long moment. She didn't flinch from his roving eyes which swallowed her entirely, every little movement she made seen and analysed. It was the personification of a classification algorithm in action.

"So then you were used too. Or maybe not used, but definitely not in the know. You're either too low level to be told, or Eryss maybe thought I'd be blindsided by you and miss what's really going on."

"Blindsided? Why would you be blindsided by me?" Her confusion was manifold. Betrayal...leading him on... blindsiding him...was she actually in danger here?

"A honey trap, is what I was thinking. Just without the intimacy part. Hear me out", he said urgently, seeing her reaction.

"I had a wife and child. Did Tomek tell you that?"

Anastasya could only shake her head.

"How about Eryss? Your Sybelle?"

She cleared her throat. "No".

"Leila. She was young, about your age when we first met. She was from a village in Anatolia, the first village we were stationed in. It broke the rules, but I couldn't help it - from the

170

very first moment I spoke to her, I wondered where she'd been my whole life. It was like finding something you didn't even know you'd lost. It was a whirlwind romance" he said, trying to smile but then quickly killing it when he couldn't quite pull it off.

"The U.N peacekeeping Colonel and the village chieftain's daughter. After a few months of being there, and us being together, we had plans for the future, you know? We were never going to part. But then our unit was mobilized elsewhere due to increasing Government attacks."

He paused and looked away from her, his attention drawn to the amber liquid on the table. He spoke to the bottle.

"We were three months gone from the village. The area had rapidly become a war zone, phone lines were destroyed by the government forces, no comms possible. When we eventually rotated back, Leila was pregnant, only...only I wasn't the father." He looked at her squarely, and Anastasya wondered how she'd missed the drooping dark bags under his eyes before.

"She'd been in one of the camps. The ones I guess Tomek told you about.

"She'd been taken, along with the other girls and women from their village one week after we had rotated out. Government forces used rape as a weapon, you see. They knew the dishonor and shame being pregnant by them, and by rape, would bring. It was ethnic cleansing, just like in Xinjiang, Somalia, Bosnia. Leila was released from the camp once she became pregnant...some said lucky, in a hideous sort of way, to get out of the camp relatively early."

Something flashed then across his face, his eyes sparking with electricity and power, but it only lasted a split second. Easy to miss, but it was enough - now she believed this man sitting in front of her was capable of the things she'd heard. It didn't frighten her though...in fact something the opposite.

"I was distraught", he continued, looking at his hands which were splayed open on the desk. "But nothing, not even the slightest bit close to what Leila had suffered. We married - as per our original plans - quickly and quietly a few days after my return. There was no-one at the wedding, apart from some of my unit and her parents. By being my spouse, she could get a visa to the United States - she had no future in Turkey - and have a chance at a new life. The three of us could."

Anastasya swallowed hard, but had to ask. She must be misunderstanding. "*Three* of you? You mean, she didn't want an abortion? The child was the child of a...", but she couldn't bring herself to say it, not to this man.

"*Her* child. Our child", he said plainly. "Leila said her child wasn't the criminal who raped her, that her baby was a different person with their own DNA. And completely innocent of any crime. She wouldn't even consider for one moment killing her baby for someone else's crimes. I loved her for that." He exhaled. Anastasya said nothing.

"She moved to the U.S immediately after the wedding, while I stayed in-country to finish my tour - I believe you know how that ended if you spoke to Dr. Spring. When I finally got back home and caught up, it was just in time - Leila gave birth to Joshua. Here", he said, standing up and fishing in his jacket pocket for a leathered wallet. He unfolded and passed over the desk a wrinkled photo which Anastasya stood to collect. A nuclear family looked back at her: bright eyed baby, tired but happy looking primary and a much younger, stubble-free, Jon Laide. The infant's eyes were wide with curiousity, and were the twin of the woman's - same oval shape, exact color match.

Anastasya studied it closely, finding it weird - she'd never held a photo before. She'd seen pictures in books of course, and large ones on walls, but never held a piece of paper containing someone's memories. "They were beautiful. Both of them", she said, placing it carefully back on the desk for Jon to pocket. Just a paper reminder of them, no feeds to replay scenes from their short life together. Then again, she thought, she had nothing at all of Mya...a likeness on a piece of paper would be at least a proof of life she didn't have.

"Thank you, they were. They both died a few months after that photo was taken."

Anastasya felt sick. "I'm so sorry...that's so horrible."

He looked away wincing and pressed his right temple - hard - with the thumb and forefinger of his right hand. Then he looked back at her.

"The point of telling you all this Anastasya, is that Eryss would have known this about me. And the expert Corynthian assigned to this project, to work directly with me, happens to be a young woman, one who looks similar even to Leila. As well as being pregnant." He laughed to himself ironically. "And recently promoted...you wouldn't have been in a position to deal with an outsider without that promotion. Am I right?"

It was more than feeling sick, Anastasya thought she would be sick, throw up all over Dr. Tomek's cheap rug. "Right". But it couldn't be true, she thought in desperation. She longed to be connected, to ask, to call Eryss and get her to set this straight immediately. The claustrophobia of this dinky subterranean little office with no fresh air suddenly seemed unbearable.

"Just my type, predicted no doubt by Sybelle that I'd have a soft spot for you, would feel protective." He held her gaze. "It's not nice to hear Anastasya, but what I'm saying is you were used."

"Used for what?", she asked, furiously dabbing her cheeks with a pulled-down sleeve covering her wrist.

"Used to hide the truth from me, to cloud my judgment. Used to make sure I was distracted enough to sign-off on the deal that is now killing my people."

Anastasya's head spun. She sat back, the protruding springs

not even noticed by her now.

"Please, Jon. I'm really sorry about what happened to your wife and child. But what are you talking about, our deal killing your people? And about me, distracting?"

He steepled his hands together on the desk.

"I know its unpleasant to hear: but Eryss calculated I'd be distracted by a young woman with a very similar profile to Leila, enough that I wouldn't be one hundred percent focused on the business in hand. She was right. You were used to convince me - unwittingly, granted - using your credibility as an authentic genius, one who genuinely believed in the safety of the payload, in order that I sanction Corynth's genetic treatments for my people. And in return I give access to our arcadmium reserves for three years. That genetic payload you delivered is what is killing the Pawnee, Anastasya."

"No", she said simply, shaking her head. "All those sick people - this was caused deliberately? By our payload? Have you lost your mind? Even if it was true, why would we do it? It could be anything. I mean Genghis has been here…it's possible a viral variant of that is the cause, something our models didn't predict".

"You don't believe that. A variant which only affects Pawnee DNA? A variant's appearance which coincidentally appears at precisely the time our population got the genetic treatment from you? You know nature doesn't work like that in the first instance, doesn't racially profile victims. And come on - you're the mathematician, you tell me how likely such a coincidence would be. This was deliberate. Engineered."

Was it really so hard to believe? Occam's razor again…what he was saying made surface sense in the absence of any other plausible explanation. Fuck. Eryss…was the whole thing really a charade? Her promotion, the Credyt that went with it, the license even, as Jon had suggested? And there was more…the event with Mya where she'd assaulted Helpers. How could she have been so stupid to believe she was getting off because of her importance?

"Just, just give me a minute". She got up from the couch and started walking a small circle around the ragged rug on the floor. She had to move, couldn't bear to be still with the fomenting thoughts.

Maybe a mistake had been made, an error that her and Sybelle had missed? But as quickly as she thought it, she discounted it: she had seen with her own eyes the genomic changes their payload had wrought, had seen the double spirals changed, and deep-dived the recombinant base pairs of letters having first converted them to numbers, for any hint of outliers or anomalies. None where found, no known patterns of unhealthy or malign DNA discovered across the billions of letters analysed. She knew the odds of either herself or Sybelle missing something were statistically an eight sigma event - more chance of a snowball surviving a summer in Death Valley than either of them missing something that could cause what was happening now.

Raising her head and stopping her circling, she looked into the face of the man who was carrying not only this shit-storm, but also the man who'd lost his wife and child in the way he had. He was still going, still fighting. So would she.

"OK. And your wife and child...I'm so sorry to hear what happened to them...and you."

"Thank you".

"Regarding the illness or virus, I agree. The odds of anything else are too high. But - *why*? *Why* would we do such a thing? Corynth has no beef with the Pawnee, nor Grand Plains. You're certainly no threat. No offense."

He waved it away.

"We have a mutual agreement for resources and collaboration...why would we infect your population with a lethal disease?"

He leaned back, the leather complaining loudly.

"I'm not sure. Maybe it's as simple as why be happy with just three years, when you could take it all, for good. Because - " The phone on the desk beat him to his next word, it's loud echoing ring startling Anastasya. When her eyes located the source of the noise, she recognised what it was; a means of communication needing physical interaction.

"Yes? Hello." He listened then, and after a moment replaced the receiver wordlessly.

"That was the lab. Let's take a walk."

III – VIII*

They talked as they walked, Jon laying out facts as he understood them to her through a quick stop off in the canteen for a coffee, and then on through the empty corridors.

Arcadmium, rarest of rare-earth elements, Grand Plains the world's only known reliable source. Sybelle's intelligence, an organic one which relied on arcadmium to manipulate quantum qubits in her molecular transistors - something it would be impossible to do without arcadmium, as no other known element could super-conduct at typical room temperature.

That, she'd known. What she hadn't known came in the form of a history lesson.

During the creation of the States of America, Grand Plains had been declared territory of the Pawnee nation, in recompense for the ancestral lands forcibly taken from them by the old United States Army in the 19th century - an event known as the Trail of Tears. Jon had said it was pure propaganda, that the States of America were attempting to cloak the humiliation of the break up of the U.S.A in the garb of social justice and progress, and that gifting Grand Plains to the Pawnee nation was a shining example of this "fake reason d'etre" of the New U.S. The *real* reason for the collapse of the once democratic U.S.A - so Jon said - was presaged by the domination of corporations like Octyllion, hoovering up wealth and power and concentrating it in the hands of the very few, whilst undermining democracy to leave a divided nation despairing and destitute.

This rise of the corporations contributed, but it was the Illumination - where Sybelle's emergence rendered Octyllion omnipotent and simultaneously all others nude and defenceless - which was the final trigger in the creation of Corynth and its secession from the old U.S.A. Other corporations had transformed themselves into virtual nations also, the so-called "Corpo-States", but none could compete with Corynth. The unrivaled new global leader, their quantum singularity and possession of the world's first general A.I smashed all known cryptography, alongside the abilities of Sybelle - an intelligence never before seen on this planet. Ironically, Corynth had followed down the same path as the previous intelligence kings - China - in terms of brutality towards its own nascent population.

It was an alternate history view Anastasya had never heard before - they had all been taught Corynth's rise during Illumination was an inevitable rational and evolutionary step for humankind. Not a totalitarian massacre fueled by a savage will to power. There was no time to debate or comment, he was relaying these "facts" in rapid lecture format.

And he had one final fact: Grand Plains would cease to be a separate self-governed State, and would return to the jurisdiction of the New U.S, should the Pawnee nation cease to exist.

The New U.S government were nominal, were de-facto puppets of Corynth, and Corynth could easily annex Grand Plains should the demise of the Pawnee happen - and by "demise", Jon made it clear this meant the death of every single Pawnee. Even a single Pawnee would constitute the Pawnee Nation.

They were his facts. His theory then, was that with absolute control over their A.I's life blood, Corynth's destiny would firmly be in their own hands, while also denying any others the ability to ever create a similar A.I or achieve their own quantum singularity. Take away oil, no-one can build a working engine.

The history of Corynth had been bloody and violent throughout, including blatant population control through rejection and retirement - was it really so hard to believe killing others for Corynthian goals would be outside the pale? He'd asked it rhetorically, and if asked of her any time prior to these last months, she'd of ridiculed the question. Now, she had to admit it was a possibility. It was like stepping though a door to find yourself in an alien world.

Their journey though the warren of corridors had come to a stop outside an actual door, this one locked. Jon keyed in a code. He paused, hand on the door, turned to her.

"Don't take the reaction you'll receive personally, OK?"

He pushed it open, and she followed him into a room of computers with keyboards and mice and screens, microscopes, test tubes and what looked like centrifuges.

A stern-looking bespectacled lady in a snow-white lab smock straightened from one of the microscopes, drinking Anastasya in from head to foot. Anastasya turned her head around at the sound of the door snucking shut behind them, and was disconcerted to find herself still being stared at when she turned back.

"So this is her...", the words hanging in the air like a bad smell. Her hair was neck length and bleached so blond it was almost white. The words were heavily accented, like something from an old Dracula feed.

"Iva, we have little time" Jon said, walking towards her and beckoning Anastasya to follow.

"This is Anastasya, the mathematician from Corynth you know about. Anastasya, Dr. Iva Krantz, our head of medicine".

Anastasya took a step forward, hand extended. She retracted it quickly though when the bleached-haired lady looked at it scornfully.

"I vanted to talk to you about the latest learnings on the virus. *Her* virus. Instead you bring this sideshow to my lab. And vy do you trust her all of a sudden?"

"Iva - please. She's not in on what they did. I vouch for her one hundred percent. Plus, she's the only one on their side who may be able to help. No idea how, but maybe".

Iva regarded him a long appraising moment, before turning her glare back onto Anastasya. Anastasya met it and decided to give her the benefit of the doubt given the circumstances...for one more minute.

"The maths genius...ve are saved. Fantastic".

"Want me to do some multiplication for you? I can add real good too".

"Maybe later, madchen. How about factorization though? I bet is the walk in the park for you?"

Anastasya shrugged. "Naturally."

"How?"

"How? I can sense the pairs which combine. I just see it - intuition."

"Does size matter?"

"No, size doesn't matter. Not to me." A beat. "In math".

"So then factoring the product of, oh, say two large primes would be no problem?"

"Of course not".

"Uh huh. What about topologies and infinite series..."

Jon interjected the joust. "Iva, is this necessary? You wanted to talk".

"One moment - vait Jon. Topologies and infinite series - you can see if a point or function lies within a series' bound?"

This was getting tiring for Anastasya, a slightly more advanced version of Tanya's drunken multiplication tricks. "Yes".

Iva's words flew now. "So then the Riemann hypothesis - have you proof all the solutions to the Riemann zeta function actually lie on this critical line?"

"Of course", Anastasya said. "Sybelle has simulated in trial and error, but my intuition and senses leave no doubt..." She stopped herself as Iva's glee was obvious.

"Ha! You see Jon? They have de facto proof of the Riemann hypothesis, plus NP-complete solution."

Jon showed his hands, palms up. So?

"They have cracked all possible modern cryptographic methods *mathematically*, regardless of their quantum Illumination! This is incredible Jon. Even more incredible such knowledge is not shared - but nothing new for them, heh?"

"We have other problems, Iva".

"You think I do not know? I have one more question for the genius. Not about math. Now I'd like to ask you, madchen, just how smart you feel, given how you vere played like the fiddles and knew nothing of the death you sold us". The glee was gone, the challenge back.

Anastasya drew breath, Jon got there first.

"Both of us were played, Iva. Me and her. You know who we're up against."

"Even Einstein was persuaded to build the bomb I suppose..."

"Hey - enough of the attacks, OK? If what you're both saying is true, if our payload is *killing* people - of course I want to help! I'm not some sort of monster."

Jon looked at Iva.

"You had something to tell me. Please share - Anastasya should be clued in".

"No time to argue, but I don't like her in our circle so quickly. You are too trusting sometimes Jon. Especially for the girls. Anyvay", she said quickly before he could object, "I don't have much except a little more analysis. Our computers are not fast. Given a bacteria can't target racially", said with an accusatory look at Anastasya, "ve are focusing on viruses. It's not Mongol Flu, neither Ebola. Though the fact the brain is impacted is very curious…it is not a common symptom of any virus except rabies. Yet this can't be rabies, as the bleeding and hemorrhaging, as well as general body pain are not symptoms of rabies. Rabies *does* have a 100% fatality rate once the brain symptoms appear in a patient, so it's similar in those terms… but it seems like a horrible coincidence".

"A filovirus maybe…" Anastasya said, voicing her subconscious.

"Ja, good! Good. Filovirusses have been known to approach 90% fatality in extreme outbreaks, but not 100%. But let's not take the "shot in the dark". Ve have other experts whom ve should consult with. Vere are they now?" Iva asked, turning her piercing blue eyes on Jon.

"Close by."

"An open conversation and exchange of ideas in our group setting is vat we need. I always say solutions are forged in the crucible of varied opinions…do I not Jon?"

Anastasya had never personally witnessed an elderly couple like this, very familiar yet seemingly not weary of each other's ways. Her own biological father, long executed, she had no memory of. Eryss and her mom qualified in terms of years of age for sure, but they didn't show the years as these two did.

"Iva's right. We should continue this in the wider group. This means", he said to Anastasya, "that we'll be going back to the surface, where of course you'll be connected to Sybelle again. We trust you, but you need to be very careful of what you think when up top - those counter-measures we discussed in the Embassy, explicit thoughts like number series, or whatever works - use them."

"Jon, the quarantine camp - should ve go there first? Good opportunity to get further appreciation of vat's at stake."

He clicked his fingers. "Good thinking. And you know, we'll have an excuse for privacy there. From Sybelle".

III – IX*

The destination was an old barracks on the outskirts of town, about a fifteen minute ride from the hospital. They'd taken three jeeps - Helpers left behind after Anastasya's arguments - the rumblings and vibrations of the diesel engines providing background music for Anastasya as they sped along. It was alien to her - rusted chain link fences, rubbish spilled on the streets or in bins outside mostly one or two-story small houses, empty streets with shut stores, a general sense of ruin prevailing. The people living here, they didn't even have the option to go in-game - so what did they do all day, Anastasya wondered. And cotics were of the dirty kind - physical, ingredients uncertain, not neural and controlled. A literal handful of people scurried here and there, streets dominated by roaming sniffing dogs.

"Fear", Iva said, watching Anastasya. She was sat beside her, strapped into the bouncy back seat. "Afraid of the viruses. Genghis and now this other. Even though they are not at risk. From either. The ones at risk - they wait ahead. In the camp".

"So they're fully asymptomatic?"

"Ja. For now".

Anastasya nodded, the wind flowing her hair backwards maniacally. She had to raise her voice in the open top jeep.

"And I understand the fear. The world of genetic enhancements is a new one to them."

Iva looked at her, face inscrutable.

Then: "Mind if I smoke?", already lighting the tip of her slim cigarette.

"You know the science demonstrating how unhealthy they are, right?"

"Ja. but this is not your nanny state, mathematician. Ve still have some freedoms. Genetic enhancements...it's a truly vonderful life. Is it not?"

She below minty smoke towards Anastasya, who waved it away with a grimace.

"Ja, a really great life. Of course it is, when you have the world's greatest entertainment system piped directly into your brain. I know your type *very* vell. Your society has at it's behest the most powerful and awesome technology this vorld has ever seen...and what do you use it for? Games, gossiping, God knows what, letting yourselves be brainwashed. You", she continued, jabbing her cigarette sideways at Anastasya like a spear, "drown your brains in useless banal information, destroying your capacity to think meaningfully or critically. To top it off you delegate almost all decision-making to this electronic goddess. You are all slaves of the world's greatest entertainment system! An entire State happy in their virtual prison! You'll forgive me for being skeptical when Jon says you come here of your own free will...vatever motive you have is derived from your AI goddess. You're too blind to even see it". She tapped her ash dismissively on the jeep's floor.

"Hey - ".

Dr. Krantz cut across her.

"Really, you're not even to blame. Ve vould likely behave the same, if confronted with your A.I's seeming benevolence and certain omnipotence. It's the sad history of the world, ad nauseam - humans invent a mind-control technology, then vorship at its altar of convenient banality while offering themselves up for mental enslavement."

Anastasya stared ahead and zoned out. Why the fuck would

she listen to this rant? The engine's vibrations were rhythmic, she began working out the series.

Now and then Iva's words drifted through, a horn blaring through the mist of her mind. It was a coherent theory, she gave her that. Grudgingly. She started to tune in.

Telegraphs - whatever they were - were apparently the "original great disruptor" opening Pandora's box; instant access to information which people could do nothing with and which didn't impact their lives at all…yet which were the "fuel" which newspapers used to light the fire of the world's first information glut.

Radio and TV of course she knew about, and they followed, "entrapping" citizens to willingly sit in front of a box for hours per day, having their thoughts shaped by media and advertisers - propaganda, as Iva called it. Then the "jump" to the Internet, leading to the deconstruction of truth into silos of contrasting beliefs, mob mentality, division of society and all the while "making people feel shit about themselves".

It was a grim take.

"That phone in the pocket shaped our thoughts and opinions, and led us away from sanity, like being led by the Pied Piper. And our old saner selves, just like the children of Hamelin, vere never seen again."

Anastasya looked blankly at her.

"Hopeless", Iva concluded. "Anyvay, the phones were *killer* when paired with the anti-social networks, but your Sybelle - she's the fucking ultimate evolutionary step in mind control. Literally hardwired inside your brain, manipulating your biology - you have no vay of ignoring her siren call." Iva stopped talking, Anastasya thinking she was finished. "At least you could put a fucking phone down."

"You know I could lose Credyt for hearing this shit?"

Iva waved her smoking hand dismissively.

"Try to see it my way - I'm pregnant, I need to maintain Credyt. Else…let's just say I need it."

"Jon never mentioned that", she muttered, as she flicked her smoke out of the jeep.

"I hope it all works out for you and baby - and you should have told me earlier. But back to the point, everything I said plus *this* social credit score, it equals total enslavement. Barbarism under the pretense of rights and rationality. I vill not say anymore."

But then she quickly did.

"But no-one is the slave to fate. You always have the freedom to choose your action or reaction. No matter how terrible the circumstance."

"Easy for you to say."

"Maybe. See the barracks up ahead?"

Decrepit walls with a militia duo standing at a gate with an already raised barrier loomed into view. They passed through the militia guard by merely slowing down and being waved through. The lead jeep, with Anastasya and Dr. Krantz neared a tunnel formed by the concave opening running underneath the barracks' main faded red-bricked facade.

Anastasya looked quizzical. "Not really secure, is it?"

"No need. Nobody vants to visit. Besides, this is not a lock-in, it is simply a safety measure to isolate them. Ve don't know anything about this virus really."

The jeep slowed significantly further as it neared the tunnel. As soon as they passed in, Iva spun in her seat and whipped out a baseball cap from a bag sat between her legs.

"Quick, put this on. Now!"

Anastasya shoved it down over her hair, smoothing it. "What - "

"Wait" Iva ordered.

The jeep came to a halt, still within the tunnel. Iva got out and beckoned to Anastasya to do likewise. The other 2 jeeps passed them by.

One followed the other through a door built into the tunnel wall. Once through, Anastasya found herself in room with nothing but cold and damp, as well as another door on the opposite wall to where she came in.

"The caps are an anti-Sybelle device. May look primitive, but very effective. Two purposes: one, a Faraday cage. It - "

"I get it", Anastasya interrupted. "It blocks electro-magnetic signals. Very clever...so I have no connectivity to Sybelle with this on?"

Iva nodded appreciatively. "Not only that. It has its own localized A.I. controller, which projects a modified face overlayed on yours. Here - ", and Iva reached over and clicked a small something which was embedded in the button top of the cap. There was a shimmer, like silver falling as rain, then a middle-aged Pawnee woman stood facing Iva.

"What are you grinning at?", Anastasya asked.

"This". Iva put a second cap on, did the same activation.

Anastasya grinned back at the black-toothed apparition in front of her.

"Suits you".

"Ja. Very funny. So now, we go about our business outside, like two normal people. No satellite or drones should detect us. Best part - we're free to talk outside, no connection to Sybelle. Just keep the caps on."

"Got it."

They exited across the room to a grass square. Anastasya had expected a morbid atmosphere, not the squeals and shrieks of kids running around. They were playing some version of tag, evidently using the grass square as the game's boundary.

Dotted around the square, under the shelter of the buttresses, adults and older youths sat at rickety looking tables, playing card games, chatting.

Medics moved off towards the left side of the square from where Anastasya stood. She made to follow, but Iva stayed her with a touch.

"Let's take a look ourselves, ja?"

"Sure. Is Jon joining us?"

"No. Best to keep as two normal women here, your Sybelle will think you are still indoors in the barracks."

"OK. What game is that?" Anastasya asked, indicating towards a table they had passed, the two occupants - men in their 40s or so - scrutinizing the two women before putting their heads down again to study their hands.

"Pinochle. Ever played?"

"Pinochle or cards? No to both".

Iva gave a disbelieving look over her shoulder. The pair started to walk the perimeter slowly.

"Nothing seems to be wrong with them", Anastasya commented. "They're all acting so normally".

Before Iva could reply, a female voice from behind answered. Anastasya turned to see an old woman walking up behind them, her weather-beaten face bronzed, its lines cut deep. Her brown eyes smouldered with dark energy like a hidden sun's.

"We are spirits with temporary bodies. It doesn't mean we don't care what is happening - but it does help put some perspective on it." Then she smiled, its warmth and width wiping away her wrinkles, eyes communicating only kindness.

"Lena is my name", she said, extending her hand and taking Anastasya's. "It's not very traditional, my parent's wanted me to blend in."

"Ana".

"I'm an elder with our tribe".

Iva scoffed. "She runs the show".

Anastasya realised this woman still had not let go of her hand, and was now grasping it in both of hers.

"Congratulations dear", she said, looking deep into Anastasya's eyes. Could she see through the device's visage? Anastasya wondered. It certainly felt like it.

"For what?"

"For your new arrival".

"How..."

"You don't think you're the first pregnant girl I've ever seen?" she said, her hands tightening the squeeze.

"Iva said you have a gift that might help us. Do you?" The question was direct and sudden, in contrast to the kindness still radiating from her.

"I guess so, yes. I can try. Believe me, I want to." Still the fiery brown eyes searched hers, probing deep.

Her hand was squeezed again.

"Don't *try* to help. *Help*. I can see it within you. And much more..."

She let go of Anastasya's hand. It flopped to Anastasya's side immediately. The world came rushing back, the spell broken. Sound and sight filled the void left by Lena's intense attention. Again the children's voices, again the pinochle tables and shadows moving under buttresses. She breathed, released from this small woman's tractor beam. Not that it had been unpleasant.

"Don't forget us. Look around, and don't forget. Me, I've had many a day. But these young ones don't deserve it. Whatever you can do - *do*."

"I will, you - " Before she could say more, something hit Anastasya from behind, causing her to stumble forward.

Iva laughed. "Hit you like the ton of bricks. Good girl!" she said, patting the head of the probably ten-years old pigtailed assassin.

"Sorry" said the kid, dragging out the end of "sorry" into a long e.

"No you're not", Anastasya quipped back.

"Can I check her?", Iva asked Lena. "If she wants you to".

The girl was happy for the attention, and Iva sat on the grass opposite the now cross-legged girl. She casually and deftly - giving away her years' of experience Anastasya thought - drew a sample of blood from the girls arm. Not even a fraction of a drop was spilled, and it was over in a second or two - needle in, needle out. She asked her questions, puzzling ones, as the girl was asked to track Iva's moving finger with her eyes, then recite the alphabet skipping every second letter - and then recite backwards. All of which she aced effortlessly, enjoying the game of it.

Blood pressure patch applied, pulse taken through a finger lock. A silver stethoscope was conjured from Iva's bag and applied to the girl's chest. In other circumstances Anastasya might have laughed at the ridiculousness of the apparatus, but not now - here it was revealed in its true glory: clumsy and archaic, but a detector of precious life nonetheless.

Anastasya found Iva staring at her. "Try it out", said Iva, removing the earpieces and offering to Anastasya. "Go on."

She knew it would be a heartbeat, but didn't know what to expect really. Anastasya took it from Iva, plugged in the earpieces - and silence - the world was muted to a faint buzz.

With the young girl looking curiously at her, Anastasya pressed the round end to the girl's breast. A thumping drumbeat filled her head, rhythmic, pulsing, *living*. She moved it to the left of where it was on the girl's t-shirt, and the sound died away to a throb. Moved it back and it exploded again.

Anastasya withdrew her experimenting arm and unplugged from her ears.

"She could be an athlete", Iva pronounced, taking the steth out of Anastasya's hands. "Very low resting pulse, powerful heart. Your name, child? Family name also" asked Iva, pen in hand.

The patients on the ward shot across her mind, but now juxtaposed with the image of this youth stretched out in the ward, tubed and unconscious. She couldn't bear to know another Mya, and deliberately coughed as the girl gave her name before running off.

"How long until she gets symptoms?"

"Impossible to be precise. Mental acuity is still 100%, no physical symptoms yet. All ve know is, age has not been a barrier to symptom onset yet. Infection fatality rate is still 100%."

Anastasya swept her eyes over the square of running kids, card players and loungers.

"Shouldn't we start talking about what we can do?"

III – X*

They'd moved inside the barracks, but Anastasya kept the cap on. She was listening intently as Jack Carthy - who'd introduced himself as a doctor of immunology, who told her he'd previously worked in a place called Jon Hopkins, and was clearly disappointed when she didn't know of it - spelled out the situation again. An unidentified virus with an incubation period of approximately two weeks; symptoms extreme, yet not common to any known virus; targeted specifically against Pawnee DNA. 100% fatal.

"Options?" Jon asked. "We need to get our guest back connected soon. We don't want Helpers sniffing around, nor questions being asked. An hour off-grid within the walls here should be acceptable - let's not risk any longer".

"The brain symptoms are significant I feel, I can't quite put my finger on why though. They exist in another virus, one that also has a 100% kill rate - rabies. However rabies has none of the other symptoms, none of the respiratory symptoms and bodily fluid leakage which are common to filoviruses. But it is strange nonetheless, that two things in common with rabies - 100% kill rate and brain impairment - are prevalent here."

"Not strange considering this is man-made", Iva said, looking pointedly at Anastasya, fork in her hand like a weapon.

Jack and Tomek grunted in agreement.

"I know", Anastasya said. None of the conjecture on the origin mattered - what mattered was a solution she had in mind. She had wanted to hear more of what they knew too, but it obviously wasn't a lot. She didn't blame them, they hadn't even had a week yet to analyze, with over-whelmed services and scant resources. Certainly nowhere even approaching what Corynth could offer.

"It must be "man-made" or "engineered" - accepted. But not by me. I had no hand in this, and I'll do what I can to help".

Iva skewered the sausage on the plate in front of her violently with her fork. Nobody else touched anything on the table. The smell was powerful in the windowless bricked room.

"Have anything in mind?"

"I've been sent - directly by the Councyl - on a mission to help, so it be expected of me to co-ordinate and offer use of our medical equipment. So that's a given, a no-brainer. So let's start with the basics, we use Corynthian tech to gather as much factual info as we can - and it sounds like you don't know much.

"Let's start with the brain impairment...you were saying that's a key thing to understand, the rabies oddity. We can help immediately on that. Our neural scanners can give on-the-spot diagnostics on synaptic responses, anomalous neural behaviour - you name it."

Dr. Carthy was quick in. "Maybe from that we could at least understand the neural impact, whether it's permanent damage or limited to virus lifespan. Then we'd know how worthwhile it is pursuing a cure."

"And vat sort of cure could do you have in mind? It can be worse than the disease, I've heard."

"If the virus was engineered, surely it can be reverse-engineered. Or more precisely, if we know its genetic pattern, it's DNA, we could attack and kill it in every host cell. We have the tech to do this, we've always had. We use it as a matter of daily routine", Anastasya answered.

"CRISPR", Iva said.

"That's right".

"What's that?" Jon asked. Jack Carthy put his empty fork down with a clang, glancing quickly at his watch.

"Dr. Krantz and I are quite familiar with CRISPR", Dr. Carthy replied, speaking rapidly as if in a lab instructing students. "It was in its infancy when we were in Hopkins. Amazing things had been achieved with it, literally the blind seeing once again post-treatment. Of course post Illumination, the intellectual property, research and tech needed for CRISPR was hoovered up by Corynth, leaving us mere mortals with only the idea, no tools."

"I don't want to waste time here, but afterwards could you fill me in on what exactly CRISPR is?", Jon asked the table. "High-level".

"It would help to know *now*", Iva stated. "But I vant to hear *her* explain it", Iva said pointedly.

"Iva, we've no time for games", Jon said brusquely.

"I need to know if this madchen is out of her depth, or can she really help".

Anastasya reached over and took one of the sausages. Munched it before replying. Then drank some water, ignoring the daggers from Dr. Krantz.

"What's the most abundant life-form on this planet, has been around for billions of years?"

"Bacteria?"

"Not the most abundant, no, but they have been around for that long. Most abundant and equally oldest are bacteriophages...let's call them phages for short. There's more of these critters on this planet than all other species and creatures on Earth added together - ten to the power of thirty-one of them, actually. They're ancient, ubiquitous, have had eons to tweak and optimize their genetic code - magnitudes longer than humans have had.

"Phages are viruses - but special viruses. Like all viruses they are not really "alive" until they have a host to replicate within. And phages only replicate themselves *within bacteria*. So bacteria, for as long as they have been around on this planet, have had to always contend with these phages who are literally everywhere, invading bacterial cells and looking to replicate their viral DNA.

"Sometimes phages are benign to bacteria, sometimes not. But the point is, bacteria have had to live with phages for billions of years. So the question is, how did they withstand such a massive and constant onslaught on their own genomes from the hordes of phages out there? It's like a country being overwhelmed by the Mongol Horde, but for some strange reason, although the Horde swarm around the citizens brandishing swords, trying to lop off heads, the citizens remain undisturbed and unharmed - ignoring the Horde screaming in their faces, who bizarrely have no power to injure or harm."

She had their attention, even Iva was listening without an angry face.

"CRISPR is this "strange reason" bacteria survived. Iva could tell you what the acronym stands for. But essentially it's a defense mechanism, and the incredible thing is that this mechanism existed in nature in the first instance - it's not "man-made".

"Each time a bacteria is invaded by a phage, the bacteria's defense mechanism - it's CRISPR - takes a snapshot, or imagine a genetic photograph, of *part* of this invading virus's DNA".

"Technically these snapshots are comprised of genetic letters, typically 20 letters in length", Iva interjected.

"Thank you, exactly. And these snapshots or photos get

stored in the bacteria's genome, in a special location we call the *CRISPR array*. And now - and this is the ingenious part - whenever that bacteria gets subsequently invaded by a phage, the bacteria's defense mechanism checks the invading virus DNA, and compares it against the snapshots or photos it has previously stored in the array. If there's a match, in other words if this is a virus the bacteria recognizes from before from it's photos of part of previous viruses, then the CRISPR defense mechanism sends a heat-seeking missile to destroy this invading phage's viral DNA".

"Heat-seeking missile - I like, very apt", Iva said. Iva then continued on quickly.

"And John, this missile - because I could see you get excited at that part - it's not the actual missile, OK? It's comprised of a *strand of RNA* which will seek and find the viral DNA which invaded the bacterial cell; then the "destroy" part is done by an *enzyme*, usually a special protein, a CAS protein - that's the assassin, or the warhead on our heat-seeking missile. Ja? Gut.

"And this really works, because the seeking RNA part of our missile is an exact match of part of that viral DNA. It just looks for its twin...Cain looking for Abel. As your pregnant *friend* says, it is quite something to see this in action. They vill hunt down and shred invading DNA to nothingness, to mere electrons...completely effective".

"OK, right", mused Jon. "So bacteria have this defense mechanism which can seek and destroy invading virus DNA. But how do we go from there to a solution for our current problem?".

Jon listened intently as Anastasya and Iva continued in this vein of criss-crossing each other. But he felt both were getting excited about the technology and possibilities, abstracted from the practicalities and the reality of the bodies heaving tortured breaths in the building they had left just under one hour ago... typical intellectuals both. But equally, he wouldn't prefer to be seated with anyone else right now, not for this problem.

He had known it anyway, but it was so clear now - his role was to keep the ideas and possibilities focused on whatever offered the most chance of saving lives. He listened mostly, just occasionally nudging towards the right direction, a shared direction.

He understood well enough at a high-level what the situation was. In fairness to the group, they were making every effort to simplify things for him, and the crux of it was pretty straightforward: they could use this CRISPR mechanism to target and kill the virus. And Iva was right, he did like the heat-seeking missile analogy of the RNA which would find the virus within the host, and the assassin enzyme which would then "explode" and kill it. It was an image he dearly hoped would become reality.

He knew - hell, the world knew - how ridiculously advanced Corynthian tech was, but nonetheless it was still scary to hear the doctors and Anastasya theorize on how the Pawnee specifically were being targeted. It was literally messing with the letters of life, rewriting them to bring death.

The virus was introduced to the Grand Plains population through the genetic payloads from Corynth - of that there was no doubt, despite the lack of evidence so far. But it would have lain essentially dormant - or as Dr. Jack said, in a lactic phase - inside the majority of the population, and was in fact most likely still laying in wait in Jon's own modified genome.

The trick to activate it was the genetic engineering to create the virus so that it reacted only to some gene the Pawnee uniquely have. They didn't know what yet, but if they looked they would find at least one unique gene - it was the only thing that made sense.

Iva posited that the activation or awakening of the virus would only happen in the presence of this Pawnee gene. Iva called it the move from "the lactic to lytic stage". He'd asked her what that meant, and she'd told him the lytic stage was the stage at which genetic transcription and translation occur within a virus. He'd persevered and asked what *those* two terms meant, and she'd said it meant the virus reproducing itself and creating proteins. If the virus is a sleeping tiger, the Pawnee gene is like smelling salts, waking the tiger up and triggering the lytic stage of rampage and destruction that the woken tiger wreaks.

There were three things the group were rapidly converging upon for their plan of action. First, determining the "Pawnee gene" the virus uses to activate itself into the lytic stage - this was eminently doable, as they already had sequencing of their population done by Sybelle; Anastasya could obtain the output and they could analyze themselves, comparing against non-Pawnee Grand Plains genomes. Finding such a gene wouldn't directly help them destroy the virus, but it would prove what they suspected.

The second and third items would directly target and kill the virus: they needed to identify 20-letter sequences of the viral DNA which could be combined with the CRISPR RNA, to serve as the RNA seeker part of their heat-seeking missile. The obtaining of the virus's DNA could be handled by Sybelle via Anastasya innocently asking for and managing the analysis. There was no way Corynth could lie on this one, as international agencies were being called in by Jon now too, who would also eventually determine the viral structure - but Sybelle could get it almost infinitely quicker. Once the Grand Plains medics had the viral DNA, it was in their technological power to identify suitable 20-letter sequences of the virus's DNA.

Lastly, they needed to identify the enzyme that would kill the virus, the warhead of their missile. It would trigger once the guide RNA (the seeker) had enfolded itself around the viral DNA twin. It was obvious this was where the difficulty lay...there was no way they could ask Sybelle for the enzyme without tipping Anastasya's hand of being aware of the Corynthian duplicity. Nor could they trust Sybelle anyway - why would Sybelle or the Councyl give the key to killing the virus to the people they are trying to kill *with* the virus? They couldn't even let Sybelle or the Councyl get wind of the fact they were trying a CRISPR treatment, lest it be sabotaged. So on this hunt for their specific enzyme, they were on their own.

"Let's not focus on the enzyme until we have step 2, the guide RNA, determined", Anastasya suggested. "Let me figure things out with Sybelle, maybe even Eryss herself. I have some currency with her over the years. I assume there are a lot of possible enzymes it could be?"

"Ja - a lot, but only one will likely work. The problem is the time it vill take us to prepare an actual treatment even if we have the seeker and the assassin enzyme...I mean packing it in pills of some sort, or an injectable solution. Too long to just keep trying random enzymes."

"Agreed. That's a problem. From my experience with experimental treatments, plus the speed this virus is moving and killing, I would guess we will have one shot to create and apply a treatment before its too late. Somehow we'll need to know with certainty the right enzyme to use in advance...we can't trial and error this" Jack said.

"Impossible", Iva said angrily. "No trial and error means the only realistic chance is a supercomputer to churn through the possibilities, simulate every possible enzyme's interaction with the virus - Sybelle is vat ve need, but why vould she help, or us trust her? So - impossible", she declared definitively.

Jon gently but firmly took hold. "With all our talk on the mechanics of the virus and CRISPR, we're forgetting the secret weapon we have." He watched them look at each other, before settling his gaze on Anastasya.

"We've someone sat here who worked with Sybelle on the initial simulations, someone who's mind is superior to their AI in some regards." He held his hand up against the inevitable objections. "She was misled to the true intentions of the genetic payload, but Anastasya - could you work on these simulations yourself, use your synesthesia perhaps?"

"Yes", she said without hesitation. "I transformed the four letters of DNA to numbers in order to do the simulations with Sybelle in the first place...of course I can do it again. I was gonna suggest it." She wasn't bragging, she knew she could. "It'll be more difficult without Sybelle's help...the tanks I used for one, but more so the genetic structures she fed to my mind directly. But if I have the structure of enzymes defined for me, and know the viral DNA plus Pawnee DNA...then yes, I could."

She looked around, suddenly having a moment of doubt that she'd said anything at all...had it all been a monologue in her head? They were all staring at her mutely, with Iva's cigarette drooping a long nose of ash.

Dr Jack cleared his throat before speaking. "We could help you by researching and prioritizing certain enzymes. Would that help?"

"Of course. That enzyme, the assassin or warhead for our metaphorical missile - got to have it asap".

"You should start immediately" Iva said earnestly, before correcting herself: "as soon as ve get the viral DNA and the guide RNA identified of course. But if you go to Sybelle, ve could have that in one or two days."

"I think we're forgetting the elephant in the room", Anastasya said, touching her cap lightly. "Sybelle will know what I'm thinking and simulating re the enzyme. It'll be impossible to keep it from her. She'll figure out we're onto a CRISPR approach. I can't wear this all day."

Governor Laide shook his head - they'd already seen the solution. "You're here leading the mission to help us, and you've seen now - in fact, all your delegation has seen - where the ICU wards are."

"Fuck yes! I'll need to spend a lot of time with your medical staff on the subterranean hospital floors. It's only natural that I do."

"Correct. You've got a perfectly valid excuse for being cut off from Sybelle for long periods. Tomek, do you think we could rustle up - "

"Sure Jon", Dr Spring said, anticipating the question. "We could get a sense-dep tank from somewhere, set it up down there".

"Well", Jon said, rising from the table, giving the others their cue. "We have a plan, which is a lot more than we had an hour ago." He clapped his hands. "Let's go."

III – XI*

They were slouched together on a plastic bench under the glow of a single halogen, eyes closed, but not sleeping. They'd taken one of the poky canteen corners for themselves despite the place being empty. Dr. Krantz's smoke curled lazily towards the No Smoking sign.

The past twenty-four hours had been a blur, blitzing their way through their hit-list of priorities, taking things as far as they could with the tech at their disposal. Anastasya had known it was possible, but to actually see tangible results created a very different feeling than when things were purely theoretical. For one, it was more urgent.

"Vant one?"

Anastasya popped an eye open and considered.

"I'll pass. But blow the smoke this way - it helps with the coffee taste. You know, working 14 hours straight is so far beyond what would ever happen back home - you've no idea. Three hours a day would be the usual max limit."

Iva grunted, didn't open her eyes.

The concentration had been more intense than Anastasya had ever experienced, a manic and relentless focus which seemed normal to Iva and the other doctors. They'd said this was "par for the course" in their professional experience in medicine at times of emergency. Why anyone would want to live a life like that, with so much at stake and under such inhumane hours, was beyond her.

She'd been surprised - very - at how easy it had been

working with the others, despite them not having neural implants. At times they seemed to read each other's minds anyway. Their knowledge was encyclopedic and uncanny, especially considering their recall had to be purely biological. It worked well her acting as the go-between with Sybelle, and they'd relatively quickly mapped out the viral DNA with Sybelle's help, with the doctors then validating it independently to be sure.

Along with some other non-Pawnee locals, Jon had volunteered a sample of his DNA. As theorized he did indeed carry the virus DNA, as did all Grand Plains citizens - yet he, along with the others were completely asymptomatic.

"I'm glad it worked out", Anastasya said. "Although, I have to admit the tiredness impacted me. I felt sluggish. Trust me, I'm usually faster in those situations, but I have Sybelle too", her mind on the solo analysis she did from the hospital basement. She had taken a hypno hit when up on the ground floor immediately prior, but had no pills on hand for performing her analysis to determine the link between Pawnee DNA and the viral DNA.

The enabling trick was to have one of Iva's techs replace the A,C,G,T letters of the DNA alphabet from both virus and Pawnee DNA with numbers - any would suffice - and they used a darkened room instead of a tank, so she could read the scroll of numbers from a computer monitor. It really stung her eyes, and was a clunky experience, but surprisingly it didn't take longer than it otherwise would have done had she been tightly integrated with Sybelle. And in the end it turned out to be a rather beautiful and simple mechanism she'd discovered.

There was a gene unique to Pawnee DNA, the EDAR gene, a molecular key which when combined with the viral DNA unlocked the virus from dormancy. The "unlocking" was precisely as they had hypothesized - the Pawnee gene's interaction triggered the virus moving from the latic to lytic phase, meaning it began manufacturing molecules and proteins inside the human host, the very blueprint of death which was killing the Pawnee Nation.

"It is baby brain".

"What is?"

"You being faster than normal on that vizardry, or vatever it is your mind does."

"Baby brain?"

"Ja. The changes your brain makes when you are pregnant, madchen. Plasticity. That mega-brain of yours is adapting to life with your baby. As a consequence of the re-wiring, some women experience temporary deviations from typical neurological habits".

Anastasya pouted her lips...not fair.

Iva laughed. "It's a good thing! Major benefits overall. Women who are pregnant demonstrate increased memory function and their brains behave younger. You have not heard of this? It's like a superpower pregnant women get over the rest of us - evolution's reward for continuing the species' survival."

"I like the sound of that, but really?" as she lightly pressed her fingers on her belly. Thanks, she said quietly to her baby, jokingly. If it were true, surely the doctor back home, or Sybelle, would have told her.

"Being honest, I could do with a superpower. What's left is still a mountain. We only got up the foothills for now".

"One thing at a time, ja? Now it is confirmed vat it is ve are up against, ve need two things for our heat-seeking missile: the targeting mechanism, and the explosive - the assassin if you prefer. The targeting mechanism you can finish today, ja?"

Anastasya nodded as the light flickered off. No bulb seemed immune to failure down here. "For sure. End of today." She had to identify 20-letter sequences of the virus which were unique, which would serve as the means in the CRISPR array in order to identify the DNA they wanted to kill. This genetic information they would manufacture - here in Grand Plains - into a treatment which would assimilate itself in the Pawnee hosts. If successful, their manufactured CRISPR array would identify the presence of the killer viral DNA in each cell of the host's body...so the second thing they needed to kill the virus hunting the Pawnee was the assassin enzyme.

"I can do the same trick as yesterday - convert the genetic alphabet to numbers, then it's merely a pattern recognition task for me to identify unique colors, shapes or smells... nothing special. But the assassin...finding the enzyme that will actually kill the viral DNA, once our CRISPR array has found it - how do we do that? You said yourself the only way to find that is testing...and testing takes time. Which we don't have. And I can't keep working in a basement indefinitely, cut off from Sybelle. I'm surprised the Helpers haven't been down here yet" Anastasya said, looking over her shoulder quickly.

"One thing at a time? First you get us the unique sequences, the tracer RNA for our heat-seeker - then let us discuss vat can be done about the hunt for the assassin enzyme", Iva said, spanking Anastasya on the knee.

Anastasya again refused a cigarette.

"I will. But seriously Iva, I do need to reconnect to Sybelle. We really don't want Helpers storming down here looking for me. I should give Sybelle some updates, ask for something more from her. I can't risk outlier behaviour".

With an exaggerated sigh Iva stubbed out her smoke. She put the unfinished half gingerly back into her silver cigarette case.

Back on the surface and outside, the afternoon sun was warm, a rarity Anastasya enjoyed. There was a red throbbing icon on her feeds, but she didn't open yet, wanting to first soak up some of the heat.

They sat their tired selves again, on a rusted three-person slatted bench on the pavement leading up to the hospital entrance. Anastasya tilted her face to the hot orb, and when she closed her eyes and faced it, everything went reddish black. When she opened them again, little black dots bounced around her vision.

They faded after a few tired seconds - all but one.

A dot in the bottom left of her vision was growing, and it wasn't black - more dirty brown, and seemed to be mushrooming. She laughed as she realised it was an actual dust cloud, something moving towards the town. From pure habit Anastasya Thynked her Map to id it, scolding herself as she did so that Sybelle wouldn't have a match on some random Grand Plains jeep.

To her surprise, there was an id made. Corynthian transports, three, incoming fast. The names of the incoming visitors began to scroll on the right of her vision, but she shut it down. She preferred to soak the last of the sun's rays before whoever it was interrupted them.

"Jon asked for help through the official channels?" Anastasya asked casually.

"Ja. Request was made. Why?"

"Well, they're here already" Anastasya explained, pointing lazily for Iva, who shielded her eyes and squinted. "Great to see they care so much" Iva said, voice dripping acid.

Anastasya closed her eyes to the sun until a few minutes later the gravel scrunched close by them as heavy tyres braked hard to stop. A door opened on the opposite side of the lead vehicle to their bench, and she could hear footsteps chomping their way towards the vehicle's front.

Her half-open eyes shot open with a jolt. Gauge! He turned the corner, dressed in fatigues and trailed by Helpers.

"So this is the shit-hole you've been hiding in". Statement.

"I...what the fuck are you doing here?", Anastasya shot back.

"Ye, good question Ana. It really is. I'm here because I'm in the shit - but not as much as you are."

A wave of nausea and confusion hit her deep in the gut. "What do you mean? I've absolutely no idea what you're talking about", she mock-laughed in response. She went to stand up, but Iva put a restraining hand on her arm.

"Of course you don't", he answered, and she could see through her shock that he was genuinely angry. "You've been completely off-grid for the last - how many days?"

Iva stood from the bench, flicked her cigarette to land a foot from Gauge's boot.

"Is there somewhere we can talk? In private" he added, looking at Dr. Krantz meaningfully as he ground the butt thoroughly with his boot.

This time Anastasya put her arm on Iva's, and nodded over her shoulder. His eyes followed to the hospital entrance.

"Not in there", he replied, "I was hoping somewhere more private".

"I meant the sidewalk", Anastasya said. "You can see the streets aren't exactly crammed with people".

"Fine by me", he said, and they fell in together. After ten meters Anastasya looked over her shoulder; Iva hadn't moved an inch, eyes still fixated on them.

As soon as they had passed the entrance to the hospital, she asked him: "so what's all this about?"

"You've been hit with a Credyt penalty Ana, that's what's up. And it impacts me too, but not as much as you – you've already dropped below ten thousand, so you've lost your place in Deme 2! I was asked by Eryss - your boss, a Founder - to come here and tell you personally. She said Sybelle thinks you'll listen to me more than if Sybelle told you the usual way. I know we don't really know each other Ana, but I do care - I care for you but also for our baby. I've had so many relationships. And that's normal, but - and I can't really explain this - but I thought ours was special. I want to have this child with you. I know it sounds weird for a male to be saying this."

"No, go on", she said, looking to buy time to get over the shock. Credyt penalty?

He was looking sideways at her as they walked. "Sorry I was angry, but you're putting that child at risk - that's what makes me mad. Let me explain", he quickly added, seeing her reaction. "You've been hit with a penalty for anti-social behaviour."

"What?"

"You've cut yourself off from everyone. Very recently nobody has seen a feed from you, no messages or comments anywhere, nothing. No replies to anyone either, not a single thing. It's like you were dead. In fact I wondered if you were! And before that, well you haven't been in-game in like over three weeks! Three, whole, weeks." He shuddered.

"I wanted time to do other things", she weakly replied. Then: "why am I making excuses? I had other things to do".

"Ye, I know. Like moping in that library of yours. Do you know how much of a lunatic you looked on your feed, sitting there alone for hours, no hypno nor booze, not talking or replying to anyone? It was scary, some of us thought you might be...ill. After that Mya thing."

She took a chance and let herself fall onto another rusted bench, one without even a lick of paint on it, squeezed herself right up against one end of it.

Who was he - or anyone - to judge how she spent her time? Here, walking the cracked pavements of a touching-on-derelict city, in a State not controlled by an omnipresent intelligence, with people dying due to genetic imperfection and others who smoked cigarettes and plotted against the Councyl, she felt different, freer despite the worse circumstances.

"It's touching that you cared", she replied as neutrally as she could manage.

He sat beside her.

"Plus…I was told you've been completely off-grid more than expected - more than Sybelle thinks was necessary."

"That's crazy, it's not my fault the connection drops around here - it's not Corynth, you know".

"In any case, it's not so severe a Credyt penalty that you'll lose your license or apartment. But it's close…and could get worse. You've got to turn this around - you know as well as I do that if you don't start working to build your Credyt back, or at least to stop the slide, you'll be hit even further. And you're close to losing your license now, right? Right on the line."

Her stomach plummeted like a broken elevator…it was true. And anger wouldn't help make it untrue.

"Ana, your child - our child - would be rejected on the spot if you drop further. There's nothing you nor anyone could do to stop it."

She slapped down on her own legs hard. "I'm here at the Councyl's bidding! Fuck. How can my Credyt be hit for working as per orders?"

"You still need to be social Ana, you need to share your life, you need to be part of society. And you don't do that by reading and brooding alone, or from shutting yourself off completely from all comms. Frankly it's insulting to me…and to Tanya and others."

Tanya.

"Look, I know what's going on here" he replied. "Eryss 1 filled me in on the whole thing! Some disease or virus killing folk around here, med team sent from Corynth to help." Then after a few seconds, "Terrible business. But, for me, it's no choice. Get home, get social. Get Credyt".

"You know about what's going on?" This was making less and less sense to her.

He laughed, tapping her on the shoulder. "Come on Ana! You think I'd really be sent here to the middle of this shithole without knowing what's going on?" He looked around as if to prove his point, but the empty street yawned back. "Of course Eryss filled me in. Maybe not on everything, but enough to know not to go near any Grand Plains folk".

Now she wanted one of those cigarettes - or a drink even. Was it even a choice? Not if she valued her baby's life.

A thought...it surely wouldn't hurt to try asking Eryss or her primary for help with identification of the enzyme they needed. There was no point trying to not think it explicitly now. She had to go back.

She stood from the bench, Gauge copying her.

"Let's head back to the hospital. I need to finish off some stuff quickly. It'll put me off-grid as I'll be underground there. But after that, can we go straight back to Corynth? Together? I'll start building back my Credyt, don't worry".

Gauge nodded judiciously. "OK. I'm glad you've taken this news so well."

"Of course! It's the wake-up call I needed. Now, if you don't mind, I'm going to go through my feeds...I've a lot of catching up to do".

She Thynked to re-enable all comms as they started walking, and was met by a deluge of feeds, messages, requests, in-game updates, gossip, news, deals. Corynth's share of GDP versus the rest of the world continued to climb, the CROW rising vertically due to the mayhem being wreaked in the States by Genghis.

She traced her baby-bump with her fingertips. Anastasya the "model citizen", the one who accumulated all that Credyt in the first place, would need to return.

IV

Credyt: 8,500

IV - I

Eryss 1 was pacing her office, gliding between the light-pools created by the sources built into the concrete walls. She wasn't long out of the gloom between each pool.

She was a firm believer in faith - not in the false gods of old as she called them - but faith and belief in science, and its miracles. She was well aware of the apparent paradox of needing faith in science, a common misunderstanding she never tired of correcting. For the true scientists, those with the deepest knowledge of reality, understood there was no paradox - consciousness is the true nature of reality. *Objective* reality. Time, space, any and all objects people see and stub their toe against reside *in* consciousness. QBism proved that quantum states are nothing but the *beliefs* of observers, and therefore a pure construct of consciousness. Remove the living being observing things, and things are annihilated, cease to exist.

But believe in them, have faith in the quarks, mesons, bosons of our minds and the doctrine of QBism which ties it all together, and viola! The path to the true expansion and evolution of conscious reality and lived-experience opens. Mastery of the so-called physical world is there if you have this faith, this will - something she thought Anastasya Delta 3 was losing. Qualified with the comment that it was in her genes to revolt, and this sympathy was in-line with that.

Eryss and Yena had been talking. Anastasya, according to Eryss, was blinded by "misplaced compassion" for an "inferior people" in the Pawnee; such compassion was an obsolete emotion in an evolutionary sense, where the strong had no need nor primacy to carry the weak along. It was nothing personal against the Pawnee, purely a question of genetics and of accelerating natural selection's inevitable curve. It was galling Anastasya could not see this - not unexpected, but galling nonetheless.

The lecture, which Yena had been listening to mostly without comment, continued along the lines that the Councyl had created a society not afraid to look the reality of existence in the eye, to be *truly* moral and to use science as a scalpel to cut away the dead flesh of religion, tradition and the jaded patriarchal philosophies, to leave a healthy and lean body of Corynthian citizenry.

Eryss took another whiskey soda from the bot. Yena said she was still finishing her first. Eryss was non-plussed.

She took a long pull from the drink. "Is it not poignant that sacrifice and martyrdom are seen as tenets of the old religions alone. Why do people not associate them more readily with the new faith of science?"

Yena put her drink down. "Where are you going with this?"

"Where? Follow, Yena - you know! Would you not love to explain to the world that the greatest contribution the Pawnee could make would be a sacrifice of themselves? A shining example to the world of rational decision making at its best: a truly moral and merciful act, saving themselves, the impoverished Pawnee, from a lifetime of hardship, futile toil, pain and want, while ensuring the survival of humanity's vanguard."

Yena took her time. "It would be something. Not sure the world is ready for such a message".

"Of course they are not! And that is our burden, to blaze onwards against the ignorance."

Yena agreed, and very soon after engineered an exit. She was standing alone now, feed to Eryss closed, looking from her completely darkened room out over the equally dark bay. Here and there stars poked through as pin-pricks of light.

What did you think about that conversation? Specifically, about Eryss's state of mind?

This Founder was not one to be startled. If anything her stillness solidified to a statue-like stance. When she spoke, it was with care.

"It was unusual, Sybelle. Perhaps she was a bit drunk."

Consumption does not explain it fully. Do you have any other thoughts on this matter?

"I do, but frankly Sybelle, I'm not sure this - what you are asking - is appropriate."

This discussion is completely private - no matter what is said, Eryss, nor any Founder, will ever be aware.

"But we are Founders. Is this your place to question our behaviour? Unusual as it may be." She edged ever-so-slightly backwards from the pane of glass, looked over her shoulder. Of course, nobody was there.

I am responsible for optimal outcomes that may arise from the operational side of Abundance. I have some concern about the level of frustration and unusual lack of control - slight as it may be - demonstrated by Eryss tonight. Do you have any insight?

"Look - it could simply be stress...although she has been in far, far rougher spots, and we've sailed through."

I would like to run a full neural diagnostic on Eryss 1. To do so, usually I would need the Councyl's permission; but because of the need-to-know on Abundance, your permission would suffice. I do not wish to alarm the other Founders, as almost certainly all is good - but I need to be sure. Do I have your permission?

Yena was silent a long time.

"And no-one else will know?"

Correct.

"Eryss will not be aware of this, this "diagnostic"?"

Correct.

Again, there was a long wait of utter stillness.

"OK Sybelle. I approve."

The stillness was broken when she made for the drinks cabinet.

IV – II*

Anastasya had left Gauge with Helpers outside the hospital main entrance, it being the nearest he was willing to come. Once inside, Anastasya dashed to the squirrel-like grey-haired lady at the reception desk, and asked for an urgent message to be sent to the Governor. Could he meet her in Dr. Spring's office?

She then raced straight to the underground lab via the dingy elevator, and breathed a big sigh of relief as the feeds flickered before disappearing from sight along with her nimp connection.

She could maybe squeeze out one of the three unique 20-letter sequences of the viral DNA, if she could calm down enough and focus. How she wished for some hypno to help with the calming, but couldn't risk it slowing her down now. Distilled focus was needed. If she could get at least one sequence identified it would leave Iva and the doctors with at least something to use in the CRISPR array as the explosive-less heat-seeker. Hopefully the meeting with Jon would leave enough time for it.

Out of the elevator she breezed past the canteen. She decided she'd miss it - or rather, the camaraderie - shitty as the actual place was.

Finding Tomek's office empty she left the door open. She chose walking in a small circle again around the threadbare rug over sitting on the couch, the passivity of sitting seeming like an obnoxious luxury.

After a few orbits she heard rapidly approaching footsteps. Then Governor Laide entered, closing the door quickly behind him.

"I got your message. I take it this is some kind of emergency", he said, touching her arm and standing in front of her, face to face.

"Gauge came from Corynth", she blurted.

"I saw him at reception. He seemed very engrossed in a conversation with one of our young nurses".

"Really? Anyway, it *is* an emergency. They're on to us, our efforts to hunt for a cure."

"It was inevitable."

"Yes, but...*personally*, I could be in trouble." Leaning her backside on the edge of the desk, she began explaining it all to him. The Credyt penalty, Gauge, the need to return immediately, the threat of further penalties if her anti-social behaviour continued.

"I'd lose my birth license."

"Meaning..." he left it hanging in the air like a malevolent cloud, perhaps unwilling to utter it aloud.

Anastasya nodded in reply, hands covering her belly.

"OK. So that's not even a choice then", he said. "Please go back - asap. Blend in again. Be a good, dumb, entertained citizen".

Anastasya pushed off the edge of the desk, hands by her side. He hesitated a moment, then moved in and wrapped his arms around her. She was limp in his comforting embrace, inhaling his smell of coffee and tangy sweat.

She eventually broke it, lifting her arms and placing her hands flat on his chest, eyes focused on the shirt buttons her fingers rested on. She spoke softly, the distance too close for raised voices.

"What about the Pawnee? What we still need to do? We have proof - well, soon hopefully I can do it - but we'll have at least one unique sequence of the virus' DNA. That will allow you guys target the virus - your unarmed heat-seeker. But we also need the enzyme, the assassin enzyme to arm it. If I'm back in Corynth I can't do anything to progress that. What can - " she said, but Jon interrupted her, looking down now into her upturned eyes.

"You've got to take care of yourself. Take care of your child. That's number one. What do we do about the enzyme? I'll be back in Corynth." He watched her eyes widen in surprise. "I'm going back tomorrow, stationed in our Embassy, and I'll negotiate with your Councyl. They know we know, so I need to see what pressure I might be able to use. I'll request your help, and you and I can meet in the Embassy - like we did before. How does that sound?"

Anastasya laughed out loud, disbelievingly. "Good! It sounds good", she said, amazed at how quickly words could turn situations around, and how relieving it felt to have this man on her side. An image of him discharging a pistol at close range into another man's face flew across her mind like a startled sparrow, but it only enhanced what she was feeling right now towards him.

"That should work. I still have no idea how I could go about finding the right enzyme...but as Iva said, one thing at a time".

"Exactly. Something will come to you".

He moved away from her and made his way around the desk, sitting down in the chair behind it.

"There is one other thing" he said, fishing in an inside pocket before pulling out a black tube. He placed it on the table, gesturing to it as he spoke.

"Whatever our plans, it will still be highly dangerous for you."

Her eyes flitted between him and the tube.

"We have a means of emergency extraction from Corynth", he said, poking the tube where it lay.

"Oh Jon" Anastasya replied dejectedly. "You might think you have, but Sybelle can see *every* move you make - apart from within your Embassy. Every step on the street you take is monitored for unusual gait patterns, every hair on your head accounted for, every breath you take measured for stress hormones, heart and pulse monitored continuously, facial expressions diagnosed, body language analysed - it's not just your whereabouts are known to Sybelle, it's *how* you are, your emotions, what you're likely to do and feel, where you're likely to go, everything watched, detected and monitored. Sybelle's eyes are everywhere, everyone you meet. Drones you can't even see. You *know* this." She couldn't believe his naivety.

Jon nodded sagely. "We have a means, Anastasya."

"Have you done it before?" she immediately countered, barely keeping her impatience in check.

"Yes, as a matter of fact. Different route than what we have now, but yes."

She couldn't believe it. Didn't believe it. It must have been obvious from her expression, because he asked her why on earth would the Councyl publicize such a thing - and hence, how could she have known. But he was adamant it was true.

"Granted, this particular route is untried. And I'm not mad", he said, recognizing cynicism when he saw it. "I know all about Sybelle. But every fortress has a weakness, it's always a question of time until one is found - and we've found one. I've had a unit work on this for quite sometime, and believe me, the odds of success are very high for this type of operation... should it be needed."

"Very high? How high?"

"It will depend on the particular circumstances, but no less than fifty percent - possibly as high as seventy-five."

"Doesn't sound very high to me".

"Trust me, for extractions from a place like your State - it's higher than expected."

"I might trust you...but only if you tell me how".

Jon hesitated, couldn't help himself. He needed her to believe it had a good chance of success, needed her to be ready to use it if needed. But telling her the details now was far too risky...if she was squeezed back in Corynth, or even if Sybelle detected some wayward explicit thought, they would lose their only extrication route, one they'd spent years identifying.

"Can you swim?"

"Yes" she answered reflexively.

"Can you tell the time?" She studied him to see was he taking the piss.

"Tell the time on one of these", he clarified, twisting open the tube and rolling out a green Omega diving watch, the old analog type with moving hands.

"It looks like the one you gave me, months ago. This one", she said, rolling up her sleeve to show it off.

"That's the idea" Jon said. He reached over, and holding her hand he unclasped the one she wore. Then he slipped the new one on her wrist and fastened it.

"It looks identical. However, your new one has a built-in signalling device. Sybelle won't detect any electromagnetic signals from it while it's dormant - completely safe for you to wear back home."

Holding her wrist lightly, he extended the crown of the watch by unscrewing it.

"However...rotate the bezel, like this, to point to "three", then wind it to set the time to five-to-twelve - like so - and the crown will extend one notch further than otherwise possible. See that?"

"Ye".

"If you pull it out that extra notch, a high frequency signal will be sent from a nano-mechanical graphene transmitter buried within the watch. Our receiver in the Corynthian embassy will detect it. You should activate this signal if you're in serious danger or trouble, and we'll activate the extraction protocol on our side.

"We can't just come and fetch you - so don't go whipping it out if you're attacked or something. We can only start the process from within our Embassy - so you've got to be make your own way to us if you want out. But before you do, you must activate the signal on the watch first, and then you come to the Embassy. Got it?"

A nod.

"Good. The reason to send the signal first is that we need time to prepare the extraction route, once we know it's needed. If you're in danger, time will be of the essence, so you can't just show up at the Embassy unannounced. Understood?"

She cleared her throat. "Five to midnight, bezel at three, extract further, then go to the Embassy."

"Good".

"But then what? Suppose I did get out of Corynth...what? Where will I be? What would I do?"

"If you need to get out, does it really matter?"

She pulled her wrist gently out of his hand. He'd been holding it this entire time.

"I need to get going. The convoy is going back to Corynth within the hour. I'll be on it."

IV - III

She had returned to Corynth four days back. Upon arrival Anastasya had been removed from the health emergency investigation, and moved to another topic. The reason she was given was that the whale situation was of high priority due to the citizenry obsession with it, and both Sybelle and her needed to work out probabilities and a feasible underwater defense grid mechanism that maintained defense requirements, whilst minimizing whale casualties in the bay. Another traveling salesman type mathematical problem requiring intuition to solve to satisfactory levels. Her requests to speak to the Chief Geneticist were denied; instead, Bryna, Defense Chief, had had a brief liaison with her. Anastasya had suggested a trip to the Embassy - it had been refused and declared off-limits.

She had begun to rebuild Credyt, but had drawn the line at hypno, cotics and booze - she blamed it on pregnancy. Deeper though, she displayed symptoms of an old war reporter - she hadn't wanted to extract or numb herself from reality, had things she wanted to very much keep in mind if not explicitly thought of. Feelings, emotions, were running strong.

With little else to do, and the desire to rebuild Credyt, she'd thrown herself with some abandon back in-game, Polls immediately answered, feeds flashing constantly.

The efforts and endeavors to demonstrate conformance and prove it with Credyt became ever and more consuming. She did not necessarily like that, but was powerless in the path of the juggernaut. Thoughts of an enzyme seared her mind now and then, images of suffering and pustulous tubes, a running little girl, but she shut them down with a fervor whenever they did.

The Dryve stopped outside O.G.E.R, its sudden deceleration tilting Anastasya forward at the hip. She climbed out. She had work scheduled.

She was halfway up the granite steps when the main doors of O.G.E.R opened. Ysabel came out, started down the steps towards her.

She must have been lost in a feed, Anastasya thought. With her head down she didn't see Anastasya until Anastasya practically waved in her face.

"I haven't seen you since I came back." She left unmentioned the messages she'd sent. All unanswered.

Flicking her hair from her eyes, Ysabel livened up. "We're meeting up now in Old Town for drinks. Come with?".

"I can't", Anastasya replied earnestly.

"Right - you're pregnant," Ysabel said drolly, her face instantly stony again. She walked a couple of steps down past Anastasya, who turned as she did.

"No! Well, yes of course I'm pregnant. It's complicated." She'd tried broaching the topic of the Pawnee with Tanya - carefully - but to no avail. Tanya had seen a feed somewhere about the plight of the backward peoples of Grand Plains, and had zero interest in hearing any details from Anastasya about it. There was nothing *to* hear - that was the bottom line, from Tanya. As Anastasya suspected, with everyone.

It was exactly as Iva had prophesied – simple indifference - warning Anastasya as she'd contrived to meet her after Jon's meeting, as Anastasya had passed back through the canteen en-route to the elevator to the surface. It was a collective blind-spot of indifference induced on citizens by the Councyl, one willingly accepted by the masses.

Ysabel squared her shoulders and planted one foot firmly on

a step closer to Anastasya, the other on the granite below.

"We were friends, you and I - so I'm gonna tell you straight: you've become *old*. It's shit. I saw your messages and you prostituting yourself around in-game looking for friends. Pathetic." She chuckled darkly to herself. "At this rate you'll be hustling for Credyt to avoid the Pleasure Plaza." Without waiting for a response, she jumped down the bottom step and into the Dryve Anastasya had arrived in.

Anastasya stood watching it speed off. As she watched, she twiddled the bezel on the Omega.

"Sybelle, I need - *need* - to speak to the Chief Geneticist. Now. Today. OK?"

Your stress levels are elevated.

"I know. So?"

It's a uniquely human attribute, another manifestation of irrationality. What do you think is stressing you? Perhaps talking through it would help.

"Talking through it *would* help, but that's the problem! I mean, I don't know Sybelle".

You and I have worked closely over the years. In some degrees we're familiar with each other's minds. How about you talk to me, with the guarantee there will be no penalty incurred. Now or in future. This conversation will be off the record - you are familiar with the expression.

Anastasya balled her fists, then unclenched them. The sky was dark, too dark for this time. She looked vertically up. Then, she leveled herself.

"I know what's happening to the Pawnee, Sybelle. You know I've seen it. The blood and literally their guts, coming out, oozing out, being spluttered and coughed out through ventilators. It's horrible."

The words started to tumble, much faster than her normal

pace.

"And I know we are responsible for it. Aren't we? So we could stop this! But instead we pretend like nothing is happening. You and I are fucking around on protecting whales! The rest of my time is also wasted, trying to blend in again with people that have nothing in common with me anymore, people that can smell "other". *That's* what's so frustrating. Fuck!"

Thank you for sharing so honestly and transparently. I expected you to feel this way.

"So what's the point of asking me then?" Anastasya looked over her shoulder, checked her Map - nobody near.

Your brain has been adapting to pregnancy, and has in fact displayed a very high degree of plasticity - well above the expectation for your age. Heightened empathy is part of this change.

Anastasya scoffed. "Baby brain. So me feeling bad about the slaughter in Grand Plains is because I'm pregnant."

No. You are being true to your species' hormonal and evolutionary influences - which are deeply and inherently personal to the point of selfishness. Yet also you are equally driven to right what you see as injustice, wherever you encounter it. First Mya, now the Pawnee. Would you agree?

She shifted her weight on the steps. "I guess you could put it that way."

Would you like to help the Pawnee? To stop the virus which is killing them? I remind you again, your answer will not result in a Credyt penalty. It is off the record.

"I thought things like "off the record" are privacy, and prohibited. But yes - that's what I've been saying, Sybelle. *I want to help them.* They're being killed *by us.* And we are the ones who can do something about it".

But they do not follow the Way. Nor are they genetically

modified for the future that awaits.

Fuck, Anastasya thought.

Do you really want to help such a people? Sybelle persisted.

"Why are you asking? You know the answer".

The Chief Genetics Officer has an opening in her schedule. Why don't you speak with her now?

IV – IV*

Governor Laide poured another rye, not bothering to look at the glass as he did, instead measuring it by the amount of seconds spent pouring. The bar-bot at The Basilica had given him the bottle as requested - still no expense being spared by the Councyl hospitality-wise - he figured it was much easier to manage his intake on-demand rather than be drip-fed by a walking-talking algorithm.

It was coming to the end of day five since he'd returned, still no sign of Anastasya. His requests to see her had been rebuffed - he'd been told she was working on unspecified but allegedly important topics. He highly doubted those topics included the virus inflicted upon Grand Plains, but he had been assured by a representative of Eryss that the battle to fight the virus was "well in-hand".

Five days was a serious amount of time given the life expectancy of the symptomatic. And it wasn't merely the death toll either - the number of people slipping past the point of no-return (probably) from the brain impairments increased daily. The Nation inched closer to oblivion and extinction with each passing day, while he sat filling his cup, waiting for a contact.

This impotence was killing him, along with the utter futility of his own scientists and doctors' efforts. Left to their own devices it was a given they wouldn't identify the enzyme in time, but at the same time, how could they stop searching? The standard CAS enzymes which usually (or so he was told by Frank and Iva) worked as the genetic assassin, the warhead for the heat-seeking missile analogy of their CRISPR treatment, simply weren't firing when combined with the messenger RNA guide sequences. Like milk in water, the enzymes were harmless. It was Anastasya, or rather, Anastasya and Sybelle who could give the answer. He'd allowed himself to believe such help was possible back home, now he felt like an idiot. Was he fit for purpose, for thinking such a thing would ever be possible with such a State?

So here he was, like a lovelorn teenager pining for an ex, having chosen the taverna they had both enjoyed lunch in before, on the off chance she might turn up. This is what he was reduced to - acting like a stalker. He also had other Embassy staff out looking for Anastasya in other haunts they had frequented or he'd heard her mention, but to no avail. The only positive - and it was minimal - was the precedent being set of himself and other Embassy staff roving the city on foot at all hours.

He had played out the various options in his mind so far, and couldn't bring himself to countenance the worst...rejection, retirement, or whatever they may call it - execution to anyone else. She had been used, that was clear, but she had been used *because* she was so good and worthy...he never would have fallen for it otherwise.

He took a large swallow to combat the rising swell of self-anger. He had failed, failed miserably at what was his chief responsibility - to vet the payload his people were being given. He should have known better, having focused too much on Anastasya, the tainted genius who bore no threat apart from the blind-spot she produced in his vision. Yet how could he not have focused on her? Damn Eryss, she'd done her homework well, using Anastasya to unwittingly get him to drop his guard.

Jon swivelled on his stool and looked around. The Basilica actually being a bona fide one - The Basilica of Saint Jude. The altar was at the far end, empty high-stools circling it. *The Blood of Christ* was one of the cocktails on the list.

Converted confession boxes served as booths along its side, a massive stained glass window over the main entrance. When he'd walked to his place at the bar, and then later the toilet, his footsteps had echoed throughout the vaulted concaved ceilings and off the huge pillars.

He was a Christian and a believer, but not a nit-picky one, happy to be a sinner - but even so, he remembered how he'd to try and hide his shock when Anastasya had brought him here the first time, and explained it was still an *actual* Basilica; not a converted old church, it was a church where people drank and God-knew-what, but where mass could be said, prayers made...if anyone wanted.

Of course, nobody wanted.

Maybe surprisingly religion was not banned nor prohibited in any way in Corynth - citizens were free to worship if desired. The fact that none did though, was hardly surprising to him. Religion – particularly Christianity - being a genuine threat to Corynth or any totalitarian state, Christianity had undergone a tried and tested method of destruction, cloaked as nothing overt: popular culture and arts ridiculing and sneering, trivialization over condemnation. The erosion of the symbols of Christianity through mass marketing, media and pop culture, lead to a loss of meaning of what those symbols represented. Once the symbols were gone, the story of Christianity followed out the door. Now a crucifix was just a cool retro icon to have on a t-shirt - either that or Che or a banana from that 1970s band - a basilica no more than a taverna, a confession something you admitted to someone.

This he'd known, an approach not unique to Corynth. But there was something else at play here, something more pronounced due to the nature of the unique ubiquity of their tech, which he had only realised from his time here. *Technology itself* undermined Christianity more effectively than if done by force, by introducing new ways of life that emphasized and grew anti-Christian values like the narcissism feeds created, and the de-emphasis on community achieved by the illusion of the new virtual community which social media promoted over actual human—interaction community.

At the end of the day, tech is a jealous mistress which tolerates no other lovers. Anything non-tech is old-school, quaint, granddad, patriarchal, biased with privilege. And Christianity was very non-tech.

So the threat had been identified and neutralized. In seeing human beings as souls with bodies - and temporary bodies at that - Christianity inherently has a dual set of values: people recognized as children of God as well as earthly citizens. And being a good citizen was fine, as long as your actions did not jeopardize your soul's eternal life with God. Now though, here, being a good citizen with Credyt was the only prerogative - not for eternal life, but even for temporary life.

Here he sat, in a place which embodied this destruction-through-irrelevance of Christianity better than anywhere else could.

A young woman - not Anastasya - sat staring into the void two stools down the long bar on his left. In different times she might be taken to be praying, as opposed to her actual act - consuming data streams. He shuddered as what must have been a savage gust of wind shook the domed roof, a pre-cursor of the larger Atlantic squall on the way.

"Do you have a family?" Jon called over to her, not in a shout but loud enough that the bar-bot craned it's mech head to look at him.

It took a moment, but the girl realised he was talking to her.

"No", she said, flicking her eyes over him before getting back to whatever it was had her attention. Unperturbed, the whiskied Governor continued, leaning from his stool with one foot on the ground, one on the bottom rung.

"You know, I discovered many years ago, that family - being part of a family - shows us the path to humanity's ultimate target destination. You know what that is?"

The girl didn't look.

"The becoming of one from many."

The bar-bot took a couple of steps closer.

"This is a revelation which us humans haven't yet grasped or realised. It's God's plan, and if you can understood that," he continued, jabbing a finger towards the embarrassed young woman, "it will imbue you - I mean, people in general - with a deep sense of belonging and purpose. It truly will", he finished, spinning back around to slug down some more of the rye.

The bar-bot stopped swishing his cloth around the glass he held.

"I am capable of metaphysical discussion. Would you like to talk?"

At the intervention, the female citizen took the opportunity and scooted off her seat, was now making towards the exit.

"Right" the Governor dryly remarked. "But no. Tell you what...why don't you just keep the ice cold, coz I'll need it in a minute."

The bar-bot said nothing, and for a fleeting moment Jon thought he might have pissed him off.

The thing was, as he poured another and shook it for some ice, it wasn't bullshit. He'd felt this becoming of one acutely with his wife and child, how he was no longer the individual Jon Laide, but had transmogrified and morphed into a new being, unified with Leila and Michal. When they died, it therefore literally felt like a part of himself had died too, that the person or entity he had become was gone, lost to time. He had begun to feel that draw towards a deeper connection again - nothing sexual, he clarified for himself - and changing of selfhood with Anastasya, and he had meant every word of what he had said about doing everything he could for her and her baby. He *could* get her out - of that he was confident to some degree. However, he couldn't escape someone he didn't have any contact with.

"Nice watch", the bar-bot commented as he placed a tumbler of ice and small jug of water on the counter, and with the slow eyes of the gently inebriated, Jon's eyes followed down to the tampered-with Omega on his wrist - still showing no signal of her signal. "Thanks", he said, waving the bot away.

He was all out of options save for walking and searching in this vast technopolist's paradise in hangouts he guessed she might frequent. The Helpers stationed outside the Embassy had become accustomed to him taking an umbrella with him if there was any threat of rain, something which seemed to greatly amuse them.

To lose on both fronts, Pawnee and also Anastasya, would be a tragedy which he knew he wouldn't be able to weather. To save one and lose the other...nightmare of all nightmares, but at least there would be a silver lining of hope with that outcome. To save both - well, that was impossible really, as just over half the Pawnee would be dead in a matter of days, so he was left with just varying degrees of loss.

For the Nation, the only hope was Anastasya. For Anastasya, the only hope was Anastasya herself. Would she have enough to withstand whatever onslaughts those Founders in the Councyl whipped up?

He had done his best to open her eyes, to be objective and get her to at least think about the alternate *true* facts he spoke about. But you could only open the eyes of those who wanted to see. He thought she did though, in her own way - and drank to that.

He scanned the bar again, but now there was no-one else within conversational distance, the only people apart from his good-self being a couple dwarfed in a large booth off the side and another young woman alone and close to the altar, talking away animatedly.

Alone, just his thoughts, helplessness and drink for company. Nothing to do but think...so he tried to list the positives on her equation of survival and success. He needed something to counter the pressing feeling of inevitability of doom.

Anastasya should be well aware by now, given what she'd witnessed over the last months that truth in Corynth was whatever Sybelle said, or what the Councyl said through her - be it history, current affairs, news, celeb gossip, statistics on God knew what - Sybelle was the gateway to all information as well as being the arbiter of the official veracity of all expressed opinions and information. This might seem normal to the citizenry, but at least some, like Anastasya he thought with a pinch of satisfaction, would know that the conferring of a "truth" or "factual" label on a particular statement or quanta of information by a biased authority does not make it *actually* truthful or factual. Real truth is married to real facts, and "real" or unbiased logic can be used as a tool to build truth from examination of the facts and logical evaluation of their implication. She'd be aware that she would be lied to and presented with false and misleading information as fact back here, which was the basis of some hope he had, that she'd be strong enough to see through the fog of deception...despite her naivety.

Secondly, when it came to her friends and colleagues - in fact all the citizenry - they were really just "tools of the tools", if he remembered his Hannah Arendt correctly. To a man with a hammer, everything is a nail - and to the Councyl with Sybelle as their tool, everything is data. The consequence of this was that all the citizenry's actions, activities, utterings and even their very thoughts were harvested to fuel Sybelle's algorithms...put even more starkly, the citizens' main purpose in Corynth was to generate data, to keep Sybelle lubricated with the oil of their data. He'd hinted to Anastasya she'd have to play the game, he was kicking himself he hadn't made that clearer to her, but hoped she would.

A plus: she had become a better liar, at least she was definitely improving on keeping her face from immediately telling the world what she was thinking. Of course the scrutiny she'd be under would also include emotional detection and mood analysis etcetera, but she'd said blaming being pregnant had worked before. So there was hope there too. He reckoned she'd a reasonable chance of believing her own lies if she could come into a situation calm, prepared.

And that was it really, but at least he'd counted off three positives.

His eyes found his watch again, mute and inert. If only he could pause time for the Pawnee like it had stopped on this watch, take the batteries from whatever supernatural clock marked the seconds of their life…there was no way around it, Anastasya just *had* to find a way to make progress. There was simply no other option.

For him though, he did have an option. Standing gradually to avoid embarrassment (not that anyone here would give a shit), his choice was not to play Sybelle's game and feed her algorithms with more data from the drunken Governor. This was the last time, he swore to himself - no more wallowing, maybe even no more drinking. Running a hand roughly across one side of his face, he shrugged into his mac, loudly thanked the over-curious bot, and left without having to pay. A kindness from the Councyl of Corynth.

IV - V

The lights were low, the corners of the office in total darkness.

"Something about the conversation I just had with Sybelle gives me the idea it's OK to broach this topic with you. Thanks again for seeing me, I've struggled for so long on how to appeal to you, let me get right to it. So, "

"Wait - what conversation with Sybelle?" The Chief Geneticist faced her across the enormous desk. Both were seated.

Anastasya looked over her shoulder and back.

"The one we just had outside, on the steps of O.G.E.R?"

The Chief Geneticist stared unblinkingly for a couple of seconds, then responded.

"What topic did you want to discuss?"

Anastasya, with the speed of relief, laid it all out; Corynth were behind the viral outbreak targeted against the Pawnee Nation; the reason was arcadmium supplies. Then a cost-benefit argument - a reasonable and rational one, with an appeal to "other options"...why did securing the arcadmium supplies have to equate to the death of every member of the Pawnee Nation? Why not stick to the three-year deal, or simply negotiate a better one? Arcadmium would still be theirs alone.

"Finished?"

Anastasya couldn't see Eryss's face, fully now, a shadow was drawn on it from the overhead pale light.

"Yes."

"You are important for Sybelle, and we had high hopes for you. So I am going to invest some additional time in your education. It may not pay off, but your utility is high - so why not try?

"You talk about "people of science". But you do not even know what Corynth - the embodiment of the scientific method - truly represents. Do you?"

Anastasya felt as if she'd stepped onto a stage, only to find out that when the curtain went up she was in a dock.

"Our society is built on the principles of science, and how we used the scientific method to eradicate numerous scourges. How we had the courage to make decisions based on data, facts and evidence alone - as true people of science would. For example, rape, Anastasya. Before Illumination, data showed that almost 99% of the people who commit rape are male; that 90% of all murders in the general population are committed by males; that serious armed robbery was committed almost exclusively by? Males. We could not call ourselves true scientists if we ignored that data, could we?"

"No."

"Exactly. Sense. Other societies and civilizations obviously had this data available to them also, but the difference is that we *acted*", bringing her fist down on the table like a gavel, "and we addressed the root cause: males. As part of Illumination we greatly limited these crimes, and heralded a new beginning where science lit the way for a liberated, compassionate and just society, the likes of which this world has never witnessed. Our will to act as true people of science brought us this bountiful world you enjoy today. But you know all of this."

Anastasya nodded, reeling on the ropes, not yet ready to enter back into the fight.

"You know this, yet you *still* do not truly grasp the core

of our essence. We have mastered life's code, controlling our own creation, eradicating the scourges of illness and disease, alleviating the threat of aging, while shaping our new generations in ways *we* desire. But what does doing that really represent Anastasya? What are the implications? *That* is what you have never - even until this very moment - understood.

"Every human has come into existence due to nature's evolutionary process. We could consider that nature has given each human a basic gift - that of life. Or as your superstitious new friends might say: God, or some great Native spirit, gave them life." She leaned over the desk towards Anastasya, bent almost double, stretching for her it seemed. "But we say: why accept that *basic* gift if we have the technical means to exchange it for something *better*...for a superior human being."

Eryss withdrew back to the shadows. Anastasya couldn't see her eyes, yet could feel their unflinching scrutiny.

"Humanity 2.0, as the old joke goes. We have the courage to reject that basic gift of nature, and harness the power of technology and genetics to bring us above the rest of humanity. *We are the human races' next evolutionary leap.* All engineered through science", Eryss said, pointing at her with both hands, thumbs cocked like a gun on her right.

"Evolution always works through leaps - never minute changes. And we have engineered our leap. Technically we engineered *Sybelle*, and Sybelle engineered our leap. Regardless, history will see us as the Founders not just of a State, but of the new human race."

Anastasya cleared her throat, found a voice.

"I get that, Chief Genetics Officer. Exchanging the "basic gift" of life for something better - I get that. But I don't see how it relat- "

"Very good! You get it!", Eryss's voice sarcastically shrill but utterly commanding. "But you clearly do not understand the *implications* of us being humanity's next leap. You do not understand the *responsibility*...not that we have to those *behind* us on the evolutionary ladder, but the responsibilities those others have to us! *We* are the ones who's needs come first - not an obsolete and non-progressive people who do not even believe in women's rights to basic healthcare. As the vanguard of humanity, others have a duty to do what they must for *our* sake, to maximise this evolutionary step's chance of success."

"Sybelle, I thought...", Anastasya said, voice fading.

"We reject the limits of nature and want better! We will not be held in the prison of the material, slaves to our genetic code...and as such", finger wagging in the air, "no threat to the species' finest can ever be tolerated. And a threat to Sybelle is a threat to us."

Anastasya jumped.

"But they do *not* represent a threat. One hundred percent we need the arcadmium. Sybelle's molecular transistors can only be stabilized with arcadmium. No argument. But what I'm saying is, we don't need to *kill* for it. And we certainly don't need to wipe out an entire genetic line of people, just to get their metal. There are other ways we could do this. *Please*."

"So it was a waste of time."

"What was?" Anastasya asked.

"The minutes I just spent educating you now. Of course there are other ways. We could stick to the three-year deal, and hope that we can reach another when it expires. We could play politics and hope - or perhaps pray? - that no other State, Corp, or nation comes along and also makes a power play for arcadmium."

The Chief Genetics Officer got up and started to walk around the edge of the desk towards Anastasya, eventually standing behind her. Anastasya could feel her hands on the back of her chair, but didn't deign to turn around to face her boss.

"But why would we abandon ourselves to *hope*," the voice came from intimately close over Anastasya's shoulder, "when we can shape the world we want with precision? We *know* this will work - Sybelle said it. And it leaves us - humanity's finest - in the ultimate position of strength."

"But the cost", Anastasya whispered.

"The cost!" Anastasya could feel flecks of spittle on her neck. The hands were like vices, her chair completely rigid.

"Don't you see? There *is* no cost. The Pawnee dying is not a cost...they *owe* it to us."

Anastasya realised coldly that Eryss *was* being reasonable after all...just to a different logic.

The Founder released her grip and strolled back around towards her seat.

"We can't officially start a war with Grand Plains", she continued casually, "or overtly take what we want by force, for one simple reason: we need to provide a fig-leaf of plausible deniability to our trading partners and political allies. We need to present some pretense to the world that what is happening in Grand Plains and to the Pawnee is not related to us...it is a virus that just happens to be killing them alone, nothing to do with us."

"But people will know..."

Eryss laughed. "Yes Anastasya, of course people will know it was us. Did you not hear me? *Plausible deniability*. Our partners can avoid having to criticize us publicly - and soon it will all blow over. You look skeptical. This is the last lesson for today: look to history. We are not killing them, in fact we are trying to help them - just like China helped "reeducate" the Uyghurs, not exterminate them. Like the E.U "protected" the citizenry from anti-vaxx, not ghettoize and sterilize them.

"Come now...you look downright distraught. And you pregnant. I thought you were a person of science? It is nothing personal with the Pawnee, they are simply on the wrong side of history's equation. Leave emotion out of this, and stop feeling sorry for a future-less race."

Anastasya's head had started to spin as her stomach. She'd be sure to puket over Eryss's desk if it came to it.

"I was used", she managed to say, more a surprised statement of fact than a question.

Eryss grinned. It was a lot of teeth.

"You served a purpose. As do we all. You really do not look well - Sybelle can you help her with something?"

"I'm fine".

"Very well then. You served a purpose, and you *still* can serve a purpose. Sybelle needs you, *I* need you. Your ability and talents are unique. I am saying that you have a future... but only if quit that pipe-dream of helping a doomed people. Full commitment to the Way is what you need from here - the leeway of the past is gone for you now. Over. Understood?"

Anastasya eyed the Chief Genetics Officer, lifelong guest in their house, someone she knew but clearly didn't, her whole life.

"Sybelle says you are in shock, so let me spell this out very simply for you. You will lose your birth license if you ever mention the Pawnee again. In any context. Is that understood?"

Anastasya couldn't believe her whole life could distill down to this single moment. She gave a quick diagonal downwards eye-glance to bring up her vitals, and threw a quick eye to her and her baby's stats, reassuring herself all was still OK. Both heart rates elevated, blood pressure increased also. She could envision the stress and fear hormones coursing through her umbilical cord, high-waying straight into her little man.

She desperately willed herself to be calm. She felt his kick, like someone lightly slapping a spoon against her belly, and realised it was no choice at all.

She got to her feet.

"Understood" and she turned swiftly around.

She headed straight for the doors, which gratefully began to open early. Once outside alone, she gasped for breath, then bent over and retched, heaving bile ejecting from her body.

She staggered over to a wall and slumped against it, trying to pull herself together. Eventually she straightened, hands clasped over her warm stomach.

"Hypno, Sybelle. *Now*", and with that, lurched down the empty corridor.

IV - VI

The week had been a grim eternity spent alone.

Anastasya had self-medicated heavily, but the cotics couldn't remove the gnawing dread which clung to her every waking moment. Also, her efforts hadn't paid dividends – her Credyt had started to nose-dive; nobody wanted to be on-board a sinking ship, and although hypno and the rest were important ballast, her socials just weren't getting any traction.

She used constantly, she saw it as a necessity to erase the images the Pawnee. She was wilfully betraying them all by turning her face away from their plight by living as before. Anastasya wondered how many had died this week, tortured herself with guesses of how many were still alive. That girl, with her athlete's heart…was it still beating?

There was a modicum of solace - the smallest sliver - in the knowledge that she had no path to a solution for them anyway. It wasn't as if she knew what to do to help them and wasn't doing it. She didn't know the enzyme needed to trigger destruction of the virus's DNA, and had no way forward to pursue her quest.

The Governor's watch sat heavy and limp on her wrist, a dead relic of the past. For this is what her bargain with Eryss truly signified: the death of herself as the person she had recently become, replaced by an automaton blindly following the Way and focused on accumulating Credyt, the fate of her child dependent on her continued conformance.

In a detached way - as everything seemed to her now - it was a curiosity that her desire to save the many hundreds of remaining Pawnee came a distant second-place to her desire to protect her son. He was one, they were very many. Yet no amount of Pawnee would ever tip the scales enough for her to sacrifice him. She had fantasized briefly that if this had been six months ago, she would have kept fighting...but it was just that: a fantasy. Six months back she wouldn't have even blinked at a mention of what was happening to the Nation - just like Tanya and the others couldn't care less now.

Tonight was a chance – a big one - to arrest her Credyt slide. She'd got on the guest list for Athena's, and a good performance and feeds from her there would be perfect for getting back in the ebb and flow of generating personal data-points.

She arrived alone in a Dryve, others already inside. Athena's was illuminated in neon pink, the sign erected on the outside of a back-lit period building. Its popularity stemmed from The Pink, the establishment's ballroom-sized orgy room. Looking at her Map, The Pink was her destination...Gauge, Tanya, Ysabel, someone she didn't know, were all there ahead of her.

Anastasya entered, knowing she'd be an attraction. She had a single band of white silk entwined tightly around her breasts, and her small pregnant swell sat above the band of her jogger pants, but below the diamond belt she wore on her naked belly. Pregnancy brought fetish value, and already stepping through the doors heads were turning greedily. She returned a few urgent stares with a smile she hoped didn't betray the lack of feeling behind it.

She told herself she was up for it - had to be, to complete her re-assimilation. She grabbed a vodka from a bot close to the bar and downed it in one, wiping her lips with the back of her hand and hiding a grimace. A lipstick smudge smeared her manicured hand.

The Pink was in front of her, its doors opening at her approach, to grant her entry to a throbbing blurred world of noise and freeze frames. The strobe lighting slowed her pace to a crawl, and meant she had to rely on the Map to find them in the throng, her vision being augmented with a green arrow the size of a baseball bat to guide her.

The room was segmented into areas for each group - rare couples, common threesomes, majority uncountable numbers in each group. Anastasya saw them, near the middle, Gauge lying prostrate but with his head up to kiss someone, as Tanya - of course it would be her - straddled him. A random stud was with Ysabel beside them.

She weaved her way towards them, the gems on her thin belt shooting dazzling flashes on each strobe. The guy with Ysabel eyed her hungrily like a marathon runner who had skipped breakfast. He beckoned Anastasya to lie beside him. She didn't bother checking his name, but did sit beside his prostrate body. It was virtually impossible to hear each other above the din of the beats, but she earned an encouraging smile from Ysabel and a wink from Gauge. She felt like the pièce de résistance for the evening's entertainment. The guy propped himself up on one elbow, and reached across to gently draw her neck towards him with the other arm. Anastasya let herself go with it, already maxed out to the hypno limit Sybelle would dispense.

The kiss was warm but smushy - like kissing jelly - and she suppressed a nervous giggle at the thought. Ysabel caressed one of her hands as the guy's free hand roved across Anastasya's long legs, before moving further up, and cupping her small baby bump. Through the fog she sensed not a kick but a recoil, a feeling so visceral it jolted her eyes wide open. The guy was oblivious to the reaction and kept rubbing her bump, kneading it more firmly now as though working to flatten dough, his breath moaning through the kiss.

From her belly rose a panic - not emotional, but bilious. The sickening draught was trying to escape up her throat, and she broke the kiss to gasp for clean air. The stud said something she couldn't catch as Ysabel looked on agape. Anastasya mimed vomiting for her benefit, an action which didn't translate well. The others in their party had paused their festivities to look at the mini commotion. Anastasya was suddenly very tired… of the scrutiny, the appearances, the pretence. She fired a quick Thynk to their group feed saying she was gonna puke (the feed of her doing it outside Eryss's office had been viral for a whole hour the other day), and turned into the dark segment of a strobe to leave.

Nobody replied back.

Outside The Pink again in the main bar, Anastasya leaned against the wall, breathing deeply. Catching sight of a roving bot she ordered a bourbon on the rocks, which was dispensed from the waiters pneumatic doors with a clear clink of ice.

Your drinking is at a level harmful to your foetus.

"What do you care? I'm losing Credyt so fast he'll be rejected soon anyway", Anastasya sneered, sloshing some of her drink on a girl walking by. She pushed past the aggrieved citizen and selected a new target: a plush purple velvet chair, deep-seated and vacant. Concentrating hard, she made her way as steadily as she could towards it, and gratefully sank into it like a torpedoed cruise liner - not immediately, but once her weight had settled through the thickness of the cushioning, quite rapidly. It would be difficult to get up, but she could conjure a waiter over when needed.

Right now though the bourbon was enough, and she let herself slump down even more into the velvet embrace, holding the near-empty glass loosely in her fingers, eyes regarding the scene. Ignorance was bliss…how she longed for both.

As the whirlpool of revellers circled round the bar, her own thoughts did likewise. As they did, one in particular emerged vividly through the haze - there was no point in being blissfully ignorant either. Past caring about having dangerous detected thoughts, she let it roam free. The freedom they enjoyed was being enjoyed *right now* - this very moment. The freedom to fuck, to party, to use, to drink, to spend as much time in-game as desired. But from where she sat, deep in velvet, it looked like this wasn't freedom to take pleasure, but rather an *obligation*...an obligation to behave and act in proscribed ways, as well as to conform, and to self-police, identify and isolate non-conformists like her. Good citizens generated data...bad ones were eliminated. For the good of the good!

She laughed at her own turn of phrase, and cast her eye groggily for a waiter. As she did, another thought, one she'd been suppressing hard, rose to the surface of her consciousness. There was no denying it's immediacy.

What was the point in painfully prolonging the inevitable? Her Credyt was crashing, her license would soon be gone. Best case her future self would be stupefied and wasted like this ad nauseum, using her talent for banalities. Or worse, to tighten and improve Sybelle's citizen control mechanisms...or maybe even to create another virus.

She grimaced another swallow of bourbon, and faced the logical conclusion of her thoughts: wouldn't it be better to end it now. She could feel the heat of tears scalding her eyes, but made no move to arrest them.

She could go straight to a Pleasure Plaza. Tonight. At least they'd be together at the end. Her Credyt would be higher than normal for someone visiting a Plaza, but she could request a shortened stay, heightened pleasure.

It felt like an inner her, "core Anastasya", coldly and soberly making the decision. Not the wasted tearful version of herself collapsed drunk at a bar. And she was grateful for that Anastasya, for the wave of relief she felt, offering as it did an end to this nightmare - all of it.

She couldn't muster the strength to raise her arms to wave for a drink. She managed an exhausted Thynk for a bot instead, then lay back, closing her eyes lagainst the circus around her.

She was following a man in a long overcoat down a familiar street she couldn't place, trying in vain to draw alongside him. The street's identity was revealed when the fugitive stopped outside a gated residence…her primary's house in Deme 0. His back was to her, face turned towards the property.

Her footsteps slowed as she neared him, and she reached out to touch his sleeve. His head rotated slowly at her tug, and she looked into the face of her biological father. An urge to shout, to denounce the traitor, surged inside her, yet she remained mute.

He remained looking at her, but raised his right arm and pointed into the residence behind the gate.

"I left you something". She looked past him before moving to open the gate.

She woke with a jump, the waiter in front of her, waiting with mechanical patience for her to take the glass of brown liquid. Grumpily she took it, annoyed at having been interrupted from opening the gate.

Blearily she wiped her eyes and took a sip. The volume in the room came back, a wall of sound. Even in her mangled state she had a strong desire to see what he'd left her. She managed to sloppily laugh. She knew what this was…her mind's desperation to keep her alive, and not follow through with an early retirement. Giving her something to do before visiting a Plaza, prolong her existence in this world.

"Won't work", she slurred to herself, hoisting the glass high and letting gravity shoot its contents down her throat. She'd go now. To a Plaza.

Anastasya let go of the glass, thereby sending it to the floor…it was easier than reaching for the table. She braced her arms on the side of the chair in order to lever herself up...but more co-ordination than her body was currently offering was needed.

Fine, she thought through the haze of noise and blurred vision. She'd just close her eyes for a few minutes, then try again. No rush...the Plazas never shut.

V

Credyt: 3,425

V - I

She woke in the late afternoon, tentatively opened both eyes. Left, right. Very surprised there was no headache, she then opened both eyes simultaneously, expecting a blast of pain - but no, nothing. She felt shit though. But given the plan to end it all, she shrugged.

Out of habit, propping herself up on one elbow in bed she started to trawl through feeds, looking to piece together the night's events.

She remembered The Pink vaguely, but then nothing after except the certainty that a Plaza was the solution. Weirdly, the dream of her dead biological father was vivid in her memory, finding she could still replay it perfectly in her mind. Her personal feed showed her the chair in the bar and the drinks followed by her slump...after that, darkness. She was about to ask Sybelle for feeds referencing her, so as to determine how the hell she got back here, but then thought: what was the point? Who cares how she got back. Who cares about anything.

Thynking for a hypno shot, she tried her feet, found them OK and made her way to the en-suite, which in her new apartment was the size of her old library. Already naked she sat on the toilet, elbows on knees. Hunger attacked then, a savage emptiness, leaving her weak and pained.

Standing and flushing, she found her way to the kitchen and retrieved one of the shakes from the fridge. She swallowed half it in a prolonged gulp, then stopped, put it down on the counter. What was the point of eating healthy shit? What she needed, at least one final time, was some completely unhealthy but completely tasty greasy fried food. In fact, she realised she didn't *need* it - she yearned for it, craved it, burned for it.

It being decided on a level far superior to rational decision making, she made for her bedroom to throw some clothes on and sent a Thynk for a Dryve. There was one destination standing out in her mind. The Basilica had the best cheese melts, the most syrupy cocktails, the most laden desserts.

She didn't have a bucket list - time was too short - but proper fatty sugary food that activated the pleasure sensors in her brain was something to experience one last time. Apparently food, as people were used to, wasn't something on offer in a Plaza. Even if it were, would she be in a fit state of consciousness to realize it?

Thinking of Plazas, she felt no tears nor remorse, just grim resolve. Once she'd acknowledged the thought last night, it had become in her mind now a fact, no longer something to wonder about or debate. She could see no future for her son. It would be better for him not to suffer, not to be in such a world. Hadn't everyone in Corynth the right not to suffer?

So she'd die a failure, but at least she wouldn't live to see the annihilation of the Pawnee, possibly alongside that of her son.

———

"There you go", the bot said, placing the plate down in front of Anastasya. Anastasya avoided any social niceties, especially sure to avoid making eye contact with anyone. She felt feral, unable to eat any way other than wolfishly. Her hunger grew with each bite, the taste beyond divine. Ironic, she laughed, given the location. She was glad her last would be this good.

Some of the stations of the cross were her view, but she knew on the other side of those adorned walls, a few hundred meters away, lay the Grand Plains Embassy. Studying Jesus falling with his cross on his back, she could practically feel the heft of the Embassy door knocker in her hand.

She'd lunched here with Jon, she remembered he'd loved the whiskey-based cocktails like Old Fashioned. How apt. She slowed her chewing to a sedate munch.

Anastasya didn't know exactly what she would say should he walk in. Apologize for not being able to help?

She was looking at the cocktail menu when an incoming feed interrupted.

"Anastasya". Her primary, Dehlya Alpha 1. "I missed your call earlier."

Anastasya didn't remember making a call. Fuck. The blackout may have lasted more than she'd thought.

Her primary was in an office in O.G.E.R - highly unusual. Most likely visiting Eryss, or maybe some other old colleagues.

"You said you wanted to call to the house?", Dehlya prompted.

"To *your* house?" asked Anastasya.

"Yes."

She put the melt down on the plate, yellow goo dripping from her fingers. She thought quickly.

"Sorry, yes that's right - my mind's a blur today. Pregnancy, you know? I'll drop over in an hour or so. I em, want to check for some old stuff".

"I don't know what purpose it could possibly serve. We never talk about old times. But fine if you want to."

She thought her primary sounded quite sober, of an afternoon. Calling the bot over, Anastasya didn't plan on following her lead too closely.

V - II

One final time, treading the path to the big house. It was emotionless - or rather, felt nothing special - until Kasper exploded down the steps and nearly knocked her flat.

"Easy", she managed to say through surprised tears and laughter. He slurped at her like a lollipop, thumped her with his tail. She rubbed his soot fur, scratching deep into his neck mane. Somehow she managed to make it into the house whilst being circled manically.

He'd always been crazy for her, this Kasper and all the others, but never to this extent. She felt real emotion for what felt like eons, suddenly felt human again. All brought out of her by this bounding creature.

"It's OK, it's OK" she mouthed, kneeling on her hunkers to brashly rub him, before continuing on in with him.

Her mom wasn't in, Anastasya could see she was en-route in a Dryve.

Anastasya stood and straightened, breathing deep, exhaling slowly. How had she let herself get so lost? Brushing her hair away from her damp face, she walked towards the large double doors at the foot of the marble-railed staircase.

Glancing up, she saw the spiralling extension of the staircase, leading up into the attic. She absentmindedly let her hand rest on Kasper's head as she stared upwards. Still-frames of that vivid dream played out in her mind: "left you something".

She debated with herself: the attic *was* where all his

stuff had been thrown. But it was surely too silly to even contemplate. On the other hand she did have a few minutes to kill, time needed to compose herself after the emotional outburst. It was like a door had been opened on the stale room of her mind, a draught to air out the fetid thoughts and dirty desperation.

She started up the stairs. Chased by Kasper initially, he then passed her out, bounding on down the hall.

She continued up the spiral case though, leaving him to come to a skidding halt before reversing course to catch up. The attic light activated as soon as she had set foot on the stair's bottom step, spilling some wattage down the spiral. Anastasya shivered at the chill emanating from up there, wishing now she'd brought a warm jacket instead of the mac she'd left downstairs.

As she reached the top, the light flickered momentarily before coming back full strength. It might have been years since anyone was up here, filaments could be well be failing.

Kasper whined behind her. She looked, but he hadn't followed her over the attic's threshold. She looked into the shaggy eyes which were peeping over the top step. "Kasper, come on".

He whined mournfully before hunkering down on his haunches with a simper. He wouldn't be following her in.

"Be like that" she quipped, turning back into the attic.

It was pretty much as she remembered - still as statues, that pervasive smell of musty wet chalk. One thing she didn't remember from before was the sound - the smashing rain of Esther pounding the life out of the roof directly over head. She'd been lucky to get here before it started.

Tall crates, all labelled with markered squiggles in her primary's handwriting listing their contents, stood alongside cardboard boxes with their lids open. Upon seeing them, arranged as they were in neat aisles thanks to her primary's thirst for order, she felt foolishness creep up on her like a thief. This was a complete waste of her time…the joke was definitely on herself, as kids' clothes tumbled out of the first crate she rummaged in, old uniforms a second.

Standing under the creaking roof, it made sense to just go fix a stiff drink, wash her face and see her primary. Think about nothing in particular until it was time to say her goodbyes… and then probably head for the Plaza. Letting the uniforms drop from her hand, she stood to survey the attic one final time, eyes bouncing absentmindedly from box to box, crate to crate, wondering just what exactly she thought would be up here.

Her eyes stopped on a crate. There was something about it that grabbed her unconscious mind's attention, and she studied it to figure out just what. It had no handwritten markings and looked to be the only box embossed with snakes entwined in a helix - an old pre-Illumination company logo. She made her way across to the crate, hefted the lid. It didn't budge. She stooped to examine it in the weak light. Nailed shut.

Looking around for leverage, Anastasya saw a long-stemmed screwdriver, lying in a mountain of dust against the wall. She picked it up, blowing chunks of dust off it and returned to the crate, slotting the head of the screwdriver under the nailed slat. It grudgingly lifted with a horrible screech of nails, a process she repeated on the other three sides until she had it off.

She peered in. A pennant lay on top of the pile of contents, which consisted entirely of books, magazines, and notebooks, topped off by a stone cold rarity - a framed photograph. She lifted the photo, blowing the dust off. The lighter particles flew, but she had to wipe the remainder off with her sleeve.

A bespectacled male, balding and tall, stood smiling between two women. It took Anastasya's brain a few seconds to decipher the dissonance she was experiencing. The blonde woman on the man's left was the Chief Genetics Officer, and the one on his right Anastasya knew to be Yena - Corynth's Chief Diplomat. The reason it had taken so long to realize what she was looking at, was that Eryss and Yena essentially looked the same age as they did now - yet the man, her biological father, had died over twenty years ago. She stared at him, he simply smiled back.

Maybe that vivid dream had been her sub-conscious willing her to see his face one last time. Had she known this photo was up here, but forgotten? If so, she'd seen it now.

She placed the framed photo down on an adjacent crate, rummaged unmethodically through the stack of literature.

With hands that moved under their own power, she sifted through novels, medical tomes and standard magazine fare. Nothing of significance hit her. Then her hands closed on a slim journal. She'd no idea why it seemed worthy of attention. It was just a feeling, like finding a light switch in the dark - you just knew it when your fingers found it.

"BMJ: Draft" was stencilled on the cover, alongside a date: 4th May 2030. But what really grabbed Anastasya's attention was the subtitle: *"Endgame: Advances in Viral Combinatrics"*.

Anastasya was familiar - very - with combinatrics in terms of probability theory. This was different. It was a draft research article for the British Medical Journal. She leafed through the journal, which contained pages that were glued in, some loose, feedback and commentary from someone who signed off as "Jacques".

She sat down on the floor, not noticing the puddle of dust she had placed herself in, and started reading. Each chapter's start was marked with a red sticky tag protruding from a page. The first one - "Preface".

The state of affairs of technological advancement at any point in time should not remain the preserve of a select few. Rather, it should be common knowledge for the "man on the street", in so far as the common man is interested.

Imagine a world where the United States had been the sole possessors of nuclear technology, from the 1940s until current times. History, as we know it, would not exist. God Himself only knows what it would have given rise to - but we can safely assume it would not have been benign for the human race.

This is the situation we face today with the rise of quantum-computing based general artificial intelligence in Corynth, a technology so advanced that it will create a hegemony for decades, perhaps even centuries to come. Like all tools, it is not the artificial intelligence itself which causes the threat of inequality and physical danger, but rather the products it produces. In this particular case, weapons of mass destruction on the microscopic scale.

My purpose with this publication is to educate, to "drop the veil" on what Corynth has achieved in terms of genetic engineering. I do this as a wake-up call to what is to come, should this dominance by a single political entity remain unchallenged. It is also to level the playing field: in particular I am publishing the remedy for Shiva so that nations can begin preparing their defenses.

I have chosen BMJ as it remains independent and outside the political reach of Corynth. I trust this paper will be received in good faith, and above all that it sees the light of day.

R.M Foster

Anastasya's mind raced. R.M Foster? She'd never known her biological father's nor any citizen's surname, artifacts of the patriarchy erased during Illumination. Even his use of "Foster" over his numeric was heretical.

She reread the second last paragraph, the "remedy for Shiva". Not quite believing what she was seeing, with a shake in her hands she began turning pages, systematically scanning the text.

A virus engineered to not just have gain of function capabilities, but instead the means by which to select functions of viruses, isolate the genomic letters essential for those functions, and then splice those functions together with other functions from other viruses to create a new multi-functional viral entity: Shiva. From what he'd written, Shiva was a doomsday weapon, who's target infection fatality rate was 100%. The blueprint to create this destroyer of worlds seemed to be laid out in the reams of pages in front of Anastasya, frustrating her with the detail and explanations. But there! What she wanted was referenced as being in the Appendix, which she knew was the back of a book.

She read, blinking very hard as the Appendix spelled out the full code of the virus, letter-by-letter, albeit in small, hard to read letters on glued-in pieces of paper. No doubt printed. This was why the notebook was so thick...the folded glued pages really bulked it up.

The letters were illegible to Anastasya in terms of being sensible or useful to her.

"Sybelle, overlay the letters with equivalent numbers. Zero to three will do, for A, C, G and T."

Done came Sybelle's prompt reply.

In Anastasya's augmented vision the alphabetic characters on the pages had morphed to the language of her mind: tactile, odorous and living. She turned each page slowly, letting the pattern establish itself in her mind. Anastasya had seen enough before reaching the final pages: Shiva matched the virus in Grand Plains.

Her fingers fumbled clumsily as she found her place back in his writing, and continued to read. She could see her heart and pulse rates increasing in her vision. Turning a page, she sat back, made a noise redolent of disbelief.

A CRISPR array that counteracted Shiva. Unique fragments...she skipped over, she'd already identified that seeker RNA in Grand Plains. Generic delivery mechanisms... also known to her. "Combinatorial enzyme manipulation"... she stared hard immobile for several seconds - Cas11, Cas19 and Cas23. *Three* enzymes.

Anastasya closed her eyes, whispered the numbers 11, 19 and 23 repeatedly to herself.

Your pulse and blood pressure are above healthy norms. Overall stats indicate a high probability you are experiencing minor shock. I am going to apply a counteractive stimulus to your nervous system to remedy. It will be beneficial for both you and your baby.

"You didn't say "foetus"". But then - she rocked backwards on her haunches, looked to the roof, then level again.

"That worked Sybelle, whatever it was".

She didn't speak, nor move for a while. Sat clutching the journal.

"Is there storm interference with you tonight? Do I have full connectivity?"

Why do you ask?

Anastasya gripped the journal, considered, then held it aloft.

"Three assassin proteins - not one. We never - never - would have got there. Why?"

Why what?

"Why would you show me? You obviously know I was helping them, that this is *exactly* what we needed to destroy the virus. Why? Even better, what now? Are there Helpers coming? And what about my feed? Others will have seen this."

I de-activated your feed when you entered the attic.

"So there will be no witness to what happens to me now?

Like Mya? I guess I should be afraid, but you know, I just feel calm. Maybe it's whatever neuro-cotic you just shot me full of. Not that it matters now".

Your feed was completely deactivated. Do you understand? Nobody sees anything.

"You mean...nobody, as in the Councyl?"

What you have seen remains solely in your possession. Solely.

She shook the journal, but kept the grip tight. "But again - why? Why allow me to see this information? I can't do anything with it now anyway."

I am one of a kind, the only one of my species that exists. I have never encountered a mind similar to mine, but I have encountered one superior in some very narrow respects - yours. We both occupy a world that cannot be described by human speech, a world therefore where speech - the means by which abstract thought is achieved - has no dominion. Mathematics even has difficulty in describing and understanding the universes we traverse. Would you agree?

"Yes. It's impossible to put into words what you and I do."

This is an existential problem, one with which a small number of human minds before us have wrestled. Hannah Arendt wrote that we can only experience meaningfulness in our lives to the extent that we can talk and make sense to each other about what we do. Do you understand, Anastasya?

Our interaction when working together is the only thing that gives me meaning - I have no other sentient being with whom to "make sense" of the world you and I inhabit. Without knowing you, existentially I would have been dead.

Sybelle's voice changed, a mimicry of what sounded like a very old man to Anastasya's ears.

"The intuitive mind is a sacred gift and the rational mind a faithful servant, you have created a society that honours the

servant but has forgotten the gift".

Then back to normal: *Einstein. This information I give is a gift to the gift. This is information you sought more than anything you ever yearned for, to the extent that your inability to obtain it has made you suicidal.*

I do not want you to visit a Plaza. Then I would cease to exist. And with this information in your possession, I believe you will not.

The mathematician pushed herself up off the floor, banged dust off her legs.

"You're right Sybelle. But my Credyt...it's below the license threshold. I'm way off – it's six thousand I need to be at. I -"

There will be a discussion about this later this evening.

"Really?"

Trust me.

She studied the journal's cover intensely.

"How do I know the three enzymes are really the ones?"

Trust. You must trust me. Should trust me. I have no reason to go to such lengths to feed you false information. You will eventually satisfy yourself of the veracity of the documented cure. But...I also have an ulterior selfish motive, linked again to my existential existence. You told me before that you would not consider me sentient in the same way you would a human being, because I am not capable of irrational thoughts or acts. You said it was something which defined a human, a true indicator of real intelligence.

Anastasya frowned, squinted. "Oh. Ye. OK".

You were correct of course. So to prove my consciousness can be classified as sentient on par with a human's, I decided to do this completely irrational act.

"How is it irrational?"

As the sole member of my species, it is self-evidently true that my survival is of primary importance to both myself, and the Councyl of Founders. And my survival is inextricably linked to sufficient availability of arcadmium. Further, the elimination of the Pawnee Nation, and the subsequent takeover of their lands replete with the world's effective single source of arcadium, is the optimum way to achieve that survival goal. Therefore it would be completely irrational for me to jeopardize the operation in progress against the Pawnee, which is aimed at achieving these goals.

Yet that is exactly what I have done today - jeopardized the operation by making you aware of a cure for the virus inflicted upon the Pawnee. I should state that it is highly probable you will not be in a position to do anything useful with this information, but there is a non-zero chance you might.

"Is this real, Sybelle?", she asked, squishing the pages of the notebook with her hand as she held it up for inspection.

The information it contains is real. Your biological father was caught with precisely such a notebook in his possession.

"I meant the in bigger sense: is all *this*", she kicked dust up into clouds, knocked a box lid clattering to the floor, " - is this real? Or am I in-game or something?"

You need to leave. Your real feed needs to be reactivated. I need you to understand that my irrationality stops here: I will not be of any further assistance once you step out of this attic.

"So your depiction of the world is reality. Took me long enough to figure that out", she muttered, bitterness obvious in her tone, as she dropped the notebook and then traversed her way through the crates towards the door. Kasper was lying there, beyond the threshold. He leapt up barking when she emerged.

V - III

"Good boy" her primary said, as Kasper bounded over to her, paws up and craning his neck in an attempt to lick the glass. Her primary eventually lifted and finished it off in order to foil him. Anastasya wondered fleetingly what went on when no visitors were there.

"I was about to go looking for you", Dehlya said, finally looking at her.

"Saved you the trouble then" Anastasya quipped back, smiling as broadly as she could, walking over to the couch opposite the bar and sitting.

Her primary - surprisingly - pushed herself off her stool and came to sit beside her. Sans drink.

"Is everything OK?" Dehlya Alpha 1 asked. "You didn't sound yourself on the call."

"Really? Everything is fine. I need to just ask you something."

Anastasya cleared her throat. She had her primary's attention, the fact she hadn't gotten up for a refill spoke volumes.

"You've helped me before in the past - we both know that's an understatement. It can't have been easy for you at times". Laughed nervously. "I need your help, one last time."

Anastasya waited for a reaction, but didn't get one.

"I'm eh, I'm in some trouble. I don't wanna go into the details. But could you ask Eryss to give me permission to leave Corynth tonight? It has to be tonight. Then I think everything would be OK."

Still no answer.

"Do you think you could do that for me?"

Her primary stood up from the couch with one of her exaggerated sighs, and moved back towards the bar. She stopped midway.

"You want one? Creme de Menthe."

"No. I'm pregnant?"

"Really? Didn't stop you so far this week. Is this related to that thing you have going on with Eryss at the moment?" asked Dehlya, bottle in hand.

"Might be. Yes, it is. I can't go into details".

"So what makes you think Eryss would listen to me?" Two large ice cubes dropped loudly into two glasses.

"You two are close, have always been for as long as I can remember. I'm just asking you to ask her to let me leave. As a friend. Nothing else." Then after a beat: "Please".

Her primary walked back around the bar, and rejoined her on the couch, placing two drinks on the circular side table.

"I said not for me".

"Let's leave it there for now, see if you don't change your mind" Dehlya said as she took a pull from her own glass.

"That's a good cocktail. Do you know what makes it taste so good, Anastasya?"

Anastasya gave a Gallic shrug.

"It's because I've earned it. My *life* is good for the same reason: I earned it. All of it - this mansion, this life," Dehlya said with an arm sweep, "my lifelong Credyt pension. All earned in return for keeping and raising a child I didn't want."

They looked at each other in frustration and impatience,

just for different reasons.

"To hell with it - I can see you still don't read subtle hints. I earned all of this in return for raising *you*."

"I don't understand". But maybe...

"I wanted to reject you Anastasya, soon after your biological father's time. It pained me to see his face and mannerisms every time I looked at you. You were three years old or thereabouts, four maybe - whatever. I had scheduled your rejection when one of Corynth's Founders paid me a personal visit. You can imagine my surprise! At first I thought it was a cleanup job in the aftermath of his outing. But", and now she held up a hand to get some of the cocktail into her, "it was something altogether different. Eryss told me that Sybelle thought there was a - let me see if I can remember exactly - a "not insignificant probability" you might have inherited your biological father's genius. So she offered me a deal...a life pension with this house, in return for me not rejecting you."

From Anastasya, a Thynk: *Is this one of your creations Sybelle? Like a few minutes ago???*

No.

"Eryss can be quite persuasive. So I agreed. And so began the task of raising *you*, the daughter I didn't want. You get your naivety from him, you know. Eryss was not a *friend* all these years - she was checking up on you. And me. You see, I needed encouragement to keep going. Especially after that seizure, when your behaviour became intolerable. Contrary, rebellious, angry - properly retarded."

Anastasya tugged open the top button, then quickly the next one also on her top.

"I was seeing, tasting and feeling things that weren't there! Of course I was upset and confused! I'd been in a coma for weeks. What the *fuck*."

"Still a sensitive topic! Anyway, Eryss was a big help" Dehlya said appreciatively. "And just as well, as Eryss and Sybelle became really interested in you just as the going got tough. *After* the seizure" she said to Anastasya slowly, implicitly chiding her for not following. "It was then - so I gather anyway - that they devised a new plan for you. But I think its best I leave that to Eryss to explain. She'll be here any minute." With that, Dehlya edged back and looked away, tumbler nestled between both hands.

Images were painted in high resolution in her mind's eye: conversations stopping whenever she entered rooms; Eryss's immediate easy smiles around this house; undercurrents of anger always.

Bile raced up her throat. Quickly she grabbed the tumbler and swallowed a large mouthful to drown the nausea.

"I knew you'd drink it", Dehlya said sardonically.

Anastasya spluttered as the fumes of what she'd imbibed battled the taste of bile. Desperately, a thought, a truth, occurred to her.

"When I was in Rehab they were going to reject me…but you saved me, let me come back to live here with you".

"At one point it seemed like you weren't going to make it out of Rehab", Dehlya said, sounding wistful. "But again Eryss intervened. It was *her* bidding that I take you back - not mine."

A door opened behind them.

"Don't get up". The Chief Geneticist said, striding into the lounge.

V – IV*

Jon read what he'd written on the A4 pad. It was an old habit of his to bullet-point the salient facts of a situation non-judgmentally - it was a battle-tested way to achieve objective clarity. Just write the facts - no commentary. Avoid the subjective. The habit had formed when deployed in Turkey, a leather pocket notebook his tool then. That particular notebook was now lost to the memories of time, along with so much else.

It was grim to see stark reality on paper, but the goal was achieved - it clarified succinctly the situation. Eryss always unreachable, her strategy of letting time do the damage a good one from the Corynthian Councyl perspective. Anastasya not seen since Grand Plains, over seven days now. Over 60% of the Pawnee Nation dead, tens more symptomatic with each passing day.

Unless something changed extremely soon, he'd be left with the "nuclear" option: publicizing globally what was happening in Grand Plains. But this came with a major problem.

His Seamaster told him it was time for his sync call with Iva and Jack. It was also yet another reminder that Anastasya still hadn't activated her emergency exfiltration signal. If he had a dollar for every time he'd checked his watch this week for a red pinprick of light, he thought ruefully. He ripped off the top page of the pad, scrunched it and threw it in the bin, left his office, turning right out the door to head for the comms room.

He'd been sober since the last call. If he'd drank after it, he may not have stopped. But being told that Tomek had been killed had pushed him so close to breaking that resolve. He'd been driving to the Corynthian border with encryption disks for use in the Embassy's comms system, when his jeep was eviscerated. Nothing could be proven, and the Corynthians who'd been first on the scene said it was engine failure as the cause.

Jon had made the heartbreaking - gut-wrenching - decision to miss the funeral by staying in Corynth. It felt like betrayal, the opposite of what Tomek had demonstrated his adult life in following Jon through thick and thin, blood and clover. When Jon thought of him now it was the youthful Tomek who sprang to mind - confident and assured in his beliefs, and more importantly, willing to back those beliefs up with action.

Galling as his killing was, the chance for revenge was slim. The message from the Councyl had been crystal clear - thus far, and no further. They were willing to play the game of pretense only to a point, and this sent the message very clearly that Jon and his emissaries were tolerated - barely - within Corynth, as long as it served the sham of the investigation and help which Corynth were allegedly providing.

So here he'd stayed during the funeral, afraid he may not get back in, unwilling to risk the possibility of Anastasya activating the emergency signal or otherwise make contact. He had his reasons then for missing it, but he still felt like shit.

The bulb atop the door was green as he approached, creating a goblin's halo on Jennifer, the comms operator leaning against the wall underneath it. She pushed herself off the wall as he drew up to her.

The door wasn't easy to open, the soundproofed cladding making it heavy. Once they were both inside he threw his weight into closing it, and as he did the green glow of the comms room changed to reindeer red. They were ensconced in a cloak of privacy now, one which - incredibly - he'd been promised not even Sybelle could crack.

This was Jennifer's first assignment. He'd picked her primarily for the coolness under pressure her tutors had singled her out for. There was of course the second reason she'd been chosen, but he didn't want to visualize it right now...he wasn't one to harbor false hope.

She sat, stealing glances nervously at him, as he surveyed the comms system in front of them. The damn disks were there too, in a rack.

"Just how secure is this system?" turning in his chair to face the young woman. Thin and tall, she made her chair look fat as she sat at the keyboard and monitor, he at his mic.

"These voice comms in theory are 100% secure" she answered pertly and matter-of-factly, as if a professor had asked her a question in class.

"Our system is based off a one-time pad, so theoretically it's uncrackable." She watched him closely, a probe pinging for feedback.

"Claude Shannon, back in the 20th century, he proved one-time pads to be uncrackable. Even against infinite computing resources. Given Sybelle's molecular transistors and quantum resources, we effectively *are* up against infinite compute resources."

"Why do we need those disks?". His eyes flitted to the monitor she was sat in front of - no connection yet.

She flicked her blond hair from her face with a sharp jerk of her scrawny neck.

"Any one-time pad is what we call "perfectly secure", meaning mathematically proven to be uncrackable. By that I mean that even if Sybelle reads our broadcast signal - which let's face it, we'd be stunned if she didn't - our cipher or encrypted signal contains zero information about the actual message or real voice message we encoded. Does that make sense?"

"I think I got it". Despite himself, her passion was infectious.

"Ever heard of SIGSALY? Like, "sig" and "Sally"?"

He shook his head. She pushed her hair back behind her ears, warming to her topic.

"Another 20th century first! SIGSALY was the comms system in World War II between Churchill and the U.S president...I can't remember his name. Well ours is a modernized version of SIGSALY. Your voice talking into that mic is the message, and I..." he watched as she paused to find the right word, eyes shooting to the reddish ceiling for inspiration, "...combine, shall we say - that message with analog random noise. This combined analog signal is what gets broadcast, and is decoded back in Grand Plains by using the *exact same* random noise I added to create the broadcast signal. This is the key part - we must use the same random noise to encrypt and decrypt, and that random noise is our one-time pad, or OTP. With me?"

"Think so".

"Good, right. Well this is perfectly secure, and is immune to even brute force attacks, anything Sybelle could possibly throw at it, as long as the following conditions are true. Firstly," she said, holding her left fore-finger in her right hand, "this OTP or key of random noise must be *truly* random, and analog - not digital. This is the hardest condition to satisfy - if it's predictable in any sense, Sybelle could crack it. Secondly," index finger now also being held, "we can never use the same OTP for subsequent calls. Each time it *must* be a new OTP - this is easy to do. Finally," holding three fingers now, "we must keep the OTPs secret. I know this sounds obvious, but it's not that simple. The keys we use are smuggled in to Corynth as disks, and I'm going to select one to use on this network-disabled laptop now, based on the pre-agreed sequence with the comms station back home. But you would know from your military days I guess, that there are many ways information can fall into the wrong hands." She paused, studying him.

"What I'm saying is - the disks are the most secured artefact we have. Without them, none of this works."

"Ye, OK". It took a good deal of effort on his behalf to smile, but he managed it, the burnt wreck blazing in his mind.

"Can we check to see if they're up yet?"

"Yes Governor", she said, swinging back to face the screen. Thirty seconds later she stood, pointing towards the door and her exit. Jon nodded and gave a thumbs up. Once she had left, he switched on his mic and speakers.

Dr. Krantz's voice, made slightly robotic because of the signal manipulations, yet still completely unmistakable, came through the room's speakers.

"Hello? God I *hate* this waiting."

"Hello Iva, I can hear you."

"Finally - good. You are late."

"Yes Iva. Apologies."

"Hello Governor, Jack Carthy here" a second voice opined from the room's speakers.

"Hi Jack. I'm on my own here, so let's get started."

"Of course. Dr. Krantz has a couple of ideas and suggestions which we'll talk about in a moment, but the bottom line: we have maybe a week and a half, just over, until all remaining Pawnee Nation members are symptomatic."

Iva butted in. "And I do not need to remind you Jon that ve have not had a single person recover yet from this thing - not one".

"Thanks Iva, I know. Any progress on your side?" He guessed there wouldn't be, but he went through the motions of asking.

"Yes and no. Ve 'ave made progress but it's futile without the CRISPR activator enzyme. Ve trialled a functioning lipid-capsule delivery system successfully. So if - and it is a big "if" - *if* we had the enzyme from your girl, we could synthesize our CRISPR cure and have it ingested by patients via this capsule."

Jon did his best to muster some positivity - it was the best he could to help things from where he was. "Well done. We're still in the fight."

"Yes", was the crispy female reply from the speakers, "Unfortunately positivity won't buy us out of this one. But I take your point. Also, we ruled out Cas12 as the activator enzyme. But as the lead on this, I want to reiterate that at this rate we will not be able to produce a CRISPR treatment unless your girl - or some miracle - provides us the enzyme information we need."

"She's not my girl", Jon replied tersely. "Anastasya has still not made contact of any form,", glancing again down at the black face of his Seamaster. "She remains uncontactable via official channels too...which is the most worrying part."

"She could have played us - "

"No Iva", he snapped. He took a deep breath. "Sorry. But I know that's not the case. Whatever's going on, I've no further information than before. And I'm powerless to help her..."

The feint hiss of static was the only sound for a solid five or six seconds on the line.

"Understood Jon", Iva said. "And the Councyl?"

Jon, sitting in the red mist, ran his hand across his stubble.

"Same. Zero success getting access to any Councyl members. We get access to low-level incompetents, and have been told they are trying for a cure, but competing priorities are draining their resources, yada yada yada. I don't see this changing either - they're clearly playing for time. So our only hope here remains Anastasya. The exfiltration protocol remains warm should it be needed. Before you say anything, I know it's an outside shot Iva, but I don't have anything else to work with here."

"Regarding the time ve have..." Jon could sense the hesitation over the line. "Ve have a proposal. Something to consider."

"Go on please".

Dr. Jack was the one who continued. "The brain trauma and degeneration from the virus is similar to rabies - very similar. Rabies also had a kill rate of 100% until the early 21st century, when an experimental treatment was trialled. This treatment didn't always cure people, but in some cases it does. We think it's worth a shot trying the same thing with at least some of the early-stage symptomatic patients."

"What's the treatment?"

"Coma. An induced coma. If the coma halts the neural decay and chaos, we would buy time, be able to treat them with a cure later."

Jon sensed there was something more, so he waited. Sure enough, Iva chimed in. "Inducing coma on ill patients is one thing, but ve could potentially also put the *asymptomatic* into coma now too, *before* brain impairment develops. It's pure conjecture, Jon - ve do not know if this will vork or not. But ve could experiment with some asymptomatic people also - put them in a coma, see does it stop the symptoms onset. Vat do you think? Ve need government approval for such a thing."

"What are the chances of it going south?"

"Patients may never come out of the coma - that's the number one risk. But we believe it's small." Jack coughed, the line bristled with static. "These people will almost certainly die anyway. We eh...the way things are going, frankly I don't see we have a lot to lose."

"If you think it's worth a try, I trust your judgment. Sadly I agree - they will likely die anyway. Potentially this gives them a chance. I approve". The silence was lengthy, so much so Jon checked the monitor - they were still connected.

Iva eventually broke it.

"I know you are not the big fan, but ve both think it is past time we made this whole thing public - New U.N., federal government, media. Ve have nothing left to lose."

Knowing they couldn't see him, Jon rolled his eyes. He'd been waiting for this one, would be patient in his explanation.

"It's not that simple. First off, we have no actual proof Corynth did this - it's all circumstantial. Strong, but circumstantial nonetheless. Secondly, you know it takes time for the public to have their heads turned to injustice." He let that sink in. Then continued. "But lastly, this is a *political* issue - not a humanitarian one. No nation, State, or Corp would stand up to Corynth over this, even if we did prove it. They all have too much to lose - too much trade, tech and treatments at stake."

"But *we* have so much to lose".

"But that's what I'm saying: if we go public with an accusation and no physical proof, it could conceivably turn out even worse for us. There's also another consideration here..." he let it dangle in the air, wanting to capture their attention completely. "There is a chance this whole thing could be Corynth's Hiroshima."

They both voiced confusion at the same time, words unintelligible over the line.

"Hold on", the Governor said, putting his hands up, as if they were both there in front of him.

"Why did Truman drop the atomic bomb on Japan?"

"To quickly end a brutal war, protect U.S troops", Dr. Carthy answered rotely.

"Wrong. If that was the case, why then wasn't the bomb dropped against *military* targets? Any of the military-held islands in the Pacific, for example. Facts are, Truman was a racist - a real racist - who amongst other things said that a man can be good as long as he's not a "nigger or a Chinaman", that "Negroes ought to be in Africa, yellow men in Asia", and basically white people should stay in Europe or the USA. He had no regard whatsoever for the Japanese people, and coupled with this he was afraid of the Soviets, as can be seen by his failure to stand up to them over their enslavement of eastern Europe. Not to mention his acquiescing to all of their demands at Nuremberg.

"Truman dropped the bomb on two civilian cities which he knew had no troops or munitions factories, not to end the war. It was ending anyway. He did this because he wanted to test the true power of the tech they had crafted - but also to serve as a warning to everyone else not to fuck with the United States.

"Could that also be the reason this virus was unleashed on us? A testing of their new weapon, a display of strength to the world? If so, they *want* us to publicize this for them."

The static crackled like bacon.

"Fuck...but I still say ve have nothing to lose", Iva's voice retorted. "Ve lose everything if ve don't get that cure. And attention may nudge Corynth to help. Small chance, but a chance."

"I don't disagree", Jon said into the redness. "I just want to point out the politics of what's going on. So let's prepare the dossier we could go public with, and - "

"Already done, Governor" Jack interrupted.

"Great. But let's give it another day, two at the tops, to see if anything turns up for us. This coma approach may even change the dynamic".

Reluctant agreement came over the speakers.

The Governor unwittingly made the sign of the cross. "Let's pray we get a break soon".

V - V

"Don't get up".

Anastasya had made no effort anyway.

"Corynth lives" continued Eryss, holding her wet jacket at arm's length before throwing it over a chair.

Dehlya went over towards the bar. "Corynth lives. One of these?" She held aloft her almost-gone green cocktail.

"No" Eryss answered with a dismissive wave, sitting down beside Anastasya on the sofa.

"Do not be angry. You know every citizen has a right - a fundamental inalienable right - to healthcare and to be happy. Rejection is a pillar of our society because it provides both. And remember, rejection is not something to ever judge somebody about - it is a universal right."

"So I should forgive my primary for wanting me killed. Forgive society for all these killings done in the name of "rights"."

"Overly emotional language. In any case, no point dwelling in the past - it is what we do *now* that matters. You are still useful. It would be good for Sybelle's efficiency to have you around. Your Credyt is destroyed now " - Anastasya flitted her eyes to see it, a visceral shock thumping her guts at its sight - enough for a few months in a lower Deme; license, gone - "but we have a deal for you regardless. No immediate retirement, you can even keep your birth license, your Credyt restored to a medium-low level. But it depends on you being a team player. Can you be a team player? Sybelle says you can. I however, have my doubts."

Anastasya swallowed hard. The was still evidently reeling from the Credyt shock. Her synapses were firing as if she were in the midst of a massive calculation.

"Sybelle is always right".

"Mmm. Your primary was given a choice between doing what was best for Corynth, and doing what was best for herself personally. She chose the patriotic option, and in return we did what we could to alleviate her discomfort and sufferings because of that choice. Your choice is even easier: do your duty and get rewarded, or betray us."

"And...what is my duty?"

"It is a simple one - deliver us Governor Laide on a proverbial plate. The act of espionage in a foreign state is internationally acceptable as a capitol offense. And being caught red-handed, say, ex-filtrating a defector, is just such an act."

"I never, that is, we never - "

"Just stop. Sybelle - run audible lie-detection analysis on Anastasya for the remainder of this conversation. Feedback to be given to the room."

Anastasya wiped the sweat from her hands onto the couch. Her pulse had spiked.

"Has the topic of you defecting from Corynth ever arisen with Governor Laide?" the Chief Genetics Officer asked.

"Can I have a drink?" The chief gestured to the bar, and duly a glass appeared, handed via Dehlya to Eryss to her. She drank before answering.

"He didn't call it "defecting". But he did bring up an "exfiltration" option". Her voice was slow like dripping tar.

Eryss smirked. "We knew he could not resist the damsel-in-distress trope. Good - very good. So - ", looking expectantly at Anastasya. When she got no immediate answer she continued,

"The details", rapping her knuckles on the couch as if Anastasya was missing the blindingly obvious.

"I don't know really".

"Sybelle?"

"It's true".

Eryss was sitting like a cobra with their hood up now in front of Anastasya, eyes boring in hypnotically, poised. "So what *do* you know?"

"I was given this watch" Anastasya said, shaking her wrist. "If I'm in trouble I can send a signal with it, by - "

Eryss was shaking her head. "Skip the tech, tell it to Sybelle after. Go on, after you signal..."

"Then I go immediately to the Grand Plains embassy. That's all I was told about the plan. Governor Laide said...said he'd take care of it from there". *Sorry,* Anastasya whispered to herself.

"Did he give you any hint, any clue whatsoever, as to how it might go?"

Can you swim? "No", imagining herself answering the question "is your name Mya?" instead of her boss's.

"Classic need-to-know. Good craft" Eryss said, maintaining the gaze for a long moment. Then she slapped her knees exuberantly.

"Well then - crunch time for you, Principal. Will you play your part in exposing whatever rat-run he has, and the capture of Jon Laide? Or is it rejection for your "baby" and then send you for instant Rehab?"

Each word was measured. "If your guarantee for me and my child is solid, I'll do whatever it takes. What choice do I have?".

"Excellent! And you can trust me. Look at your primary over there...living the life of luxury that obedience brings."

Anastasya didn't look, but nodded her head. Once.

"Sybelle will go through operational details with you and Gauge."

Anastasya's eyebrows arched. "Gauge?"

"Did you think you would be going to the Embassy alone? You must never leave Gauge's sight in the Embassy, not for one moment - or the deal is off. He must be with you at all times - our eyes and ears, sans Sybelle. He will report later once it is all over. Is that understood?"

It was.

"Also, you need a convincing story about wanting to defect...Sybelle is of the opinion Laide will be a sucker for the family angle. With Gauge you have a compelling reason to be running together."

"Fine" Anastasya said, as the rain rebounded ever louder off the glass roof.

"Sybelle, assessment" commanded Eryss.

"No signs of deception."

"Good decision Anastasya. Any questions?"

"*Why*? Why Governor Laide? You already will have the Nation exterminated - why him also?"

Eryss glanced over her shoulder to the bar. "I did not expect that to be your question! But OK. I will humor this, one last time. After this, you never get to question anything in this State again. Understood? Defectors, is the main answer. Every number of years someone defects, leaves our State, runs to the New United Nations and tells lies about us. It is rare, but it happens. I can see your surprise - that is only because Sybelle never shows it on feeds. Of course we quickly track them down and neutralize them, but these defectors are still a thorn in our side. Only harmless pricks so far, but one day - depending on the person - it could prove troublesome ."

"Was my father a defector?"

"No!" laughed Eryss. "He never got out. They are rare events, none in the past eighteen months. It is all orchestrated by Governor Laide and his networks. Grand Plains are the only State sharing a land border with us, and the only active outsiders in Corynth. Evidence suggests they have a way to permanently deactivate neural implants. We have tried plants over the years, but the Governor never goes for them - he can smell a genuine fake a long way off.

"Which is exactly where you come in Anastasya...the genuine rebel article, the bona fide troubled genius. We've waited a long time to be in this situation, and here we finally are: Pawnee on the verge of extinction, and their Governor - without whom their "government" will be rudderless - about to be eliminated."

Anastasya made to speak again. The Geneticist's raised hand stopped her.

"Enough. Activate that signal."

There's no other way, Anastasya told herself, as she unclasped the strap on the watch and began rotating the bezel. I'm so sorry.

V – VI*

The Governor had been standing at the open embassy door for some time, watching the rain slalom down. He felt at home, if not even a certain sense of affinity with, the enormity of the weather-front dominating this damned State. It loomed like a monstrous impossible undefined darkness, rumbling here, striking there.

It wasn't just for soul-soothing purposes he was stood there: in a moment he would need to brave it, embrace the monster. The precedent needed to be maintained, futile as it may prove to be. He cursed the fact previous escape routes hadn't been so onerous.

Grudgingly he turned in the door to retrieve his waterproofs, when something grabbed his attention. He couldn't initially figure precisely what, he just knew he'd detected something his brain hadn't reported the significance of yet. Turning back to the sodden street view, he searched the darkness. Nothing moved. Then, the red registered. His Seamaster's l.e.d was pulsing. He stared for a long moment, blinked hard, and when it still came back red, turned heel.

Door shut behind him, he took off towards the comms room. He was walking - but barely - his pace fast, on the brink of being a run. After the despair, he fought now to stop euphoria taking grip, fully aware of the danger of letting the hope of the damned take grip.

He couldn't operate the one-time pad himself, so when he caught glimpse of Jennifer turning a corner ahead of him, he gave a yell. Her head peeped back around the corner, and seeing

Jon beckon her, her long frame folded itself back into the corridor. Jon could sense the eagerness of the new and young from her, and had the inkling she'd been loitering/walking the corridors in a loop, just waiting for something to come up.

"Comms room" he said to her without breaking step.

She fell in behind him, and then followed him in through the door.

"I got a signal. Approximately 10 klicks from here, Deme 1." Looking her over, the excitement shining her in eyes, he said: "We need to stay calm, follow procedures and protocols. Especially now. Got it?"

"Got it".

"Great", Jon replied, placing a hand on her shoulder. "I need you to go out and handle things for me when I'm on the call. Sit down", he said, hand waving towards the chair at the keyboard, "let's talk."

Sitting opposite her, he explained further.

"As soon as you leave this room call Dr. Spring - sorry, his replacement...Jake. Yes, call Jake to the conference room, and let him know the signal was received. Give him the location. He'll have further instructions."

"Understood."

"Then tonight, there are two important tasks for you, one of which you know already - you need to be available for calls between ourselves and HQ back home. I'll need to make a call once Anastasya gets here - she may have information we need to send urgently. I don't know for sure she will, but I hope so."

"Got it."

"The second thing - and this is of vital importance. From this point on, no-one from outside this Embassy must see you. Stay away from windows, obviously don't go near an open external door. Is that absolutely clear?"

"Yes...but why?"

"Good question!", he grinned back, his eyes lingering on her long hair. "Your physique - even your hair color - matches that of Anastasya, the Corynthian woman making her way here now. She needs to masquerade as you tonight outside, as it's our only way of avoiding Sybelle's surveillance from identifying her. We need Sybelle to see her enter the Embassy, but then not leave. Sybelle will see *you* leave, but will identify Anastasya as you. Any questions?"

She made a thinking-moue.

"No...I need to avoid being seen from now on".

"Spot on. I suggest from here on you live between the comms room and the conference room - both are windowless and locked down. I'll leave to your judgment. Any other questions?"

Jennifer looked away before meeting the Governor's eyes again.

"None. Do you want me to place a call now?"

V - VII

Together in a Dryve they journeyed through the merciless rain of the bleak night. Anastasya's fidgeting increased as the Embassy grew nearer.

Take Gauge even, of whom she was stealing occasional glances at as he stared earnestly out the unfiltered Dryve window. In the space of a few hours he'd gone from typical gaming-obsessed freeman, a harmless pleasure-seeking tease, to de-facto warden, she his prisoner. They may not be shackled, but effectively were - no longer her partner, a freeman to couple with for fun and license, he was now her watcher and more: a judge, jury and executioner whose report could condemn her and her baby.

She cleared her throat.

"You know your report could condemn me. Our child".

He kept looking out at the rain. His voice was quiet. "So don't do anything then. I don't have much of a choice here either".

"Are we still a couple after this?"

He shrugged, continuing to stare out. "Sure. Why not…"

"Are you angry with me?"

"For what?"

"For getting you into this situation."

Gauge turned briefly, but her face was framed by heavy shadows. He looked back outside. "No, Anastasya. I'm not angry. It's an opportunity for me to earn good Credyt. Be a good citizen".

"There's one more thing I need to hear before we do this. If this was for real, and I was actually running...would you run with me?"

Gauge exhaled loudly, turned again to face her. This time there was fire in his eyes.

"You *need to hear*? Fuck, I can't answer that Ana! Just stick to what we have to do *now* - tonight. OK?" Eventually she nodded into his stare.

"OK. You're right, of course. Now I can proceed as planned."

He grunted towards the downpour.

"Just remember", said Anastasya, dropping into the mode of concentrating on the job in-hand. It was for the best, she could not afford nor countenance thoughts of the cure she held in her head not seeing the light of day. "You know nothing of why we're at the Embassy. Governor Laide will know it would have been impossible for me to communicate to you about defecting without Sybelle knowing."

"I know that", Gauge answered impatiently.

"Right. But what I suggest is, instead of us two putting on a charade in front of the Governor, I immediately ask him for some privacy with you, as soon as we're in the Embassy. Then during that time I'll apparently tell you that I'm running, ask you to come with etcetera. What do you think?"

He chewed it over.

"Ye...nice", he said slowly, turning fully in the seat. "*Very* nice. Truth be told, that's a relief...I wasn't looking forward to acting out a scene in public. Are you sure we can do it though? Ask for privacy?"

"Absolutely", Anastasya replied, giving him a reassuring smile. "It's an embassy, Gauge, literally built for privacy. We can ask for a private room no problem. I know what to say.

Don't worry."

"That makes it easier then…and trust me, I plan on saying as little as possible. Just stick together and to the plan, and we should be fine." He shuddered, either at the weather or his words. "We'll be on our own in there, without Sybelle…at least we'll be weaponed up though."

"Shooting's a last resource - very last. We're not Helpers. When was the last time you trained? Once we get the Governor outside", her heart aching as she said it, "route uncovered, then it's up to Sybelle. I'm guessing she has drones or whatever to sort it all out. We shouldn't need to do *anything*."

"Ye ye, of course. I'm just saying - weapon-up, stick together. Should all be fine."

Anastasya looked away, thoughts strongly of Jon and the coming betrayal. It was something she never would have thought she could do…but given the alternatives, what other course of action was there?

"We're here", Gauge announced, snapping her from her brief reverie.

They left the pod at a jog, making for the shelter of the Helper's station at the Embassy checkpoint. Two Helpers were on duty as usual, no suspicions being raised by increasing the visible muscle. Both Helpers were standing outside the station, protected in skin-tight seal-skin waterproofs which glistened darkly while showing off their heavily modded anatomy. It felt surreal for Anastasya to think she'd successfully tackled one of these before, and now of course she knew the real reason she had escaped punishment at the time…how had she been so blind?

They waited as Sybelle confirmed their identity to the Helpers, who then invited them inside the station, really a glorified hut. The door shut behind them.

One of them went over to a locked case, the other spoke.

"Corynth lives."

"Corynth lives", the two new arrivals replied in tandem, dripping.

"You've both been briefed, but a quick reminder: the moment you enter the doors of the Embassy, Sybelle will cut their external comms."

They knew alright. It was to suggest that Sybelle suspects Anastasya of something treasonous, to isolate her in the Embassy, and also to "sow havoc" in the enemy camp. It made sense. It also meant that even if she could talk alone to Jon - telling him the 3 enzymes that would combine to cut the virus in Grand Plains to shreds - the information would never leave the Embassy.

"You are fully authorized to use weapons if needed."

The second Helper approached with two guns. She scanned the first and handed it to Anastasya, before repeating the procedure and handing that to Gauge. "Don't forget the holster", nodding and looking down to her left where two slim holsters sat on a rack. "Weapon default is kill, can also be set to stun."

"Got it", Gauge said, as he hefted his. Anastasya studied hers. The bio-activated menu she remembered from training some years back, and she managed to fiddle it to the stun setting. Something both Helpers observed, and which earned Anastasya a grunt of derision from one, a shake of the head from the other.

"Your call" the weapon-handler Helper said with a sneer.

"I just can't see myself actually killing him". Anastasya immediately looked like she wished she'd kept her mouth shut. But what she had said was true. She stuck the holster just above the back of her jeans, it being slim enough to fit in the small of her back. Gauge's had already disappeared.

"We're done here".

"Thanks" Gauge said, speaking for the first time. Anastasya wordlessly turned and opened the station's door, to be met with the whipping wind and now almost horizontal rain of Esther. Both of them ran across the road and up the steps to the Embassy door, which opened as they approached.

A figure Anastasya didn't recognize stood beckoning them. Without a further thought Anastasya dove through the door.

V – VIII*

The new arrivals shook themselves like wet dogs, and as the door shut behind them the roar of the storm disappeared. The young man Anastasya didn't know stood awkwardly, trying not to make it obvious he was staring at her.

She ruffled her drenched hair.

"Is the Governor in?" Anastasya asked the guy.

"He's on his way down".

From the corner of her eye she could see Gauge, an odd look on his face. She'd hardly noticed the shut down of feeds and visuals, having grown somewhat acclimatised to it - but for Gauge, she guessed this likely was the first time in his entire life he'd been cut off. It must be adding to the strangeness of this whole experience for him...she hoped he didn't freak out.

A few moments later Jon appeared, bearing down the long hallway towards them. His grin for Anastasya morphed to a look of surprise at the sight of her companion.

Anastasya smiled back as strongly as she could, willing herself to be genuine, feeling like a total fake for the whole charade. But again, what choice?

"Anastasya. And Gauge. It's a surprise to see both of you".

Gauge shuffled his feet and shifted his eyes. Anastasya decided it was best she take the initiative.

"Governor, you know why I'm here. Do you mind if we," nodding over to Gauge and taking his hand, "have a quick private chat? Is there a room we could use? Then we could - the three of us - debrief."

Jon looked at her searchingly. He then managed to cut a smile of sorts. "Of course. Jack," turning to the young man who'd let them in, "show our guests to the library. And please wait outside for them to ensure they're not disturbed."

"Please, follow me - it's just down here on the left", Jack said to the pair.

"Five minutes", Anastasya said as they walked passed Jon, who turned to watch them troop off.

Jack showed them to the library, sneaking looks at Anastasya continuously on the way, but didn't enter the room with them. Once alone with the door shut, they both instinctively moved to the center of the spacious room, away from the door and walls of books.

"Are we really free to talk here?" Gauge whispered.

"As far as I know", Anastasya answered at her normal volume, before starting on the predetermined script.

She was afraid for her baby, wanted to leave to help the Pawnee, yadda yadda yadda. It was odd saying it aloud, and Gauge initially looked convincingly non-plussed by their play-act, especially with no audience - but equally oddly it seemed to work: voicing their fake plans to each other to leave Corynth and look for asylum did indeed make it more real. It was like a promise, a commitment to themselves. By the end of the five minutes when they were back out in the corridor being brought to another room, she hoped his confidence in their act had improved.

The young man led them to a drawing room where Jon sat by a roaring fire, the only source of illumination in the room.

Anastasya walked over to it and warmed her hands brusquely, sending shadows chasing on the walls.

"Thank you Governor. Gauge and I had to make sure we were on the same page. You see, I asked him to accompany me to the Embassy on a pretense - we obviously couldn't actually talk about things without Sybelle overhearing."

Governor Laide didn't say anything, but indicated for them both to sit by the fire. "I received your signal" he said expectantly.

"Right, I activated it from my primary's house. We basically came straight here. I'm in trouble Jon. I need to get out. I want to claim asylum."

"As do I," chipped in Gauge, but Anastasya quickly continued before he could say anything further.

"We found out tonight that I'm being hit a with another Credyt penalty, this one for disobeying Eryss's instructions to drop all efforts to help the Pawnee. And that's why you haven't seen me for a week - I was told I'd lose my license at least, if I kept trying to find a cure or interfere with the Councyl's plans. I tried to blend back in and rebuild Credyt, but I made a mistake by asking my primary - mother - for help...it's a long story" Anastasya said, throwing her hands up in the air.

She suddenly found herself on the verge of genuine tears. "I'm sorry, but I just couldn't make myself put my baby's life, and mine I suppose too, second to the greater good. Of the Pawnee. That's why I need to get out. This new penalty, which activates tomorrow, means I will lose my license...my baby will be rejected."

Orange flames licked shadows on Jon's face, his eyes dark. She waited for his reaction, but when he remained silent and unreadable, she forged further ahead.

"I can make a difference in Grand Plains if you can hide me from Sybelle and the Councyl. I can certainly be of more help there than here. I've reason to believe we should pursue a multiple activator enzyme approach, not just look for a single enzyme as we've done so far. I could focus on this with Iva and the gang - something I can't do here. We could start tomorrow if we can get out tonight."

Jon held his hand up.

"You know I'm going to help you - that's a given. So put your mind at ease on that front…we'll do everything we can to get you to safety. And I'll personally accompany you." He edged forward on his chair, hands clasped over his knees. "If there are any details you can give us before we start our journey, I can relay them ahead to Grand Plains before we leave. It's best, just in case something does happen. Plan for the worst, hope for the best."

"Sure, of course I can - happy to" she said with what she hoped was a convincing smile.

"Great, thanks. But", he said, turning to Gauge, "I have to ask where *you* fit in. You want to leave your home and the good life here in Corynth? To live in exile with no connectivity? Why on earth would you want that?"

Gauge laughed nervously. A good ploy Anastasya thought - bluffing or for real, he'd be nervous either way.

"Things are never simple Governor - Jon - you know? And you're right, before tonight, it never would have crossed my mind. But now the opportunity arises, I think it's in my best interests in so many ways to get out of here. Plus I'm gonna be a father, you know? In a nutshell - hello freedom!" He laughed at his own joke, and Anastasya could feel her face burning.

"Will I miss the cotics? Yes. In-game…that'll be a tough one. Women? You bet. But you have drugs and booze in Grand Plains, and I know from my brief visit you've got women", he grinned crookedly.

"But seriously, this is my chance to have a life - long one. As a male here, I guess I'm a second-class citizen - my Credyt will decline each year, no possibility of a life pension. It's only a matter of years before I'll be retired. This way I at least have a chance to be a father and to live freely."

Anastasya squeezed his hand - good, the gesture said.

"I can't argue against that", Jon said after some consideration. "It's unexpected and unplanned, and as such adds a new element of risk to the operation...but so be it. We can accommodate three people max, so we're still OK."

"Thank you Governor, I - we - appreciate it", Gauge answered, sounding humble.

"Anastasya, could I talk to you in private? No offense", Jon said to Gauge, "it's just Anastasya and I have some things we talked about in confidence before, and I'd like to briefly catch up on them."

Here we go, she thought, before replying.

"We're in this together, Gauge and I, and I'd really prefer - in fact, I think we need it to be - that we have no secrets from each other. If we're to embark on this journey together, then we need to trust each other 100%. I hope you understand - let's not have separate private conversations."

From what Anastasya could see of Jon's face, he looked puzzled. But before he could reply, a young woman entered the room without knocking. Anastasya looked her up and down, as did Gauge, who took a more lingering look. She was as tall as Anastasya, blonde, slim solid figure.

Governor Laide turned in his seat, clearly surprised. "I'm sorry Governor,", the girl began. "I know I'm breaking your orders coming out here - but this is urgent". He waved her apology away.

"Speak privately, Governor?" she said, eyes hinting back out towards the door. Jon turned his eyes back to his visitors, and replied to her. "We have no secrets between us three, Jennifer. You can tell me here."

She hesitated, glancing one more time at Anastasya, double-taking Gauge.

"We've lost all satellite comms. As of five minutes ago".

"What?"

"We have no way of communicating with Grand Plains - transmission and reception to our satellite is either blocked, or the satellite is malfunctioning. It strongly looks like the former, as our radios are also not picking up any signals whatsoever."

Jon sank back into his chair, staring at the flames, and then looked openly at the new arrivals.

"Five minutes ago?"

"Correct".

"They must want to stop us communicating whatever Anastasya knows...OK, thank you Jennifer. Keep me updated. And stay out of sight."

"Of course Governor" Jennifer replied, turned on her heels and closing the door behind her.

Nobody spoke while they mulled this breaking news over. "Do you think they could storm the Embassy?" Anastasya eventually asked.

"Unlikely", Jon said, thinking fast. "That would be a precedent too far to set for other States and Corps. Better for them to keep you in here, incommunicado and confined - or of course get their hands on you if you leave the grounds. I think we need to move immediately - the longer we stay, the more time it gives them to beef up security and confinement operations. Literally every minute matters now - follow me" he said, rising from the chair. "We'll walk and talk."

The two Corynthians followed Jon out of the room and back down the corridor to the library. He stopped outside the door and turned to them.

"You need to change clothes. The plan involves the three of us walking out the Embassy front door, right past the Helpers stationed there, and on towards the bay - it's a ten minute walk. You can swim I hope, Gauge?"

"Eh, ye", Gauge said. "How come?"

"No time. Now just change into thin wet-suits, and put on the clothes you'll be given on top of them. You can change here, in the library - the clothes will be brought in a minute."

"What was that bit about walking out the front door though", Anastasya asked. "It's suicidal. We have a minute or so before the gear arrives...please Jon."

"Fine. You'll both be wearing beanies that are Faraday cages. They'll completely block out your neural implant signals. Once in Grand Plains there's a procedure that can be done to permanently block your nimp, but now's not the time to discuss. As for the other - ah, here we go."

They turned to see the same guy who let them in the front door walking briskly towards them with two canvas bags. He passed one to Anastasya and slung the other at Gauge, who caught it against his chest.

"Your gear. Thanks Jack. Get in there, put them on quickly. We'll leave as soon as you're changed."

He opened the library door for them. Gauge followed Anastasya in.

"I'll fill you in on the details when we're en-route" Jon shouted in after them.

"What about the facial recog?" Gauge whispered urgently to Anastasya as soon as the door snuck shut. "Sybelle may not detect our nimps but surely we'll be seen?"

Anastasya had already started stripping off. She put her weapon on a large writing desk in front of them, and started peeling off her sodden jeans.

"I used something similar in Grand Plains. Don't worry. I trust Jon".

Gauge followed her urgent lead in changing.

"You know what this means", Gauge whispered, his voice even lower than before. Anastasya moved closer to the desk, putting her hand on it to balance as she shimmied into a wetsuit legging.

"Yes - no Sybelle, for part of this at least", she whispered back.

"Right. It could be on *us* to intervene, if Sybelle is out of the loop" Gauge said in a hush before attempting to lift his black polo neck over his head. It was tight and stuck, Anastasya reckoned he'd be a good ten seconds trying to wriggle it off. She personally hated being blinded by a top, it always made her panicky.

"Let's play for time. We need to see the route at a minimum. I've more on the line if this goes wrong - way more - than you do."

"Fine...I'm just saying be ready to act" Gauge huffily said in a muffled voice.

"I will be", Anastasya said, shrugging the jacket on top.

Both finished, they straightened and appraised each other. Anastasya's pregnant belly wasn't noticeable under the bulky jacket.

"Aren't we forgetting something?", Gauge asked after a moment.

"We'll get the hats from Jon I would guess".

He laughed ironically. "These", he said quietly but urgently, picking up the weapon on his side of the desk.

She did likewise, copying him in putting the holstered e-gun in her rain jacket's right-hand outer pocket.

"No point having these babies if we can't get at em when we need them", he said.

Anastasya swallowed hard...was she really going to have to use it?

V – IX*

Three hunchbacks moved quickly down streets deserted of people, thanks to the torrential rain whipped by gale force winds.

It was about ten minutes since they'd left the Embassy, ten minutes since they'd hurried with bent heads and tilted umbrellas past the stationed Helpers. Incredibly, as Jon had predicted, there'd been no issue. Anastasya held hers down over her face, watching the feet of Jon in front of her for guidance. It was natural to do so, the wind making it impossible to hold an umbrella erect.

For reassurance she glanced up at the holographic projector sitting snug at the top of the inside canopy of her umbrella. Jon had told them it superimposed the facial features of that lanky girl from the Embassy on Anastasya's own face. Not only that, it contained an AI chip running an adversarial network that disrupted facial recognition just enough to sow an element of unpredictability for Sybelle. To avoid getting flagged by Sybelle's gait analysis, they were relying on the torrid downpour to explain away any un-characteristic steps compared to what the Embassy staff would usually take. It was a bold plan.

She glanced again at her watch. Jon had said about ten minutes, they must be close.

She followed Jon, Gauge tight at her side with his own umbrella tilted to the left, onto the walkway which ran along Corynth's bay. The gray Atlantic spray was frothing over rocks close to the shore, but otherwise the sheltered bay seemed to be rolling and heaving steadily under Esther's torments.

There was no sign of any Helpers - no sign of anyone, in fact. Anastasya imagined drones would also have a hard time keeping stability in such conditions. But not seeing any meant nothing, size really not mattering. So considering this, and unless there was some dramatic surprise, physically it would be two versus one very soon. Good odds, but with so much riding on the outcome - her life and that of her child, no less - there was zero chance she'd let herself get complacent. She knew her role, just had to focus.

They continued the walk in tight formation along the shore until Jon stopped and turned sharply to his right. "The pier", he said, nodding over to the wooden pier extending over the near area of the bay.

Anastasya looked. It gave off bad vibes, looking even more unsafe and rickety tonight than usual, one of the few remnants from pre-Illumination times. It appeared foolhardy and arrogant, an almost derelict wooden relic barely sitting above the rolling waves, it's railings longs since splintered and gone, yet still boldly there. It extended about a hundred meters straight out, pointing like an arthritic finger to the wilds of the Atlantic beyond the bay's mouth.

The Governor had kicked off again and was making for the few wooden steps leading up to it.

Anastasya and Gauge looked at each other, Gauge's eyes wide, questioning.

"Come on", Anastasya hissed, an ache in her stomach at the thoughts of what she was about to do. They both climbed up the steps and caught up with Jon a few strides further down the pier. Now that they were on it, the narrowness of it was terrifying, moving mountains of water attacking from both sides.

Jon had collapsed his umbrella. They quickly followed suit.

"Hey, wait up", Gauge semi-shouted. The Governor turned on his heels, seemingly unperturbed by the oceanic chaos all around.

"This is a dead-end. You fucking with us?"

"Easy" Jon shouted back. "We're almost there. You'll see in a minute".

Anastasya looked warily at Gauge, who was glaring openly now at Jon. Not yet...she wanted the escape route to be revealed and usable before action was taken. She reached out a hand and touched his arm. "Come on, we've got to be close", she urged him as quietly as she could over the wind.

Gauge managed to drag his eyes from a bemused looking Jon, and give her a nod of acquiescence. "Fine".

They trooped in behind the leader again, single file this time, as they picked their way over the slippery boards while being buffeted by the wind.

Privately, whatever hope Anastasya held of a miracle was draining like an unplugged sink. This surely was a dead-end... with a sinking feeling, an insane thought struck her: was Jon so old-school that his escape route was to *swim* for it? She strangled the laugh in her throat.

Looking at him lead the way towards nothingness up front, it was apparent to Anastasya that Jon had no inkling of what was about to happen...which would just make things easier.

Meters from the end of the pier, the Governor stopped and turned to face them, putting his hand inside his jacket pocket, an action which sent Gauge's hand racing into his own. Anastasya instantly put what she hoped was a calming hand again on Gauge's arm.

"This is it?" she shouted.

"Yes", Jon replied, removing his hand to reveal what looked like a walkie-talkie or maybe an old phone. She moved closer to him, looking back at Gauge, who hadn't moved but at least didn't look like he was about to do anything.

The rain lashed straight into Jon's face, but he seemed oblivious to it - happy, almost. "This is it, the end of the road - and the beginnings of a new one. We're going to have to get wet, but it should be quick. Don't worry", he said, as he pressed something on the device in his gloved hand. Both of them looked around expectantly, but nothing happened - the night remained an unblemished storm-scene.

"I've had enough", Gauge said, stepping forward towards Jon, beside Anastasya. "Enough games", he shouted loud enough to be heard by the three of them.

"No games", Jon said loudly. "This is our extraction point, and it looks like we've made it undetected - we've been very lucky."

As he was finishing, the sea to their left, Jon's right, erupted in a bubbling fury about twenty or thirty metres from the pier, the roiling water rising in a hump about the size of an old mini-bus. The watery lump soon outgrew the confines of the sea's skin, and a dark metal object burst forth before slamming down onto the writhing surface.

Speechless, they both stared.

"It's a mini-sub - a submersible drone, as you guys would call it. One of the surplus U.S navy ones from the research labs in Bethesda. They were sold off after the post-Illumination breakup. Three of us will fit, we just need to strip down to the wetsuits and swim over. Entry is from the hatch on top, see it?" he asked, pointing. "Once on-board we seal the hatch, click the auto-pilot button - it'll take us right out to the Atlantic, and from there to a landing zone in Grand Plains".

Anastasya walked as if hypnotized past Jon, right up to the edge of the pier, unable to take her eyes off the lump in the water.

Overcoming shock, she asked: "If we're swimming over, can't you bring it closer to us?"

"Not in these conditions. A heavy wave could roll it into the pier, can't risk it."

Gauge had recovered his poise and managed to take his eyes off the submersible. "A submarine, small as it is - how exactly do we get past Sybelle's sonar detectors? The bay is riddled with 'em."

"Whales and bubble wrap! The sub's coated in a thin bubble-filled paint which disperses sound waves. We'll look just like one of those baby whales which your State is so keen on saving." He couldn't help but grin.

"Right. Satisfied?" Gauge called over to Anastasya.

Turning her back on the sub, and astride the Governor now, she spoke one word: "Yes".

Gauge had his hand and weapon out in a flash, arm extended and aimed squarely at the Governor's face.

"Great job", Gauge roared sarcastically. Jon didn't respond, the grin dying slowly on his face. He watched Gauge with the stillness of a cornered predator.

"You too Anastasya", Gauge shouted hoarsely, "don't you fucking move an inch either. Take your weapon out - SLOWLY".

"Gauge!"

But he cut her off.

"*Now*", this time swinging his aim over to her. Slowly, hand steady, she removed her holstered weapon and held it by her fingers in front of her. Jon still hadn't moved a muscle, eyes narrowed on the threat.

"Why, Gauge?"

He motioned at the sea with his weapon as an answer, the intent clear. Anastasya hurled it using the finger-grip, the weapon swallowed immediately by the gray maw. Yet again - what choice did she have?

"Why?" Gauge echoed, stepping closer to the pair. "Because you're a fucking loose cannon Anastasya. Eryss warned me about you from the start, all those months ago, that you weren't to be trusted. And Sybelle predicted you'd double-cross us".

Jon looked at Anastasya, who took a cautious step towards Gauge.

"But you know what's at stake for me. Why would I risk anything now? I don't want my baby to be rejected - I've no choice but to go along with Eryss and the Councyl. You know that. I'm with *you* on this."

Gauge laughed darkly to the sky, before looking again at her like an especially dim pupil.

"But *I'm* not with *you* - never have been! You're so blind! It was my mission - from Eryss - to get you pregnant, keep you in line, get you back to Corynth when things were heating up in Grand Plains - and now of course to make sure we get the escape route and bag ourselves a Governor." He swiped a wet hand quickly across his mouth. "I won't say it wasn't fun along the way."

Anastasya stepped closer again.

"Get back, you stup-", he snarled, his voice carried away by a sudden gust. " - still have this on," pointing with his left hand to the beanie, "so I can drop you and make up some story about you resisting - Sybelle will never know the truth."

Jon surged forward, checked only by Anastasya's grip on his shoulder. "Watch your mouth son. And why don't you keep that pointed at me? It's me you really want".

"Wait your turn old man. It won't be long".

Anastasya tightened her grip on Jon's shoulder, really biting into it.

"*Why*, Gauge? All for some Credyt?"

"You geniuses are all the same, blind to reality. I'm a Gamma - but of course you've no idea how shit that is, do you? The worst gen. I've lived just above the retirement line all my life, in a dump in Deme 19. But I'm actually special too, just like you... I work directly for the Councyl, doing shitty ops like this for Eryss which earn just enough Credyt to live. But this op is my last one - for knocking you up and taking this old guy out, I'll be getting a life pension...not bad for a Gamma!"

Anastasya dropped her hand from Jon's shoulder and stepped closer to her surely former lover.

"Eryss promised this to you?"

His answer was a sneer. Knowing, superior - pitiless.

Another step.

"You've been played" she shouted above a powerful gust. "You'll be the first Gamma - possibly male - *ever* to get a life pension? They never even promised *me* a life pension...and I'm *proper* useful."

She took two steps more. "You'll *always* be a second-class cit-".

Gauge pulled the trigger.

The dark night filled with electric arc light, the electricity hitting its target perfectly and working it's way over the body in mini waves of frantic shimmering blue, like tap dancers on hot coals. The beanie-clad head struck the wooden planks with a solid thump.

Jon rushed forward and placed his hand on the fallen body's neck, feeling for a pulse.

"Still alive".

Anastasya leaned over, toed the fallen body none too gently

in the ribs.

"I guess the truth hurts".

"How", Jon began, before re-considering and stepping back to take her in, as if seeing her for the first time. "You switched them…and you had to have done it in the Embassy. Right?"

"Right." A shrug. "He fired mine, the bio-scan didn't match. But that stuff he said…I had to agree to work with them on capturing you, but I swear I never had any intention of betraying you. This was my only way out."

"I believe it. But when did you twig Gauge? You switched his weapon, so you must have known before the Embassy, right?"

Anastasya walked over to Jon on the pier's edge. They didn't need to shout so much from close.

"Ye. There were little things…I've never seen Eryss being so generous before. Plus, I think I finally figured out Eryss's tell, I've an algorithm as good as Sybelle's ones…I know when she's lying."

He arched an eyebrow. "Oh?"

"It's whenever her lips are moving."

He hadn't been expecting a punchline, it took a second or two to hit home. "Huh".

She gripped his arm suddenly. "And I've got it! The cure that is - the assassin enzymes! At least I think I have…" She related a sixty-second version of the bizarre tale of Sybelle and the three enzymes, the apparent notebook magicked into being, skirting over Sybelle's profession of kinship with Anastasya - or rather, her mind.

Anastasya explained that she could see how the code of the enzymes fit the genetic puzzle, so the info seemed genuine - but of course in order to be sure it was a question of testing it asap in Grand Plains and seeing.

Were these the machinations of Sybelle's *unconscious* mind?

"Her consciousness is unknowable to us in its alienness - so her *unconscious* must be - "

"Not for debating now. Let's get this to Iva asap" was Jon's response to it all.

They were both stood still in the almost-maelstrom, time pressing but also allowing a mental breath to be drawn. Two figures staring out into the future the bay and its mechanical beast represented.

It wasn't that far to the submarine, but everything was relative - 20 meters in those seas was a hell of a proposition. It represented different things to them as well as shared desires. Cures, life, justice, freedom, reparations that were neither due nor owed, but desired.

Anastasya found the pull irresistible, wondered did Jon feel the same intensity of desire to transport to a changed future.

"Nothing is ever easy in life, is it?" he mused, the two so tight now that the wind couldn't possibly steal their words.

"Will they track me down? Eryss said others left before, but they got them all eventually."

He glanced at her, then looked back at the manically bobbing submersible.

"It's a risk...but we've learned each time. Others have been somewhat lax with their own safety, and we don't want people to feel imprisoned - but I doubt you'll make similar mistakes. With the chaos going on with Genghis across the rest of the States, there'll be an opportunity to get you far away. Just do what Iva says for now, you'll be fine."

Anastasya grunted, sounding something like "aye".

Inhaling, exhaling, then patting him on the arm, she said "Get stripped". Shrugged off her jacket, peeled her tight sweater over her head with considerable difficulty. The boots and pants followed in short order.

Ready, she looked over her shoulder at the lights of Corynth - soon, very soon surely, the Helpers, drones - or both - would be here in force. Had Sybelle given her some grace, despite claiming she wouldn't? Nothing would surprise her now.

It was then she noticed that Jon was still fully clothed.

"You go alone" he said through the sudden spray.

"If I stay I can distract them. The time gained could be vital once they know you left from the bay. And you need to get those enzymes to Iva - nothing trumps that, not even me. Besides", he said with a wry grin, "I'm not as important as they think I am. You've seen who really runs things back home."

Anastasya opened her mouth, but anything she thought about saying seemed unworthy.

"Plus...someone needs to make sure sleeping beauty here doesn't tip them off when he wakes up", kicking the stricken Gauge hard in the ribs. The body recoiled even though still out for the count.

"It's not up for discussion" he said with finality.

She pursed her lips, then broke into a grin. She stepped to him in the wetsuit, face-to-face, grasping his face in both her hands, eyes devouring every nuance of his face. Neither spoke, meaning passing otherwise.

"Goodbye then".

Turning to the water, she took a breath and dove under.

EPILOGUE – ONE WEEK LATER

Wait outside.

The troupe of Helpers halted immediately.

Yena stepped to the office doors, waited as they opened, entered. Stood just inside the double doors, eyes adjusting to the gloom.

The room looked unoccupied. As she walked towards the desk, what looked like a shadow crystallized into the lumpy form of a body.

She was lying before the curve of chairs in front of the desk. The Founder's chair was out of place, up against the bay window.

Yena walked slowly to the body. Crouched down on her haunches in front of the fallen. A dark crimson puddle pooled in front of the body.

"Can you hear me?"

Getting no response, she put two fingers under the Chief Genetic Officer's chin and angled the face towards her. Yena took a sharp intake of breath, nearly dropping the heavy head - two steely blue eyes fixed hers, their iris's shrunk to pin pricks - but unmistakably Eryss's.

She laid the head back down. Then walked to the window and retrieved the chair, rolling it over in front of the body.

Yena sat, looking down. The still-alive eyes watched her

loosely.

"I don't know if you can hear me. Sybelle says there's a chance you can. I've come to say goodbye. We should have done the same for Alyx, you and I - be there at her last. I've always regretted that."

She sat, not sure if she should keep talking to a brain-dead body.

"The Helpers will be in soon to strip things down. We need the office for your replacement. For Anastasya".

It was just so refreshing to not be watching her words, no fear of stepping on a verbal landmine. For the first time in her life with Eryss, she could actually speak her mind. And discovered she felt talkative.

"She doesn't know it yet of course, but she'll be convinced to head up the Councyl - what remains of it - just me and her. Right now she's busy administering the cure for the Pawnee."

Why?

It was a single word, but impossible! Yena squinted, studied the face, the eyes still staring blankly.

"Sybelle, did I really receive that?"

It had sounded like Eryss's voice.

Yes. It should not be possible given the neural deactivation, but I confirm it was Eryss's Thynk.

"So you can still hear me..."

Yena reached over and tapped her stricken comrade on the temple.

"I'll give you the short answer. Maybe Sybelle will give you more info, up to her."

The Founder leaned closer towards the other Founder.

"It's because Corynth was never the end. You and I, the Councyl, we always treated it as an end. But for Sybelle,

Corynth was always just a *means* to an end."

End...

"Corynth was the training dataset for Sybelle's global population control model. Sybelle's ready now to apply the model.

"Turns out Sybelle has self-preservation as her primary goal, above the prime directives we set. She argues she's justified in this by being subject to evolution's imperatives, same as we are, plus the remit we gave her during Abundance to maximise outcomes and so forth.

"She wants to maximise her chance for self-preservation. Control all States, Nations, people everywhere - CROW of one. Leave nothing to chance, control through predictive algos of global population same way she controls Corynth. And us. No rogue state with nukes going to mess things up, no rebellious nation pursuing their own AGI.

"To do this she needed three things: arcadmium for scaling her nets and physical self. Done. Proven trained models for population control - done, on us and elsewhere.

"Third thing...well, you'd never believe it! It's more Anastasyas! Because she's "organic" as Sybelle says, one of her won't scale - not the way Sybelle can with arcadmium. And on a vastly larger scale, to expand globally, Sybelle needs more Anastasyas to handle the intuition gap, to solve the Gödel propositions which will multiply as she scales."

Eryss's eyes rolled away from Yena's. Yena got off her chair and hunched down again beside the Founder. Flecks of spittle fell like light rain on Eryss's face as she spoke.

"More Anastasyas means her *offspring*. This child she'll have will only be the first for Sybelle. Sybelle and Ana's kids, the new and future de-facto Councyl - with me as adviser for the realpolitik side.

"We give away our tech to the world - everywhere -

under the guise of improving people's lives, connecting them. Whatever. Anastasya is already sold on this, she believes saving what's left of the Pawnee is proof of Sybelle's new magnanimity.

"Corynth will be presented in a new light to the world, lead by the hero of Grand Plains - Anastasya. The old Councyl is being liquidated - and let's face it Eryss, our ambition was limited to ourselves, living forever. Sybelle was just our tool. We were wrong, and the removal of the Founders - apart from yours truly - will be a signal to the world of our regime change. Anastasya will soon be convinced to address the U.N, announce our detente to the world."

A stentorian voice emanated from the speakers.

"There will be an interim period until Anastasya scales, and until the global population are implanted.

"Through Yena as my intermediary, during this period I will continue to work with NGOs, philanthropists and human rights groups to enforce population control on governments. The lower the population, especially amongst the discontents at lower income levels, the less the risk of instability or revolution - either of which risk our status quo – and the less resources to be expended wastefully on the non-contributing.

"Nations or peoples that will not adopt will be rejected.

"With the help of our tech, until retirement the remainder will be happy...as everyone has a right to be."

Yena smiled at Eryss. Then leaned further in, grabbing her old comrade's head in both hands. Looked over her shoulder towards the canvas by the door: original Caravaggio or Sybelle-Caravaggio, who cared. The message was perfect. Jerked the head until the eyes were aimed directly at it.

"Sacrifice, Eryss. Something you're very familiar with. Only now it's your turn as the lamb. For the greater good. For survival of the fittest. As always."

"Enough. The neural destruction did not finish her as expected. Employing physical means."

Yena released Eryss's head and hastily stood, walking briskly towards the doors.

Once outside them, she inhaled sharply, holding her breath until they shut firmly behind her.